NEW YORK NIGHTS

T0349956

ALSO BY C.J. DUGGAN

Summer series
The Boys of Summer
Stan
An Endless Summer
Max
That One Summer
Ringer
Forever Summer

Paradise series
Paradise City
Paradise Road

Heart of the City series
Paris Lights
New York Nights
London Bound (coming 2017)

NEW YORK
NIGHTS

A HEART OF THE CITY NOVEL

C.J. DUGGAN

hachette
AUSTRALIA

Published in Australia and New Zealand in 2017
by Hachette Australia
(an imprint of Hachette Australia Pty Limited)
Level 17, 207 Kent Street, Sydney NSW 2000
www.hachette.com.au

10 9 8 7 6 5 4 3 2 1

Copyright © C.J. Duggan 2017

This book is copyright. Apart from any fair dealing for the purposes of private study,
research, criticism or review permitted under the *Copyright Act 1968*, no part
may be stored or reproduced by any process without prior written permission.
Enquiries should be made to the publisher.

National Library of Australia
Cataloguing-in-Publication data:

Duggan, C. J., author
New York nights/C.J. Duggan

978 0 7336 3664 6 (pbk)

Series: Duggan, C.J. Heart of the city; Bk. 2

Romance fiction.
Man–woman relationships – Fiction.
New York (N.Y.) – Fiction.

A823.4

Cover design by Keary Taylor
Cover photographs courtesy of Shutterstock
Author photograph by Craig Peihopa
Text design by Bookhouse, Sydney
Typeset in 11/16 pt Minion Pro by Bookhouse, Sydney
Printed and bound in Great Britain by Clays Ltd, St Ives plc

MIX
Paper from
responsible sources
FSC
www.fsc.org FSC® C104740

For all the people brave enough to book that ticket

Chapter One

Let's get one thing clear. Being an au pair is nothing like in *The Sound of Music*. To start with, I'm certainly not a nun, I have zero musical abilities, and I failed sewing in high school. There's no handsome Captain von Trapp and there's definitely no choreographed frolicking.

All that aside, it had sounded appealing. The plan was I would sacrifice x amount of hours caring for someone else's children, then stroll through a foreign city during my downtime, immerse myself in some culture, learn another language, study maybe, truly find myself, all before falling in love with a wealthy fisherman called Pascal who enjoyed crafting small objects out of wood with his bare hands. Come nightfall, we'd make an incredible paella with the freshest seafood while we sipped wine, arms interlinked as we toasted to us. I mean, we all have to have goals, right?

The reality was somewhat different. For one, I landed a job in my painfully small hometown in Australia, so the chances of meeting a handsome fisherman called Pascal were pretty slim. Instead, my days consisted of shampooing a toddler's hair or wiping the bottom of a five-year-old, and defrosting meat for an early dinner. It was hard to feel like an adult when sitting at a tiny table with my knees around my ears, trying to convince the children how delicious each mouthful was. 'Look, they're little trees, eat your little trees,' I'd say, coaxing them to eat broccoli.

And as much as my employers made me a part of their family, there was never that feeling of freedom, the kind that let me wander into the lounge to flake out on the sofa and idly channel surf, or to fling open the fridge for an impromptu snack. There was no inviting friends over for dinner and definitely no bringing guys around. It wasn't all bad, but it had been my whole life for the past three years, and I had needed a change.

Now, seemingly a million miles from home, I sat on a plush white sofa, shoulders squared, surrounded by white walls and fresh white flowers. Everything was white, save the glass-and-gold coffee table dividing me from them: Penny Worthington and her equally cold daughter, Emily Mayfair. Like her mother, Emily's smile didn't reach her eyes; there was no warmth there. She swept her blonde bob from her face and looked down at the paper she was holding, no doubt a background check they'd organised through a private detective. I wouldn't have put it past them.

'Won't be long now, we're just waiting on one other,' said Emily. Even her name sounded like she had married into money: Lord Mayfair or something equally distinguished. So distinguished I had been rather taken aback. The Worthington's driver – yes, they had a driver – had picked me up from the Park Central Hotel and driven me to a beautiful brownstone in Turtle Bay Gardens. I'm not sure what I had expected; I'd always thought of New York as cramped apartments with fire escapes and air-conditioner boxes hanging out of the windows. Instead I saw an enclave of row houses, gardens arranged to form a common space with a stone path down the centre and a fountain modelled after the Villa Medici in Tuscany, or so Dave the driver informed me.

'Oh, Emily, I think we'll just begin. You know what Dominique is like.'

Dominique? Who was she? Was Emily the mother of the children I was meant to be caring for, or the less-punctual Dominique? And more importantly, why was I about to be interviewed by three women? I took a sip of the water I was holding, kindly provided by the maid. A driver and a maid; they made my previous employers, the rather self-sufficient Liebenbergs, look middle-class. I chose to hold onto my glass of water for fear of leaving a condensation ring on the coffee table. I was certain that act alone would mean instant dismissal.

'So, Miss Williams, tell us a bit about yourself,' Emily said, skimming the pages before looking at me expectantly.

Oh God, how had I not prepared for perhaps the most obvious question of all? Somehow I'd thought I could simply wing it, turn on a bright and cheerful – not ditsy – façade and fake some confidence. I started by making eye contact with the maid, who promptly came forward and took away my empty glass. But before I could begin the Sarah Williams story there was a distant commotion; doors were slamming and a voice spoke loudly out in the entrance.

Penny Worthington closed her eyes, apparently silently summoning the strength to remain calm. Emily sighed deeply. The maid prepared to throw herself into the path of the impending cyclone.

'Hello Frieda, my love, how's that gorgeous man of yours?' A loud and heavily pregnant blonde woman burst into the room. She shimmied out of her jacket and handed it, and her purse, to a mortified-looking Frieda.

'He is well, thank you, Miss Dominique.'

'Frieda, how many times do I have to tell you? Call me Nikki; every time you say Dominique it's like you're running fingers down a blackboard.' Dominique, or rather Nikki, brushed wisps of hair out of her face. She had none of Penny and Emily's poise or elegance but as soon as Nikki turned I saw the same perfect nose and blue-grey eyes. There was no mistaking that she was Penny's daughter.

'Hello, Mother.' She pecked Penny on the top of the head. 'Sorry I'm late.' She waddled around the couch and sat beside Emily.

'You're always late,' said Emily through pursed lips.

'Well, you're always in a bad mood, so neither one of us can win. Ugh, Frieda, my love, can you please get me a water? I am so fat.' She sighed, turning to look at me with a big smile. 'And you must be Sarah?'

I knew within an instant of her turning that smile on me that I loved her. Warmth and authenticity just radiated from her.

I stood, leaning over to shake her hand so she didn't have to bend over her belly. 'And you must be Nikki?'

Her smile broadened as she looked at her sister and then at me. 'Oh, I like you, you don't miss a beat.'

I was flooded with relief, inwardly saying a prayer that it was Nikki's children I would be caring for and not Emily's. My eyes skimmed her belly, thinking maybe this was the reason I had been called here so quickly; maybe Nikki, clearly the black sheep of the family, needed help with her soon-to-be-here baby.

'We haven't begun as yet, Dominique. We had just asked Sarah to tell us about herself.'

Something told me that there would be no way in hell Penny would resort to calling Dominique 'Nikki'.

'Oh, come on,' Nikki said, rolling her eyes, 'don't you know enough about the poor girl? How many more hurdles must she jump before you give her the job?'

Penny and Emily had matching glares, and it wasn't just because they had the same eyes, although that probably helped.

'Let me ask a question,' Nikki said, propping herself on a cushion that looked like it was more for show than actual use. 'What brought you here, Sarah?'

It was a question that was not easy to answer. Being dumped from the Liebenbergs' employment had not exactly been part of the plan, but neither had following them to Slovenia where they were opening a remote medical practice. Admitting as much, however, might make me seem unreliable, and an au pair is nothing if not reliable; I would have to think of something better.

Nikki looked at me as if trying to tell me that she wanted my answer to be perfect, so I responded honestly.

'I've dreamed of New York City all my life. I am so grateful to Dr Liebenberg for setting up this interview for me, I know he is a very good friend of your family.'

Penny stared at me; there was a long, uncomfortable silence as I waited for her to say something, but she was giving me nothing. I cleared my throat and glanced at Nikki, who smiled and nodded, encouraging me to continue.

'The moment I stepped off the plane I knew I'd made the right move. I feel I'm more than ready for this new chapter of my life.'

'And you believe you can handle a challenge?' Emily asked, her perfectly sculpted eyebrows raised in interest.

'I'm the eldest of four from a working-class family so I've been surrounded by children all my life, in times when it wasn't easy. But my family worked hard, banded together and pulled through. I don't shy away from anything – my stomach doesn't turn, and the tears don't flow. I mean, I'm not a robot or anything, but I come from tough stock. I will love the children and I will care for them, something that was never more apparent to me than when working for the Liebenbergs. I cared for their boys, Alex and Oscar, since they were babies, which was a challenge, but I loved my time there.'

'Dennis did provide a rather impressive recommendation for you,' Penny said finally. 'And I am going to be completely honest with you: if it wasn't for that recommendation, I seriously doubt I would have let you through that door.'

Okay, ouch.

'You see, I don't much care how many brothers and sisters you have or how hard it was for your father to put food on the table – that doesn't affect me one way or the other. Nor do I care for any girlish fantasies you have about traipsing around New York City. What I care about is you being fully present; in your mind, in your heart. That your dedication is solely to my grandchild.

'You are to ask no questions, you are to simply do what is required and nothing more. If you are successful, you will be given a full induction on what is expected of you. You will sign a non-disclosure form.'

'And how am I to know if I am successful?' I asked, perhaps not as confidently as I would have liked.

'Well, we have a fair few questions to go through first,' said Emily in a no-nonsense tone.

'And another interview,' said Penny.

'Another?' Nikki and Emily both looked at Penny, confusion creasing their foreheads. Well, creasing Nikki's anyway; something told me Botox was keeping the wrinkles at bay for Emily.

Penny gave her daughters a pointed look. 'Yes, another.'

'You don't mean—'

'Are you sure that's a good idea?' said Nikki, cutting off Emily's question.

Penny sighed, the first proof of her having any human emotion. 'We can't hold off any longer, we have to get him involved.'

The three women looked grim, like they were about to encounter the bogeyman. Their dread was palpable, and although I had just banged on about being able to handle anything, now I wasn't so sure.

'Get who involved?' I asked tentatively.

Penny's eyes cut sharply to mine, and I regretted my words immediately.

'First lesson, Miss Williams: ask no questions.'

I glanced at Nikki, hoping to find some comfort in an eye roll or a wink, but I saw nothing more than her sad, worried expression.

I swallowed, nodding my understanding even as I thought, *What the hell have I gotten myself into?*

Chapter Two

I knew I'd screwed up the interview. I would be hearing 'if you are successful' for the rest of my days. I went down the steps of the brownstone and made my way back to the car, feeling deflated despite the VIP experience. The driver was holding the car door open. Such a different world, I thought, as I smiled my thanks to him. Not really knowing the rules, I had tipped him on the way here, and I supposed I had to tip him again. I was seriously going to run out of money at this rate. Maybe there was something in my NYC guide about tipping etiquette for private chauffeurs. I flipped through the pocket guide, wondering how this could be my biggest drama right now.

Then the door opened. 'Slide over, sweetie.'

Juggling my book, I did as the voice said, too shocked to think. Then I recognised the body of Dominique as she got in beside me.

'Where are you staying?' she asked, holding her belly and catching her breath.

'Park Central Hotel,' I said, looking at her, slightly worried we might be taking a detour to the hospital.

'Oh, nice. Hey, Dave, drop Sarah off first then drag me home. I know how much you love going to Brooklyn.'

A smiling pair of brown eyes flicked up in the rear-view mirror. 'I would drive to the ends of the earth for you, Nikki Fitzgerald.'

'Aw,' she said, tilting her head and offering a high-wattage smile.

'You live in Brooklyn?' I asked.

'Much to my mother's disgust.' She laughed.

Silence fell as Dave indicated to pull out into the street.

'Hey, don't worry about that interview, it's just a process my mother and sister like to go through to ensure they are in control, when they're actually not. The job is yours.'

'You really think so?'

'They haven't even interviewed anyone else, and if the recommendation came from Dennis Liebenberg, you could be an axe murderer and they would be hard-pressed to go against it.'

'Well, I'm not an axe murderer, so hopefully that would go in my favour, too.'

'I should think so,' she said, examining me. 'I would pack my bags if I were you, I don't think you'll be staying at Park Central too much longer.' She turned away to look out her tinted window.

I was afraid to hope, but then I thought, if I was going to be the au pair to her baby, shouldn't she have a say?

'When are you due?'

Nikki sighed, her hand going to her belly. 'Never. I am never, ever having this baby. I feel like I've been pregnant for twelve months already.'

'Your first?'

Nikki burst out laughing. 'Oh no, but definitely my last; I have four more rugrats waiting for me back in Brooklyn. As much as my mother complains about my location, I am sure a big part of her is relieved that I don't visit with the grubby-fingered little munchkins often. I mean, you've seen how white that place is, that couch would be smashed within seconds.'

If not for the physical resemblance, I'd have sworn Nikki was adopted. She had a warm, genuine aura about her; she had alleviated the thick tension when she entered the room. I liked her, but I couldn't help but swallow at the thought of five children. Was I destined to become the au pair for them? Was this what the cryptic interview was about? Capture my interest and then hit me with the big reveal?

I cleared my throat. I knew I wasn't meant to ask questions but I wouldn't sleep tonight unless I had some more clarity. 'So have you had au pairs before or is this your first time?'

Nikki looked at me and frowned. Now she resembled her mother. Then her face lightened as she broke into laughter. 'Oh God, no, I'm not hiring an au pair. No no no, I would never subject any poor soul to my brood. Oh, you poor thing, is that what you thought? No wonder you've gone white.' She continued to laugh, which didn't make me feel any better because that left a far worse alternative: I was going to be an au pair for Emily Mayfair, ice queen. I felt sick.

'Oh, okay, so how many children does Mrs Mayfair have?' I asked gingerly.

'Emily?'

I nodded.

'Emily has a boy and a girl, precious little poppets who have been sent away to the best boarding school that money can buy. Don't stress, my sister's au pair days are well and truly over.'

Now I was confused. Why was I even here? Who could I possibly be employed by? I knew they were being cryptic but this was just getting ridiculous. The no-questions rule be damned, I had to know.

'So, why are you here?'

'Exactly.'

Nikki smiled. 'Well, you're about to find out. Dave, can we take a detour to Lafayette, please?'

'Are you sure?' Dave asked.

'Oh, it's okay, he's not there today,' Nikki said, waving dismissively as she tapped away on her phone.

'And Mrs Worthington—'

'It will be our little secret.'

Dave mumbled under his breath.

'Don't worry, Dave, she hasn't put a tracking device on your car . . . yet.'

As much as I was looking forward to the mystery being solved, I didn't want to get Dave fired. I leant across the leather seat. 'You know, I think I'll just wait until tomorrow's interview. I mean, what's one more day anyway?'

'Absolutely not, I don't want anyone else for the job, and I certainly don't want you having a night to think about it and change your mind.'

'Why would I change my mind?'

Dave's eyes flicked up again, meeting Nikki's briefly before she looked out to the streetscape again. 'Oh, no reason,' she said unconvincingly.

Now I was worried. From the moment Dr Liebenberg had spoken of helping with a 'situation' it was obvious that I was signing up for something strange. What was this place on Lafayette? If I woke in a bathtub of ice without my kidneys, I was going to be seriously pissed.

Chapter Three

I wish I could say the beauty of the rustic building made me feel more optimistic about things, but I was tired, hungry and over it as we rode the elevator to the ninth floor. It opened directly opposite a set of rich mahogany doors with a gold 9A in the centre. Nikki walked towards the doors while I stood in place, widened eyes taking in the luxurious space. The white and grey marble floors gleamed, reflecting my totally inappropriate outfit choice back to me. The click of Nikki's low heels bounced off the ornate high ceilings. I tried not to let my mouth gape, because, well, that would just be embarrassing.

Then I remembered, whatever the feeling churning inside me, I was in New York fucking City!

Nikki had already announced herself via the video intercom and now she confidently pushed the unlocked door and made her way through, leaving it open for me. She grinned as I followed her, sensing that I was rather taken aback by the scale of the apartment.

'Three-and-a-half-thousand square feet, Brazilian hard-wood flooring, twenty-six-foot-high ceilings, roof garden.'

'Wow!' I said.

'If you think this is impressive, wait until you see the star attraction,' she said, gesturing for me to climb the sweeping stairs that wrapped around the wall. As I ascended, my attention was diverted to the massive windows with their sweeping city views. I misstepped a few times and made sure to grip the balustrade to make the climb without serious injury. With a view like that I didn't begrudge the detour anymore, I could sightsee from the apartment. The whole day had been a bit of a magical mystery tour; from Seventh Avenue Park Central Hotel, to a Turtle Bay Gardens brownstone to a Manhattan penthouse. Yeah, just another Monday.

On the landing of the second floor we were greeted by an older lady, the penthouse equivalent of the brownstone's Frieda, except this woman seemed a little more guarded as her eyes swept me over.

Nikki slid off her scarf and handed it to the woman. 'How is she?' Nikki whispered, not an easy feat when she was trying her best to recover her breath from the ascent.

'You shouldn't be climbing those stairs, Miss Nikki, I will not be mopping up if your waters break. I could have come down to you.'

'No, don't wake her.'

'She's awake.' The woman waved her words away as she went to the closest door.

Nikki's eyes were alight when she looked at me. 'Come,' she said, and stepped into a nursery bigger than my parents' lounge, dining, kitchen and bathroom combined. A light grey shaded the walls and was highlighted by white furniture and pink fabrics, and another giant window that overlooked the city. A rocking chair next to the window made for the most out-of-this-world nursing corner. I stood in the middle of the room, taking it all in, hardly believing that people could be born into such places. It was such a far cry from my world.

Nikki crept forward, peering into the white cot that had pride of place in the centre of the room. As she tucked her hair behind her ears, a beaming smile spread across her face. 'Hello, beautiful,' she crooned. 'Look who's awake.'

I walked closer, but before I could cover much distance, Nikki reached in and carefully lifted the baby from the cot. Bigger than a newborn and far more alert, at a guess the baby was three or four months old.

Nikki shifted her into her arms with well-practised ease. 'Did you have a good sleep, Gracie girl?'

And almost as if on cue, the crinkled little pink face yawned. We all smiled, even the cranky maid, who watched from over Nikki's shoulder.

Nikki looked at me, as if seeing me for the first time. 'Now, Grace, I want you to meet someone very special.'

She came over to me, rocking the baby ever so gently.

'This is Sarah. Don't tell anyone, but she's going to be your new au pair. You are going to be hanging out with her a lot, and she's new to New York, so you're going to have to take care of her, okay?'

Grace's wild, roaming gaze shifted around the room, flitting from Nikki to the ceiling, and then my way – I could almost feel my heart tighten. A jet-black mop of hair and those blue-grey eyes I had seen before; the worldly, distinctive gaze of a Worthington.

I held out my hand, placing it in the little curve of her soft, wrinkled fingers. 'Nice to meet you, Grace, I hope you can keep a secret.' I smiled, admiring the perfect bow of her lips, and her button nose.

Nikki laughed. 'Don't worry, she won't tell anyone.'

'What? Not even me?'

A deep voice pulled our attention to the nursery door, where a man watched with interest. It wasn't the shock of his voice or that he'd appeared out of nowhere that caused my breath to hitch in my throat. It was that his unnerving blue-grey eyes were looking right at me.

'Hello, Ben,' Nikki said, turning her attention back to Grace. 'I thought you weren't going to be in today.'

'No such luck,' the man said as he walked to the other side of the cot. His demeanour made Penny Worthington seem like Mary Poppins. He scooped a soft teddy from the mattress and looked at it thoughtfully.

'You say that like you don't want to see me,' Nikki teased.

'Just how often do you use this place as a drop-in centre?'

'Can't an aunty come see her favorite niece?'

My eyes shifted to Ben with a new interest as the penny finally dropped: this was Nikki's brother, Ben Worthington. I quickly turned away when he looked at me, focusing on Grace, now fully awake and squirming in Nikki's arms.

'Don't let Emily hear you say that,' he said, his hardened eyes changing as he regarded his daughter. Love softened his face, transforming him, making him more human and no less handsome. His hair was dark, as were the circles under his eyes, and there was stubble along his jawline. His tall, lean frame was encased in an immaculate business suit, but his look was tempered by something unkempt. I tried to stop them, but my eyes kept straying back to him. I had never felt more awkward, but then it suddenly hit me: Grace was the 'situation', and I was to be the au pair for this little baby. Ben Worthington was my potential, rather intimidating, new boss; the one I was meant to meet tomorrow. He probably had no idea.

Until Nikki let the cat out of the bag.

'Ben, this is Sarah, the one Mother has been grilling about the au pair position for Gracie.'

Ben's eyes went from soft and lovely to harsh, flicking to me then to his sister.

Nikki read the change, and handed Grace over to the maid. 'Ruth, can you take Gracie, please?'

Perhaps I should have been grateful that Nikki was on the receiving end of those eyes, but I felt even more uncomfortable when the siblings continued to speak as if I wasn't there.

'A little young, don't you think?' he said.

'Don't start, she is more than qualified. You read the profile.'

'It's just paper.'

'Well, what are you going to do then, Ben, because you can't keep up what you're doing; it's ridiculous. Ruth may be a wonderful housekeeper but she can't be your nanny, too. Have you even held your daughter today?'

His rage was palpable. If looks could kill I would have been seriously concerned for Nikki's safety. But she refused to back down, ignoring the vein that bulged in his neck.

'Go home, Nikki, and worry about your own brood.'

Nikki breathed out a laugh. 'You are just as selfish as Dad. Come on, Sarah, I'm sorry you had to witness this.'

I was more than happy to follow her out and get away from him. At least I had clarity once and for all: come Thursday, I would fly home and write this off as an experience.

We had barely made it to the stairs when Ben's voice stilled us.

'I didn't ask Sarah to go, just you.'

Nikki looked at me from the step below; she appeared as shocked as I was. 'What?' she asked.

Ben leant casually on the doorframe, sighing wearily and rubbing the stubble on his jawline. 'Might as well get this over with, saves having Mother and Emily on my doorstep tomorrow.'

'Yeah, well, nobody wants that,' agreed Nikki. She stepped up to be level with my terrified expression. 'I'll wait for you downstairs, and then Dave can drive you back to the hotel,' she told me.

'I'll make sure she gets home.'

'It's no trouble, I'll wait,' Nikki said adamantly.

'I don't know how long this will take.'

How long could it take for him to say I wasn't suitable for the position? I could tell Nikki was thinking the same.

'I'll wait,' she said pointedly.

Ben shook his head. 'You're stubborn as a mule.'

'I could think of worse traits.' Nikki turned to me. 'Go on, I'll be downstairs.' She spoke like I was about to go off to war. Maybe I was.

As she started to descend the stairs, leaving me alone with Ben Worthington on the landing of his penthouse suite, I switched into another mode. Adopting a new bravery I turned and met his expectant stare, ready to hold out my hand and properly introduce myself, but I was curtly cut off.

'This way,' he said, pushing off the doorframe and stalking down the hall.

All I had to do was follow.

I really didn't want to.

Chapter Four

I sat on one side of a large glass desk, illuminated by the sun that streamed in through the floor-to-ceiling windows. There was no way I could work in here, the view was far too distracting; and by 'view', I mean Ben Worthington. He sat opposite me, studying his computer screen, bringing up my credentials and, knowing his mother, a risk-assessment analysis report from a third-party specialist. As much as I had wanted my New York adventure, I was done. I was over the smiling and biting of my tongue as another set of cold grey eyes cast judgement on me. I just wanted to work, and I'd be great at it if they just took the brooms out of their arses and let me.

I blinked out of my thoughts and found Ben staring at me. His brow curved quizzically as he sat back in his ergonomic leather chair, linking his hands together over his chest.

'You have something to say, Miss Williams?'

I felt like I was in the principal's office, getting in trouble for schoolyard fighting. As much as I could appreciate there was a pecking order in the world, and when it came to this city I was on the bottom, I wanted it to be known that I was going to be a doormat for no man, woman or job. If that meant leaving on the next flight to go be a checkout chick at Coles then I was at peace with that.

'Mr Worthington –'

'Ben, call me Ben.'

I paused. Was that an olive branch of sorts? 'Okay, but only if you call me Sarah.'

He nodded. 'Agreed.' I thought he might have found a little humour in the strangeness of our situation but apparently not.

It was weird. He couldn't have been any more than early thirties and yet was so serious. I guess lighthearted whimsy didn't equate to fatherhood responsibility and multimillion-dollar penthouses.

And then I thought, where was Mrs Ben Worthington in all this. Would we have to wait for her too? Or would that happen at interview 2.0? I didn't think I could bear it. I noticed a few photo frames on the desk, but they were facing away from me.

'Are we waiting on anyone else?' I asked.

'No, no one else,' he said.

Okay, so he made the decisions in this family, that was no surprise.

'Ben, I don't want to seem ungrateful, but –'

'You want a definite answer to the position.'

'Well, yeah, that would be —'

'Do you often have things just land at your feet, Sarah?' he asked.

'No,' I said, a little taken aback.

'Well, you graduated school and then happened to walk into the Liebenberg job pretty much straightaway, yes?'

'Yes, I was fortunate to be able to use that as a stepping stone to work and continue my studies in early childcare and —'

'So you've never really had to fight for anything you've wanted in life thus far?'

'Um, am I being punished for having it easy? Because I assure you, despite what your pieces of paper say about my so-called character profile or case study or whatever, you don't know me or my capabilities at all.'

'Are you saying Dr Liebenberg's recommendations are not accurate?'

'I dare say that it doesn't matter what I or Dr Liebenberg say, I think you already have your mind made up.'

'You think so?'

'Yes, I do. I think you and your mother and your sister have it all figured out, and I'm sure that I will have nothing to do with you or Grace.'

Ben swivelled in his chair as he watched me increasingly lose my patience; him sitting there so cocky only fuelled my fire.

'And furthermore . . .' *Oh God, 'furthermore'? I was on a roll, all right.* 'I may be young, and not a part of any elite dynasty in my country or yours, but I can look after Grace, I can care for her, protect her, love and nurture her through every milestone because I have done it before and I know I can do it again. Whether it be in New York City or Timbuktu, I'll always bring my A game, and whoever doesn't want that as a part of their child's life, well, I think that says more about them as a parent than it does about me as a carer.'

Holy shit, did I really just say that? Did I just question his parenting skills? Someone hand me the hammer and nails for my coffin.

Ben glowered at me, deeply unimpressed by my speech. 'Well, Sarah, I think I have learned all I need to know. I'll see you out.'

'No, it's all right, I can see myself out,' I said, quickly standing, ready to get the hell out of there. If I never set eyes on another Worthington again it would be too soon.

Regardless of my rather adamant request, Ben took it upon himself to walk me to the door. He opened it and stood aside. 'Well, I hope you've had some time to see the sights at least.'

I paused, annoyed that now he opted for small talk. 'I'm booked into my hotel till Thursday, so I have a few days.'

Ben shook his head. 'No, that won't work.'

'I know it's not much but I thought if I got a hop-on, hop-off bus ticket I could pretty much cover a fair amount of ground —'

'I'm going out of town tomorrow so if you check out by seven tomorrow morning, Dave can pick you up and I can do an induction before I leave for the airport.'

'Sorry, but what are you talking about?'

Ben paused, a small, knowing smile creasing the corner of his mouth. It was the first time I had seen him express any form of humour and, no matter how arrogant it was, it suited him.

'You start work tomorrow, Sarah.'

'What?' Sure that I had heard him wrong, I stepped through the doorway. I turned back and met his amused expression.

'You're hired,' he said, before closing the door and leaving me to pick my bottom jaw up from the floor.

~

'Wow, just wow,' was all that Nikki could repeat over and over again. She was still in a state of shock.

'I don't like the fact you're so surprised,' I said, stirring the ice in my Coca-Cola as we sat in a booth at the bar in my hotel.

'What? Oh no, it's just that we tried a kind of intervention before you came aboard and it was an absolute disaster. Ben tends to rebel against any form of forced solution so today was a massive victory. What on earth did you say to him?'

'I didn't say much to him; if anything, I questioned his ability as a parent.'

Nikki spat her drink across the table, then coughed so hard and long she earned alarmed looks from the other patrons.

'Jesus, Nikki,' I said, patting her on the back.

Her eyes watered. 'You said what?'

'Oh, look, I can't remember, but it couldn't have been that bad or I would be booking that forty-eight-hour hop-on, hop-off ticket for the tourist bus right now.'

My little joke was lost on Nikki as she took a small sip of water, trying to clear her throat. She looked at me intently. 'Listen, Sarah. It's not for me to say this, but I feel that I need to at least give you a heads up before you start working for Ben.'

I swallowed, crazy theories running through my head: *He's a serial killer on parole and wears an ankle bracelet. He's a cult leader who believes he's the second coming of Christ.*

'Just don't ask any personal questions,' she said. 'And don't judge him if he isn't the father you might expect or want him to be for Grace.'

I didn't know what to say to that, and I desperately wanted to ask a question but knew it was against Worthington policy. But wasn't I entitled to know a little more about the situation I was stepping into?

'What happened? I mean, for there to be so much secrecy.'

Nikki smiled sadly. 'Doesn't every family have skeletons in its closet?'

Chapter Five

I t was finally happening.

I thought perhaps the reality would sink in once I put my suitcase near my hotel door, but it didn't. I was still waiting on the phone call from Penny Worthington to say there had been a miscommunication and my services would not be required. So, as much fun as it was to be sitting in my room immersed in paranoia and unable to sleep, what better way to combat that than to wander the streets of the city that never slept?

I had chosen my hotel purely for the location. Turn left and you were at Central Park; turn right and you were at Times Square – the best of both worlds. Considering it was night time, I chose to turn toward Times Square, where the night seemed like day anyway, flooded with an array of lights, billboards, speakers, screens, and foot traffic. I couldn't wait.

My spirits had well and truly lifted by the time I passed a giant red sculpture on the sidewalk, the letters L and O stacked on top of V and E, a young couple in front of it manoeuvring their selfie stick to capture the moment. I would have offered to help, but the last time I tried to be of assistance to a couple of Korean tourists with a selfie stick I accidentally dropped and smashed their phone. Incidentally, it turns out that 'shibal' means 'fuck' in Korean.

Immersing myself in the New York experience, I picked up a hot dog from a corner vendor and made my way merrily along Seventh Avenue, the crowds thickening into a shuffle the closer I came to the elevated seating area. I turned the corner to find myself in the heart of Times Square, a place designed to make your pupils dilate and your heartbeat race. I took in all the Broadway theatres, the cinemas, the electronic billboards, the superheroes in costumes posing with tourists for tips and the endless queues for show tickets.

I positioned myself to get the best backdrop of Times Square, streets peeling off behind me, the most famous billboard in the centre. I didn't have a selfie stick, or a well-meaning tourist to help me, but with my camera in selfie-mode there was enough to make out exactly where I was. It was my first official blatant tourist snap I would be texting directly home.

Got the job!! xx

~

The bedside phone was ringing, and a way-too-cheery, American-accented concierge was bidding me a good morning. Ugh.

I stood under the hot shower, gargling the water that streamed over my face and willing it to wake me. Death by New York cheesecake. Worth it. But for my first day on the job, I had to be on my game. From now on it would be nutritious, healthy, wholesome living. New job, new start, new boss. As much as I had considered it a bit of a win that after everything, Ben Worthington was the one who had made the decision, there was one minor technicality: Mrs Ben Worthington, who I was sure I was going to meet today. I had meant to ask Nikki yesterday, but like her, I'd been in shock about landing the job.

I dragged my bags down to reception to check out, allowing myself a good ten minutes to linger out the front of the hotel. But Dave was there sooner than I expected, exiting the car and coming around to open the door for me.

'Morning, Miss Williams,' he said.

'Morning, Dave.'

Dave was a solid man, not much taller than me, with a cheery, professional disposition; you couldn't help but immediately like him. He was a welcome sight on a morning I wasn't feeling at my most certain.

'Looks like we'll be seeing a lot more of each other,' he said, sliding behind the wheel.

'I guess so,' I said.

'Well, welcome to New York City. It's probably gonna take us a bit to bust through this traffic, but I took it upon myself to program the trip for you, musically-speaking.'

He laughed in a high-pitched *hick-hick-hick* that made me giggle.

'Well, crank it up, Dave,' I ordered.

I don't know if this was a signature move of Dave's to welcome newcomers, but as he pressed play on his stereo and Alicia Keys started blaring through the speakers, singing about New York, I couldn't think of a more poetic way to cruise through the bustling, congested streets. It was damn near perfection as I lowered the window and let the morning sunlight and sounds of the jackhammers and distinct subway smells assault my senses.

I don't know at what point I lost my bearings, it was difficult to decipher what was what with the crisscrossed grid of avenues and one-way streets. I wasn't sure which way it was to the penthouse or how much longer it would take this time of the morning. So I held my tongue as the neighborhoods became leafy and quieter. Dave stopped kerbside in a quiet street lined with towering terraces. Without a word, he got out of the car and moved to the boot to collect my luggage.

'Ah, Dave . . .' I scrambled for the door, almost falling onto the pavement, I was so panicked. *Oh, my God. I'm about to get traded on the black market.* 'Um, this is not Lafayette Street,' I said, hoping he would look at the buildings in front of us, slap his head and say, 'My bad, let's go.'

Dave only looked at me, confused. 'Ain't nobody told you?'

I knew it – I was going to be an au pair for Emily Mayfair; there was a secret baby and I had been lulled into a false sense of security.

'Mr Worthington's work residence is Lafayette; his home is here, in the Village.'

'He lives here?'

'Some of the time.'

'In the Village?'

'Greenwich Village.' He nodded. Dave looked at me as though afraid I might run off or something. It was just taking some time to get my head around the location change. All of last night I had pictured what my life might be like in a penthouse apartment. How that would work, what it would be like to make a place with sharp modern corners safe for what would eventually be a toddler. I had analysed every detail and now the rug had been pulled out from under me. Again.

I sighed. 'Is there anything else I should know before walking through one of these front doors?'

Dave laughed, lifting my suitcase out from the boot and setting it on the pavement. 'Yeah, it's number sixty-five.'

Chapter Six

The house was a classic federal-style building on a quiet block in the heart of the historic Greenwich Village, a far cry from Lafayette Street. A house that belonged to Ben Worthington – apparently.

Certain I would be greeted by a staff member, I was surprised when the door was pulled open by Ben himself. Gone was the classic-cut suit – he wore a thick-knit navy V-neck jumper and tan trousers. His hair was damp and, if the nick on his chin and the smell of aftershave were anything to go by, he was freshly shaved. He seemed on edge, like my presence was an inconvenience to him.

'You're late,' he said, stepping aside and allowing me to enter.

I wanted to argue traffic, or remind him I wasn't the driver, but I said nothing; something told me there was no use. I dare say few people disagreed with him.

Ben waved me into a parlour where long, graceful windows looked out onto Washington Street. A gas fireplace with handsome marble detailing anchored the room that was, thankfully, not completely white, like Penny Worthington's cold home. This felt warm and inviting, a stark contrast to the owner, who stood next to me with his hands in his pockets, as if he didn't know what to do with me.

'Your house is lovely,' I managed to say, inwardly cringing at myself. *Really, Sarah? You've seen one room.*

'Well, I'll give you the tour. You can leave your bags here if you want.'

Ben led me down the hall in silence. At the back of the long, narrow house light from the garden filled an elegant, double-height living room and spacious kitchen, which featured every modern convenience known to man. My gaze drifted up the crisp white walls to the ceiling. Wow.

My new home was a four-bedroom, two-and-a-half bathroom townhouse, with a lower-level media room; Ben merely pointed to the descending staircase, so I guessed that was his man cave and out of bounds to me. A beautifully intricate oak staircase led to the third floor, which was dedicated to the master suite. An entire bloody floor – talk about luxury. This was also obviously a no-go zone as we continued to the fourth floor, where two large bedrooms and a bathroom were located. One bedroom was a plain, sparse area with a queen bed and next to it was a gorgeously decorated nursery, all in soft pinks and whites, a plush chair near the window overlooking the garden. The only thing noticeably absent was a baby, a question that Ben read on my blank face when I looked at him.

He shifted a little, seemingly uncomfortable about having to talk. 'We thought we would give you a chance to settle in, get your bearings, before Grace comes home.'

We? As in his wife?

'That's very thoughtful, thank you.'

If he was pleased by my gratefulness he didn't show it and, when my gaze roamed past him to the doorway of the spare bedroom, his eyes followed.

'So this is my room?' I asked.

'Ah, not exactly.'

I turned to him, my interest piqued, and he pointed to the ceiling.

'One up.'

A smaller, poky staircase led to the fifth and final level, to a room that was smaller than the fourth-floor bedroom, but filled with light coming through large bi-fold doors that led out onto a roof terrace.

'This is my home office, I guess, but I think it will probably serve you better, give you some extra space.'

'It's beautiful. Can I take a look out here?' I asked, indicating the terrace door.

Ben shrugged. 'It's technically yours.'

Stepping out onto the roof terrace was like entering a hidden urban oasis. I could already picture myself lounging out here on the built-in seating among the potted foliage, drinking coffee and snacking on a bagel as I read leisurely in the New York sunshine. I resisted the urge to bounce.

'Are you sure? I mean, if it's your office, I don't want to —'

'I'm sure. I can set up anywhere, and I don't want to be traipsing through the fourth level and disturbing Grace, so it's yours.'

I turned from Ben, smiling as I looked over the neighbouring buildings that sliced into the skyline. I didn't know how much downtime I would be afforded, or how demanding this baby would be, but surely it couldn't have been any worse than the time Oscar was a baby, and I had a two-year-old to contend with then as well. Still, that was at home, where support was only a phone call away. Here I was on my own, with a family I didn't know. But if I was going to make a go of it and get everything I could out of this amazing opportunity, I would have to put on my big-girl pants and do all the things that were expected of me, even if it didn't come naturally. And even though we hadn't gotten off on the greatest foot, I would give Ben Worthington the benefit of the doubt; giving me this amazing room was a great place to start. To think how happy I'd been when the Liebenbergs allowed me to put cheese on the grocery list that one time. Now here I was with my own little piece of New York paradise.

'Well, I better show you how the security system works before I go.'

'You're leaving?' I said, perhaps a bit too high-pitched.

'As I mentioned yesterday, I have to go out of town for work.'

'Oh, okay, but you'll be here when Grace arrives – wait, when is she arriving?'

'Emily will bring her home in the morning. I won't be here, but she'll give you the rundown.'

Was he serious? His sister was about to hand over the responsibility of his baby daughter to me and he was acting as if she was about to teach me how to use a television remote.

'But you'll be back? Or will Mrs Worthington be here?'

I regretted it the moment Ben's stare locked with mine. A sudden chill swept over us on the rooftop and it was more than just the morning sun moving behind a cloud. This was bitter cold. Penny Worthington had stated, rather firmly, that there were to be no questions. This was clearly one of them.

'No,' was all he said, as he stepped back through the doorway and went inside.

I followed him down the stairs, watching his straight spine as he led me down the hall. I could tell he didn't know what to do with me, that he hadn't planned out the part where this creature would be residing in his house. Not that he knew what to do with himself. This was his home, but he seemed just as much a stranger in it as I was. The home had no photos, no bills magnetised to the fridge, let alone an indentation on the couch. It was a show home, and at a guess, I'd say he lived mostly on Lafayette Street – that was where he belonged.

'Have you lived here long?' I asked, thinking it more a matter of small talk than prying into his affairs.

'Not long,' he said, standing at the kitchen bench, tapping on his iPad, not even lifting his attention to me.

Turned out Ben didn't do small talk either.

'Did you renovate it yourself or . . .'

He sighed. 'What?' Only then did he look at me. He was clearly annoyed, but I continued regardless.

'I said, did you renovate?'

'Yeah, it's what I do,' he said bluntly.

'Oh, you're an interior designer?'

His brows lowered as if I had somehow insulted him. 'No, I'm an architect.'

Okay, so I was getting the picture, slowly. I couldn't imagine him dealing with clients and collaborating with others. He practically screamed hermit, like a best-selling novelist or something. Maybe he was a real dreamboat at work and just abrasive with strangers who asked questions in his home.

I figured there must be a broken home situation, that would explain his mood, and why he didn't stay here: bachelor penthouse on Lafayette, and a family home in the Village. As long as there wasn't a *Jane Eyre* situation with a crazed wife locked away in a secret room somewhere, I was sure everything would be fine.

Ben passed the iPad to me. 'Okay, this operates everything you need in the house: lighting, heating, cooling, alarm system, television. Food delivery and home maintenance services are there too, and they're linked to my credit card should you need to buy anything, which you will.'

My eyes widened at the apps before me; long gone was the good old list of emergency numbers on the fridge.

He touched a button. 'Here are the contacts for emergencies,' as if he had read my mind. 'This is mine. Don't call it unless it's absolutely life or death, do you understand?'

'Okay.'

It was unbelievable; I had the world at my fingertips. Penny's and Emily's contacts were there as well, which I sure as hell would not be calling, but Nikki's was there too, which made me feel a little more at ease. There was also ambulance, police and fire department, which I prayed I would not need.

'And if I should want to go out, and do some physical food shopping? How do I —'

'I've programed the local area in maps, so you can get an idea of what's nearby.' He pulled out his wallet, thumbing through an impressive collection of hundred-dollar bills. He handed me a couple.

'Use this for incidentals until I link you with a credit card. I don't have a full-time maid, but the cleaners come once a week. Just take care of the house and I'll let you know if I'm going to be in for dinner.'

Okay, chief cook, maid and dishwasher as well as babysitter; I could deal. 'And Grace?'

'I'll email you,' he said, pointing to the envelope icon at the bottom of the screen.

I felt like I was checking into a high-end hotel; everything was in transactions and buttons. It felt so impersonal. Maybe the reality would seem less cold once Grace arrived.

'So if I need to ask you anything, would it be better to email you?'

Irritation passed over Ben's face. Something he hadn't thought of? 'If you really need to know something, yes.'

Okay, that was something. 'And will you be home tonight? Did you want me to organise dinner for a certain time?'

'No, I won't be home tonight,' he said, stepping away from the counter. 'I'm going to get ready to head to the office, just make yourself at home.' He probably thought he was being welcoming, but he wasn't, it was more like 'do what you gotta do'.

'Okay.' I sighed, swiping through the iPad, thinking to do a test run of the lighting and gadgets in the lounge area, just to see if there were teething problems before Ben left.

'Lounge light on, and dim,' I said to myself, dragging my finger along the screen, and sure enough, the lighting dimmed. 'Beautiful.'

I tested the TV and stereo system without drama. I tapped into the email, thinking that maybe there might be a nice welcome message. There wasn't.

Okay, so I could unpack, go for a walk maybe. I pulled the fridge door open; wow, he wasn't kidding, he really didn't stay here much. The fridge was absolutely bare. I'd do a food shop too.

I tapped into the note section on the iPad and started to make a list. I was a great lover of lists and if the iPad was going to be my Holy Grail of information then I might as well use it.

I returned the iPad to the charging dock, thinking that would be the most important note to self: keep it bloody charged. I headed down the hall to the formal parlour to grab my suitcase, but as I veered into the lounge, I saw my things were gone. I did a bit of a double take, wondering if I had left them there, but I knew had.

Well, what do you know, he's a gentleman after all, I thought, turning to make my way up the stairs, only to pause as I heard the sound of footsteps coming down. Ben glanced at me, making him slow his descent as he affixed his cufflinks to his expensive shirt.

'Thanks for taking up my stuff,' I blurted , trying to seem like I wasn't just openly staring at him in the navy suit that fitted in all the right places.

'All right, I'm off,' he said, stopping next to me. Even though we shared the same step, he towered over me, looking down at me with a speak-now-or-forever-hold-your-peace expression.

My mind was whirling at a million miles an hour; everything was happening so fast that no questions sprang to mind. But I just knew there had to be something and I knew that, once he walked out that door, I would think of something and it would be too late. With no clear indication of when I would see him again, I felt a ball of anxiety lodge in the pit of my stomach.

Instead of using the opportunity to ask one last question, I only managed, 'Have a great day.'

Ben's mouth twitched slightly, seemingly suggesting I was a bit lame. Rather than returning the same pathetic parting words, he nodded once and continued down the stairs, slamming the door behind him without a backward glance.

Chapter Seven

I resisted the temptation to pump up the stereo and slide sideways in my socks and undies, Tom Cruise style, simply because it wouldn't have surprised me if Ben Worthington had a state-of-the-art nanny-cam system. So I stayed fully clothed and above board, opting to take my time to unpack my suitcase. I'd have all day to myself and I didn't know if that was going to be something that happened often, so I was going to savour it. There was a certain part of me, not too deep down, that was terrified of being responsible for a tiny human being, which is stupid – I mean, hello, au pair? But this was all so different to the Liebenbergs, and the standards thus far were so incredibly high. I wanted to wrap Grace in cotton wool and never leave the house, which was entirely possible as everything was only an app away. Zombie apocalypse? No problem.

Padding barefoot to the charge dock I tapped the icon likely to be the most important part of my day – food!

The little knife-and-fork icons dotted on the map were like shining beacons, as was one interesting patch on the screen. *Washington Square Park*. According to the map, it was pretty much on my doorstep. Only then did I allow myself to truly get excited about where I was. I headed to the staircase, skipping every second step. I was going to end up extremely fit with these stairs.

Camera, lip gloss, sunglasses, street map and cash in bag and I was all set. As of today I was an official New Yorker, roaming the streets to gather supplies and live like real New Yorkers did; well, the ones who lived in multimillion-dollar townhouses with au pairs. But, hey, someone had to do it.

I was positively giddy as I crossed the road toward the park entrance. Jazz music filtered through the air as I passed small tables set under the shade of trees and surrounded by intensely focused chess players. I smiled, thinking about how I could bring Grace here for strolls; maybe I would even learn to play chess? There was no mistaking I was in New York in this park – there was a certain vibe here. The arch, the fountains, the artists, the performers, the students, the lovers, the loners and me: all pieces of an utterly enchanting puzzle. I slipped off my shoes to cool my feet in the sunken fountain while watching the water jet into the air; breathing it all in.

I think I'm going to like it here.

~

For the first time since I had landed, I felt an inner peace sweep over me; maybe it was the heat on my skin that I could still feel even as I walked in the cool of the tree-lined streets. Passing rubbish bins and striding over uneven pavements seemed utterly charming to me. My big plan for the afternoon was to shower in the lux double marble shower, washing away my New York City fountain feet and sweat from wandering the Village. I made a mental note to perhaps go down to the Magnolia Bakery on Bleeker Street for the 3 pm sugar fix I just knew I would be craving. Life was so utterly brilliant right now.

As I delved into my bag for the keys of my new Washington Street residence, closing the distance with a spring in my step and song in my heart, my smile fell from my face. Standing at the bottom of the steps, I lifted my sunglasses to look at a very angry Emily, holding a baby capsule.

'Where have you been?'

It was a funny thing to see such controlled rage. Letting Emily into the townhouse, I could tell she was dying to stomp inside, throw down her bag, maybe slam a door, but that's just not possible when you're lugging a baby capsule through a narrow hallway.

I sighed deeply, calming my nerves, as I followed her to the back of the house. It was no doubt killing her not to be able to lecture me the entire way, but I knew that her silence would be short-lived as she delicately placed the capsule down in the lounge, making sure she hadn't woken Grace. She even afforded the sleeping baby a small smile, one that almost made her seem human . . . almost.

All that changed when she turned her full attention to me.

'Mother is furious that the interview was cancelled today.'

'Well, I didn't —'

'No, that's right, Ben went over everyone's head,' she said, as if she was just as put out by him. I couldn't quite understand what the big deal was – surely he could make his own decisions about his own child. Control freak, much?

'Well, while you were being paid to slouch around the streets, some of us had actual things to do.'

'I didn't think Grace was going to be here until tomorrow.' That's what Ben had said, right? Now I was starting to doubt myself.

'Ha! Well, I'm sorry to cramp your style, but you want the job, you got the job and the job begins right now.'

It felt like she was punishing me for having gone for a walk on what I had thought to be my day off. Emily picked up Grace's baby bag and placed it on the counter in a huff, and I knew I was about to be thrown into the deep end.

'You'll have to get used to plans changing abruptly here, and as for any of that downtime you apparently so enjoyed today, well, you can kiss that goodbye.'

Jesus, Emily needed to go back to bed and begin this day again. This couldn't be just the way she was, right?

She sighed wearily. 'Have you been shown around, know where everything is? Did he do that much for you?'

'Yes, it's all right, I got the rundown. And if I need anything I'm just to contact him so –'

Emily raised a perfect brow. 'I seriously don't advise that, not unless it's life or death.'

'Yeah, he pretty much said that.'

Emily scoffed. 'Some things will never change.'

~

When Emily left I felt an overwhelming relief sweep over me, until Grace started to cry. It had been a long time since a little pink squealing thing completely took over my life, but the memories of looking after Oscar when he was born were coming back to me. For the first two months, at least, I didn't get a chance to finish a hot drink; all my meals went cold, and I was too tired to be bothered that I was covered in vomit a lot of the time. Still, every baby is different, right? And I would like to think I knew a thing or two.

Even with the beating of my heart, and the worry about picking her up and bundling her into my arms for the first time, I did my best to soothe Grace with gentle rocks and pats, shushing her. After all, like sharks in bloody waters, a baby could sense your stress, so I would have to make sure that I was as calm as I could be, and hopefully she would be lulled into being settled into a deep slumber.

Wrong!

Whatever plans I had, whatever I thought it'd be like or what I'd be able to do, it was time to forget them all. Grace was going to dictate how the following hours went, and she had very different ideas from me. I had imagined strolls in Washington Park, sitting on the roof deck under the shade of an umbrella, reading, as I idly rocked Grace. I would sit in the nursing chair reading stories to her before tucking her in and turning off the light, switching on the baby monitor and pottering around for the rest of the evening. Perhaps I'd cook something nice with some home-delivered groceries, watch a bit of telly or listen to some music. In every one of my fantasies, Grace was fast asleep.

I was obviously deluded.

I may have had to care for Oscar, but I always had a wingwoman nearby, or within calling distance, in Lorraine Liebenberg. If Oscar cried, we worried together, sharing the load and the cuddles. Even on the days that Lorraine went back to work, I didn't feel overly anxious about my duties because I didn't feel alone, not like I felt with Grace. Sitting on the couch, watching her beautiful little face bloom with a tinge of red as she cried, the sound echoing in the light-filled townhouse in New York City, I had never felt more isolated.

Surely that extra day without Grace would have made all the difference? I would have had enough time to mentally prepare myself for the official start to my employment after a deep, peaceful sleep. Instead I was frantically googling tips on how to settle fourteen-week-old babies, as if there was some downloadable PDF with all the answers. I was learning to swim after plunging head-first into ice cold and incredibly deep water.

I settled on following my instincts and warmed a bottle from the baby bag that Emily had dumped on the counter. I kept pressing the refresh button on the envelope icon on the iPad, thinking that maybe there might have been a message from Ben, a heads-up that Emily was coming, and 'oh, by the way, here's a list of everything you'll need to know when taking care of my daughter'. But who was I kidding? Did he even know, did he even *care*?

Every high-pitched wail sounded like absolute heartbreak, and they only caused me to be more clumsy and frantic while trying to operate a microwave you needed a degree to understand. By the time I figured it out I halfexpected children's services to be knocking on the door, or a neighbour complaining of noise pollution. Gone was the zen-like calm I had adopted as I juggled a screaming baby around the kitchen, testing the temperature of the bottle on my wrist.

'Good, here.' I offered the teat to Grace's lips and she quickly latched on, sucking with brute force. A relief I had never known suffused me, as the sound of silence filled the air – well, aside from the sucking of the bottle, which I hoped would last forever. I glanced at the microwave clock and tried not to let reality kill my vibe – I was only officially ten minutes into my new job.

God help me.

Chapter Eight

It's amazing what you can achieve with one functioning arm, while the other holds a frowning, squirming baby. I was currently rummaging through Grace's wardrobe for things that would make life easier.

'What? Don't look at me like that,' I said. 'Fed, burped, changed – life is good, Gracie. Life. Is. Goo—' I paused as I breathed in, sniffing, before looking at Grace.

'Oh no, you d'int.' I lifted her closer. 'Oh, Jesus.' I turned my head away, my eyes watering. 'I just changed you,' I said, trying not to inhale too much in the confined space of the wardrobe. I stepped out into Grace's room and fresher air, making a beeline to the change table that was, to my relief, fully stocked. The house may not have had adult food, but as far as Grace was concerned, I didn't have to stress so much. Nappies, wet wipes, baby powder, disposable bags all within reach, which thankfully made for a rather swift though still nasty nappy-changing experience. I would have to get used to this, somehow.

Getting Grace back into her onesie, I wondered if this level of organisation was in preparation for me, or had Grace not spent much time here? Much like the rest of the house, her room had an unlived-in feel, and I wondered if an interior decorator had put the final touches on it – or had Grace's mum? Did he choose window treatments and colour palettes as well? It was hard to say; this didn't feel like his home but the apartment on Lafayette did, all sharp, modern corners, expensive artworks and signature-piece sculptures. The coldness of glossed, steely surfaces was accented by expensive rugs and accessories to make it feel impressive but not welcoming. I was glad that this was where home would be for us, it meant a reprieve from Ben Worthington and a little more comfort. This was the perfect place to get to know Grace, to watch her personality emerge and develop, just like the open-mouthed gummy smile she gave me as she fought to keep her legs from being buttoned up. I smiled and cooed and did all the things that were universal when talking to a baby. It just couldn't be helped, the sheer delight that pierced your heart when a baby with a wandering focus decided you were interesting enough to captivate their attention. And should they like you and you were lucky enough to be granted a smile, or a laugh, then that was a bonus. It made the screaming and the smells worth it.

'Well, Miss Grace, what say we order some food and get acquainted with our new home?'

Her gummy smile remained and her legs kicked at me.

'I'm going to take that as a yes.'

～

On the third day, the only break in my routine was the arrival of a deliveryman who had handed me a small box that I had to sign for. Enclosed was a short note.

For when you're out.
-B

Inside the box was a phone. A bit rich, I thought, seeing as, unfortunately, the only person who was checking in with me daily was Penny Worthington and, oh, how I dreaded those calls. More than that, I dreaded the visit she was going to make tomorrow to 'see how things were going'. The way she had said it made me think she secretly hoped that I was a blubbering basketcase and that ol' Grandma Worthington would have to step in and save the day. Then she could tell Ben 'I told you so.' And although I wasn't exactly a blubbering mess, there was no disguising my fatigue. Grace seemed rather adamant that sleeping wasn't her thing, and with sleep deprivation came anger and frustration.

For all the passive-aggression that Penny Worthington exuded, I hoped that she at least had some sage advice for her noticeably absent son. Between the cries and the smiles I couldn't believe that Ben could abandon his daughter like this. Did he think that credit card details attached to an app were enough to raise a child? I know Nikki had asked me not to judge him, but it was too late, he was well and truly judged. And where was Grace's mother? Maybe she really had been locked in a secret room somewhere.

I was heading into dangerous territory, one created by lack of sleep and seclusion. As for the sleep-whenever-the-baby-sleeps advice, well, it doesn't quite work that way. I lay on the loungeroom couch, baby monitor on the coffee table. But paranoia dragged me from my repose up the stairs to her room, creeping in to check that she was breathing.

Pink, warm, asleep, her dark lashes making half-moon shapes against her fair skin. I gave a sigh of relief.

'How could anyone want to leave you?' I whispered, before creeping out of the dim room, ever watchful of the cot as I closed the door, leaving it ajar before turning and slamming into a wall – a living, breathing wall that caused me to scream. I fell back against the nursery door only to be caught by hands, large hands belonging to—

'Jesus, Ben!' I screamed, my annoyance snapping from him to Grace's cry. 'Great, just great,' I said, going into the room and trying to settle her. It was no use, her heart raced as much as mine, and she was wide awake.

'Aw, Gracie, I'm sorry, I didn't mean to wake you,' I said, scooping her into my arms. The dampness of tears against my neck made my heart ache, knowing I'd caused it.

'Is she all right?' Ben stood by my side; he tentatively reached out to touch her but fell short, pulling his hand away as though he didn't know what to do with it. The dull light of the room cast his face into shadow, but I could see the deep lines on his face, the shadow of his stubble. My instant reaction was to snap at him. It had been three days, what did he care? But I held my tongue, focusing all my energy on settling Grace. Now I was the one who seemed uncertain: do I hand her over to him? Would he want that? Would that upset Grace more? I followed my gut, reading Grace's droopy eyes as I rocked her from side to side.

'I'm going to try to put her back down,' I whispered.

Ben glanced down to my arms then to my face. He nodded and exited the room.

Couldn't even tuck in his own daughter, I thought bitterly as I placed Grace in the cot. I paused to see if she would stir or cry when my arms left her but she remained asleep, and once I was confident she would stay so, I crept away.

This time I saw Ben standing on the landing when I pulled the door almost closed, anxiously rubbing his stubble. If I was tired then he was exhausted, the circles under his eyes told me as much. I had gone from anger to almost feeling sorry for him.

'Do you want a drink? I was just about to make some coffee.'

He seemed surprised, like he was weighing the answer to a serious question. He rubbed the back of his neck as if he was in pain.

'No, thanks,' he said, loosening his tie. 'I'm going to jump in the shower.'

'Are you staying for dinner?'

Obviously another serious question that had him thinking intently. God, how did this man run a successful business?

'No, I'm heading out,' he said, slipping his tie out of its knot.

I tried to keep my composure. I had no right to feel anything. My job was to care for Grace and I accepted that. I just wasn't used to this situation, maybe because I had been lucky and a bit sheltered with the Liebenbergs – at the end of the day, there was never any doubt they loved their children and were devoted to them. But here, I was unsure. Committing to a drink or a meal seemed to pain him, let alone engaging in human contact. The man was like a robot, existing in a fabricated world. I bet Ben was even cold to touch, like his eyes, his heart.

My eyes drifted to his exposed collarbone beneath the unfastened collar and it wasn't coldness that swept over me. I could feel my cheeks flush, even more so when my eyes returned to his, watching me with guarded interest.

'Well, if you're sure. I can always leave you a plate of something for later.'

Ben nodded. 'I'm sure.' Before I could respond, he turned to the stairs, heading to the third floor, and as he disappeared, Grace began to cry.

I sighed. 'Coming, Gracie.'

Chapter Nine

I tried to prepare a *MasterChef*-inspired spaghetti Bolognese . . . okay so it was from a jar . . . thinking that maybe something quick and easy would get me through until Grace stirred. Every moment of the last few days had been a fight for survival, a race against the clock. This was my new life. I had thought that maybe Ben would be some help, but I was wrong.

He appeared down the hall, clean-shaven, freshly showered and dressed in a button-down blue shirt and slacks. 'Everything under control?'

Maybe it was the trashed kitchen, or the wisps of hair falling into my eyes, curled by the steam from the pasta, that inspired his question. Or maybe it was my manic fumbling, trying to take everything off the stove so I didn't burn the house down when I went and picked up Gracie, who was gurgling and cooing happily enough through the monitor.

I drained the pasta in the sink, placing the saucepan to the side and wiping my hands and the condensation from my forehead, trying to appear like I had my shit together. I didn't want him to think otherwise. I could just imagine the conversations around the Worthington dinner table: 'And you should have seen the kitchen.' Chortle, chortle, chortle.

Well, screw them all. 'Fine, thanks,' I said with what I hoped sounded like confidence. Feeling his eyes staring at me over the counter, I let Grace be, grounding myself and doing a bit of a clean. I rinsed the dishes, keeping myself busy so I didn't have to look at him. 'Your mother is coming by tomorrow.'

I felt the shift in him, heard it in his sigh. 'Oh, joy,' he said. That's when I did look at him because now we had something in common: the dreaded visit of his mother.

'Well, I'll be at work so . . .' He shrugged one shoulder casually, and in a flash my moment of mutual bonding had changed to hating him because, unlike me, he had a means of escape, and I was so envious.

'Don't let her get to you,' he continued.

I stilled my scrubbing, and narrowed my eyes.

'This isn't her house,' he said, and with that he slipped on his dinner jacket and exited the room.

He'd probably intended his words to make me feel more at ease, but they had no such effect.

~

As romantic as it was to be sleeping on the fifth floor with access to the roof terrace, I felt strangely separated from the rest of the house. And although that was probably intentional, it didn't exactly help. Baby monitor or not, I was terrified that I might sleep through Grace's cries. But the fear soon slipped away when a bone-deep exhaustion settled over me.

It felt like I'd barely shut my eyes before I flinched awake from a dream. A dream that had me thinking I had slept through the entire night, only to run down the staircase to Grace's room to be met with Penny Worthington holding Grace, looking at me with a hateful, disapproving stare as she shook her head. It was a terrifying dream, but no more than the realisation, having glanced at the time, that only three hours had passed. But they had passed with not so much as a peep from Grace. This was unusual.

I dived out of bed, taking to the narrow stairs, my heart racing, wondering if nightmares did come true and I would find Penny Worthington in Grace's room. So when I opened the door and found Ben, I felt only momentary relief. He was sitting in the chair by the window, nursing Grace and reading her a bedtime story. I hadn't heard her cries. I had slept through them. I was so fired.

I stepped into the room, wringing my hands together. 'Ben, I'm so sorry I didn't—'

He held his hand up, continuing the story he was reading by lamplight. I stood there feeling awkward, listening to the story unfold, afraid to move. I wasn't sure what I should do. A sleeping Grace lay limp in the crook of his arm. Ben read on as if I wasn't there at all. Had I not been mortified about my slip-up, I might have taken the chance to appreciate that Ben was holding his little daughter. It was a truly beautiful sight, something I hadn't seen all week. I desperately wanted to creep away, wait on the landing for him to come out and dress me down for not being on my game. Maybe I had oversold my ability. I had thought I could conquer anything, having looked after the Liebenbergs' boys, but being on my own with all this, far away from home, it was almost like I was set up to fail – exactly as the Worthingtons had expected. Maybe Penny's visit was bang on with timing: day four meltdown mode and she was going to be here to catch the show.

Ben closed the book, placing it to the side as he gingerly edged himself out of the chair, his concentration fierce as he moved carefully. I stepped forward, instinctively wanting to help, but thought better of it. He was managing just fine, and Grace was certainly in a sound sleep. Ben walked over to the cot, placing her slowly down, supporting her head in the most loving way.

It was only when she was settled on the mattress that he glanced at me, silently asking for help. I walked over, grabbed the blanket and tucked Grace in securely. I was glad the light was dim, and he couldn't see how red in the face I was, how embarrassed I was that he'd had to come and do my job because I had slept through her cry. That I wasn't there when she had needed me. What if Ben hadn't been home? I shuddered to think.

Ben gestured with his head toward the hall. I squared my shoulders, psyching myself up for the onslaught that was to come, the verbal lashing I deserved. He didn't have to tell me, I knew I had let him down. Hell, I had even let the Liebenbergs down. Seemed like their glowing reference and belief in my ability was seriously misplaced.

I began, wanting to be heard first. 'Mr Worthington I am so, so sor—'

'Mr Worthington?' he repeated, his face screwed up as if the sound of it left a bitter taste on his tongue.

I stammered, thinking that it was a better to show respect at a time like this. Clearly not.

'Ben,' I corrected, and he seemed somewhat more at ease. 'I can't even tell you how sorry and embarrassed I am . . .'

Ben crossed his arms, forehead furrowing as he stared at me, listening to every word that tumbled from my mouth. I hated the way I sounded, I hated how I had put myself into this position, that with each stammer I was only proving how incapable I was.

Seriously, Sarah. Just stop talking already!

As if he was reading my mind, he cut me off again.

'Sarah.' He said my name as if pained, and he pinched the bridge of his nose. 'Do you always talk this much?'

I closed my gaping mouth, instinctively wanting to respond but knowing that by talking I would be proving his point.

Ben looked at me as if he was bored, or maybe he just wasn't a confrontational person by nature, and wasn't keen on having to fire me in the middle on the night. Surely this wouldn't be a problem for him, so why now was he choosing to be so coy about it?

'You didn't hear Grace because I turned the baby monitor off.'

'Why would you do that?' I asked, a little annoyed. Was he deliberately trying to give me a heart attack?

'Well, I figured you wouldn't want to be subjected to a chapter and a half of *Charlotte's Web*, even though I must say it's getting really good. Charlotte has promised Wilbur that she will help him, but he's not going to know how until morning, so, yeah, cliffhanger.'

I stared at him. Was he for real? Maybe he was taking the piss or deliriously tired. Maybe I was too.

'You know that book has a pretty sad ending, right?'

'Uh, spoiler alert.'

'Hey, look, sorry, but just be warned, there will tears, and most probably not Grace's.'

'Geez, now I want to skip through and read the ending,' he said thoughtfully.

'No, you can't do that, you have to allow yourself to get emotionally invested in the story and the characters, otherwise it will be just meaningless and hollow.'

Oh my God, were we really talking about *Charlotte's Web*?

'Anyway, you shouldn't have done that, it's a work night and you probably have to get up early in the morning. It's my job to get up to her.'

'You looked like you needed a rest after a few days of single parenting, so I thought I'd let you sleep. I know how that feels – sleep deprivation is a whole new form of torture.'

My interest piqued. Was there no Mrs Ben Worthington? Maybe there was, and he had full custody, or she was off on a girls' bonding getaway, or couldn't handle Penny Worthington's visits.

'It must have been quite the juggling act with work,' I said, in a way that wasn't exactly a question.

Ben leant against the wall, but he didn't seem defensive, merely contemplative. 'Nikki's been a great help, but she has her own crazy red-headed brood to deal with.'

I smiled broadly. 'Red hair?'

Ben smiled. 'Fire red. Her husband's Irish, a wild woolly ginger. Imagine my mother's horror that a man with no money and no social status had infiltrated the Worthington bloodline.'

'This sounds like a plotline from a Jane Austen novel.'

Ben laughed, moving away from the door out of fear of waking Grace, but that wasn't my fear: my fear was that he would stop, that he would shut down one of the most unexpected and endearing traits I had seen in him. When he laughed, his whole face lit up and his hardened edges softened. That someone could look so different had me transfixed. I wanted to make him laugh again.

'It's a sweeping saga, all right,' he said, plunging his hands into his pockets and moving toward the stairs. My heart sank a little, thinking he was heading back to bed, although since he was fully dressed, it appeared he hadn't even made it that far.

'Have you been home long?' I inwardly kicked myself. *That's none of your bloody business! No questions.*

If Ben seemed annoyed by the question he didn't show it. 'Only an hour. I just crept in here to check on Grace, and there she was, looking at me with those big eyes of hers.' He was staring into the distance as though he were in another place, and he smiled just like the first time I'd seen him walk into Grace's nursery on Lafayette. It had given me hope that this ivory-towered monster of Manhattan had a glimmer of softness. Despite being able to do little more than read her a bedtime story, he loved her deeply, that was evident. I saw it in his eyes, which matched Grace's. I saw it in the way he carried her as if she was made of the most delicate china.

It was something to behold, and I was saddened when he blinked and shuttered the emotion, snapping back into the Ben Worthington I had come to know.

'I've turned the monitor back on, so if Grace wakes for a feed or —'

'I've got it, thanks,' I said.

Ben turned down the stairs and I stepped forward and grabbed the banister.

'So does this mean I'm not fired?'

Ben looked at me with a curious mixture of confusion and amusement in his eyes, one that made me feel foolish for asking.

A ghost of a smile passed over his mouth, but it disappeared as quickly as it had come, and he plastered that serious expression onto his face. 'Only if you spoil the ending to *Charlotte's Web*,' he said and continued down the stairs, leaving me smiling and wondering if I had seriously just dreamt the entire exchange.

Chapter Ten

It was a beautiful sunny day and I had longed to take Grace for a walk in her pram. I had wanted to go to Bleeker Street and pick up some cupcakes from the Magnolia Bakery for afternoon tea in the park, then maybe sit out on the roof terrace with Grace in her bouncer while I read to her. But I couldn't do any of that, not with Penny Worthington about to arrive. I had to focus on making sure everything was perfectly in place. The fridge and cupboards were stocked with nutritional food; I had fresh fruit in the bowl, and fresh flowers on the table. There was bottled water and freshly ground coffee. Mercifully the cleaner had been the day before, so if Penny wanted to run a white glove over a mantle she was welcome to do so.

There was only one way to get things done in a five-storey house with a baby: strap them to you. As if continually climbing the stairs wasn't hard enough, transporting Grace around in a BabyBjorn carrier was giving me a serious cardio workout. Luckily, Grace seemed to love the motion, and why wouldn't she? I would have given anything to be carried around for the day, especially after surviving on less than four hours of sleep.

'Okay, Grace, if you're not going to sleep tonight, that's fine, but I really, really need you to be happy today, like seriously happy, when Grandma gets here.'

Grace stared up at me as I folded the laundry, screwing up her face as if over being strapped to my chest. She grizzled a little and rubbed at her face.

I sighed. 'Just one day, please.'

But before I could panic about Grace's trembling chin and reddening face, the doorbell rang. On cue, Grace let the floodgates open, wailing at the top of her impressive lungs. *This could not be happening.*

Leaving the pile of folded washing on the bench, I endeavoured to soothe Grace, swaying from side to side while trying to free her from my body.

'Here we go, Gracie, you're free, is that better? Don't cry, we have company.'

And as if to press the point the doorbell sounded again.

Jesus. Impatient, much? Unlike Penny Worthington, I didn't have a doorman or maid service, there was just me. No wonder she was expecting me to fail. She was probably already rolling her eyes at her driver.

'Just a sec,' I yelled, which was probably incredibly uncouth of me, but by the third doorbell ring I didn't care – by now Penny would be able to hear Grace's screams, so what did it matter? Before she even set foot in the house she was judging me, and I was doomed. I adjusted Grace against my shoulder and opened the door, only to find not Penny Worthington, but a man – a much younger man, though unmistakably a Worthington. Possibly with even more striking and clearer blue eyes than his siblings, but maybe that was the sunlight? His hair was brown, with a little length to it, and even though he was a step down from me I could tell he wasn't that tall, probably my height – five-four. He was impeccably dressed in a tailored suit but without the formality of a tie.

His surprise mirrored my own as I snapped my mouth closed, looking past him to see a car waiting for him: definitely a Worthington.

'Well, this neighborhood just gets better and better looking,' he quipped.

'Sorry, can I help you?'

'Oh, sorry, I'm Alistair,' he said, holding his hand out.

I shook it the customary three times. He had said his name with some kind of expectation that a light bulb would go off. It didn't; I was still very much in the dark.

He laughed. 'You have no idea who I am.'

'Sorry, I don't.'

'That's okay, my ego is only slightly damaged. I'm Alistair Worthington. I'm Ben's baby brother.'

Okay, so that I did not guess. 'Oh, right, sorry, I'm not fully up to speed on who's who in the zoo, so to speak.'

Alistair looked at me as if trying to solve a puzzle. 'You're Australian?'

Grace's cries had become louder, and I was amazed he could even pick it out. 'Guilty,' I said, rocking Grace as a means to soothe her.

Alistair's eyes shifted to her and he smiled. 'This must be Grace. I've never met my niece before, I've been away.'

'Oh, really? I'm sorry, she's just tired. Do you want to come in, Ben's not in but —'

'Oh no.' He held up his hand. 'That's okay, I just thought I'd take a chance and call in. I was surprised that the door opened. Sorry, I didn't catch your name . . .'

'Oh, Sarah, I'm Grace's au pair.'

When Alistair smiled there was no mistaking his being Ben's brother, he was just a younger, shorter, clean-shaven version. And he didn't look like he bore the weight of the world on his shoulders.

'Well, things have certainly changed. I never had an au pair who looked like you when I was a boy,' he teased.

I didn't know quite how to respond to that. Luckily Grace was squirming enough in my arms to give me a distraction.

'More's the pity,' he added. 'Lovely to meet you, Sarah, and Miss Grace, I'm sure we will be seeing much more of each other.' He bowed his head and readied himself to leave. 'Oh, by the way, can you do me a small favour? Don't tell Ben I stopped by, I want to surprise him.'

'Okay, well, did you want to surprise your mother? I'm actually expecting her sometime today.'

Alistair's smiled broadened. 'Oh, you poor thing.'

I wanted to wholeheartedly agree with him, but thought better of it.

His eyes went from me to Grace. 'I'll tell you what, since you're doing me a small favour, I'll do one in return,' he said, reaching into his suit pocket and retrieving his phone, then dialling with a devilish look in his eyes. He placed his finger over his lips.

'Frieda, is Mother there? It's her prodigal son, Alistair.'

I jigged Grace more intently, urging her not to cry; her face changed from thunder to smiles and I knew I was onto something as I continued to bounce and make silly silent faces, praying she would stay happy.

'Hello, Mother, yes, I'm back in New York, just landed.' He winked at me. 'Just wondered what you were up to today – I thought I might take you out on the town?' He listened intently, his eyes shifting to me and Grace in the doorway; even Grace seemed to be transfixed by the conversation.

'Oh, you don't say? Well, surely this Sarah won't mind if you leave it for another day?'

My heart dared leap from fear to hope.

'Of course you can, slip into your best Chanel, I'm on my way . . . Okay, excellent, see you soon,' he said, and ended the call.

'Well, as much as I am relieved, I'm also partially offended that it didn't take much to sway her away from us.'

Alistair laughed. 'Don't be, she hasn't seen me in months, so it's been a while since I've taken her out for lunch. There was no way she would turn it down. Now you're free for another day.'

I sighed. 'Thank you, I appreciate that. I haven't even been here for a week, so we're still finding our way, aren't we, Gracie?'

Grace shoved her fist into her slobbery mouth.

'Well, if that's the case, you won't need Mother on your doorstep. I'll make sure she's suitably distracted until you settle in,' he said, giving me another boyish grin.

'Thanks, Alistair.' I could hardly believe that, aside from Nikki, there was another nice Worthington in the world. I had been convinced there was no such thing.

'My pleasure,' he said. 'Remember, you never saw me.'

I shrugged. 'I didn't see a thing.'

Alistair laughed. 'Well, we'll make a Worthington out of you yet.' And with that he slid into the car and was driven away.

~

Meeting Alistair Worthington was the unexpected delight of my day; well, that and the freedom of no Penny Worthington visiting. Even Grace's mood seemed to have picked up, now that she wasn't feeding off my vibes of impending doom. We didn't get to Magnolia Bakery or the park, but we did manage to lounge under the umbrella on the roof terrace. Me, Grace and a bottle of formula on the daybed: things were definitely looking up. Sure, most people my age were probably binge drinking and partying and sleeping their lives away. But all was not lost: come the weekend and my days off, I wouldn't have a baby permanently strapped to me. I would go out exploring, because, to be frank, the thought of Ben and me being in the same house all day did nothing for me; a supreme conversationalist he was not and I was harbouring a terror of the weekend dynamic. In the Liebenberg house my weekends were treated as sacred and were respected, aside from the odd one here and there when I had to work. I wasn't entirely sure how weekends would work here. Could Ben change a nappy? Sterilise bottles and prep formula, handle the endless crying should it strike Grace not to be all smiles?

As each scenario ran through my mind, I felt sick. Maybe I would stick close this weekend, lurk in the shadows. I remembered the words of warning from the au pair agency when I was sent to the Liebenbergs: don't overstep barriers or blur the lines by falling into the trap of helping. I had to keep that in mind. Besides, Ben was a strong, capable businessman who navigated tough waters; I mean, Penny Worthington was his mother, for God's sake. Alistair himself had said he had an au pair; had there been a maternal influence on Ben at all, could he be blamed for the way he behaved?

Things were just so much simpler where I was from. We grew up without much money: Dad was a labourer, while Mum did cash-in-hand work cleaning hotel rooms. I thought about Mum being in Frieda's place with Penny Worthington and it made me mad. There was a distinct difference in our social statuses, and from day one, Penny and Emily had made me feel my place; the only people who hadn't were Nikki and Alistair, even in our brief meetings.

The more I thought about it, the more adamant I was that there would be no lines crossed. Ben would just have to step up and be a dad, his arms weren't painted on.

And as the mood pushed me in the right direction, I picked up the iPad and started researching my weekend's activities. After all, I did have a tourist wishlist to fulfil and come Saturday I was heading to my number-one spot.

Hello, Tiffany's!

Chapter Eleven

With Grace down for a nap that I knew I would pay for later in the night, I curled up on the nursing chair. I wondered where Ben had gotten his tattered copy of Charlotte's Web from – it was by far the only thing in the entire apartment that seemed to have a bit of personality, a history. Even in Grace's room the walls were blank – so much wall space and nothing hanging there, like a rental property. It would be a little while before Grace could provide any paintings for the fridge, but it wasn't out of the question to reconnect with my roots and get back into painting again. It'd be nice to create something for Grace. Painting was the one activity I'd loved to share with the boys back home; on a sunny day we would sit in the garden and they'd attempt to tell a story with scribblings about cars and family portraits with mythical pet dogs, rainbows and chimney smoke, while I tried to tap into a lost part of myself from my high school days, painting semi-abstract art with blocks of colour. At the start I was way out of practice and frustrated enough to think that the boys' paintings were turning out better than mine, until one evening when Dr Liebenberg observed one of my paintings drying on the clothes horse in the laundry and declared his love for it: 'It's exactly what I've been looking for, for the office. It's perfect.'

At first I'd thought he was just being polite, but when he asked me how much I wanted for it, the smile fell from my face.

'Every artist has a price,' he'd insisted, and for the first and only time in my life, someone bartered the price up. Every amount I mentioned, Dennis Liebenberg laughed, then wrote out a cheque, scribbling his signature with his barely readable doctor's handwriting, tearing it from the stub and passing it to me.

'You have to own what you do, Sarah.'

I've never forgotten those words of wisdom; I've also never forgotten the shock of reading the cheque: three hundred and fifty dollars, substantially different to the twenty-five I'd originally asked for. I'd thought him mad, but, hey, each to their own.

With the support of Lorraine Liebenberg, I'd nervously gone into Rosie's Café and asked if it was possible to display my work on the walls in return for a small commission if they sold. Rosie seemed unfazed and allowed me to hang my work with my signature and a price tag in the corner. I had thought myself quite the artist, even if the rest of the town didn't seem to be as enthusiastic about my art as Dr Liebenberg. As far as I knew, the pieces were still for sale in ol' Rosie's Café. A bit of a blow to the ego. But it was nice to know there was a Sarah Williams original hanging over the fireplace somewhere in remote Slovenia. How many artists could claim that?

I was positively giddy about looking online for supplies. Entering in the details of my credit card, I decided to start out small, a basic sketch pad and pencils, easy enough to slip into my tote bag and transport anywhere.

As I clicked on the button to complete my purchase, the doorbell rang. I checked my iPad. Surely express delivery wasn't *that* express?

I revelled in the freedom of running without a baby attached to me, making sure I got to the door before the bell rang a second time and woke her. I promised myself that the first thing I was going to make with my new materials was a 'Do Not Disturb – baby sleeping' sign. And that would go even for Penny Worthington.

I hoped this wasn't her, swinging by for a post-lunch visit with Alistair. This time I thought to spy through the peephole on my tippy toes. I smiled broadly and opened the door with glee.

'Hello!' I said, a little bit too high-pitched.

Nikki Fitzgerald stood before me, looking dishevelled yet still pretty with her ash-blonde hair unruly around her face and dressed in what looked like a maternity kaftan, sunglasses and carrying an oversized bag.

'Quick, I have one hour of peace so I have to make the most of it,' she said, causing me to step aside as she waddled through the door and dumped her bag on the floor like a teenager's backpack after school. She shucked off her shoes and placed her hands on her lower back with a groan before perching her sunglasses on top of her head and parting her curtain of hair. Her cheeks were flushed, and I could tell she was struggling to lug around her belly.

'Are you okay? Do you want a drink?'

'Yes, please, you will be my best friend,' she said, supporting herself on the banister.

'You're not going to go into labour, are you?'

Nikki laughed. 'I should be so lucky, and why does everyone keep asking me that? It's like everyone is scared to be around me or something. I'm beginning to get a complex.'

'Hey, we're just looking out for the pregnant lady,' I said, holding up my hands and heading down the hall.

'I like you, your accent is funny,' she said.

'Funnier than an Irish accent?' I asked, veering toward the fridge.

'Ah, yeah, Seamus, bless his tartan socks. I swear when we first started dating, I couldn't understand a word he was saying.'

I laughed, pouring a lemon squash from the jug. 'And now?'

'Now? Now I'm his interpreter.'

'Well, I look forward to meeting him,' I said, handing the glass to her.

'Thanks.' She gulped the lemonade, the ice cubes tinkling against the edge of the glass. She drank like she had been stranded in the Sahara, smacking her lips together in appreciation. 'Oh, that's lovely.' It was only then that she seemed to be back in the moment, skimming her eyes around the lounge. 'Where's Gracie?'

I sat down opposite her, pulling my legs to my chest on the plush leather lounge. 'She's down for a nap.'

'Is that child ever awake? I swear, every time I come for cuddles . . .'

'Trust me, she's awake plenty. Maybe come for cuddles any time between one and five am, apparently those are the party hours.'

Nikki laughed, sipping another mouthful. 'No wonder Emily offloaded her quick smart.'

I so wanted to ask about Grace's mum. As much as I had settled in and felt comfortable hanging out with Nikki, there was always this disconcerting feeling pressing on the back of my mind, one that I just had to have answered.

'You know what really irks me?'

Nikki's question pulled me from my thoughts. 'What's that?'

'My darling brother is an architect and he couldn't even install a goddamn lift for his favourite pregnant sister to access the roof terrace on a beautiful sunny day.'

'I know, right? Did you want to go up? It's beautiful today.'

'Oh, you tease. Honestly, I don't think I would make a single flight. I guess we'll have to settle for the garden. Come, we'll sit outside, and you can tell me how you're finding the Big Apple. I now have fifty minutes left to listen.' Nikki stretched out her hand in the universal sign for 'Help me? I'm huge.'

'If you ever get lonely in this big, beautiful, architecturally sound townhouse, you should bring Gracie over to Brooklyn for a day out. One afternoon at my house with the horde and you will think loneliness is a godsend.' Nikki flexed her swollen feet as she reclined on the sun lounge.

The courtyard was immaculately landscaped with retaining walls, overgrown ivy and charcoal grey pavers. The foliage was so well-established that the sun had a hard time piercing through the canopy. It was like being in a jungle with a distant city soundtrack. If you wanted a hit of vitamin D, the roof terrace was the way to go.

'That sounds awesome, I'd love to.'

Nikki and I chatted about our days, but, unsure if my Alistair secret was just for Ben or if it applied to all Worthington siblings, I decided to leave that little detail out.

'I love the sound of your painting,' Nikki said. 'I wish I could do something like that, but I don't have any talents.'

'Everybody has something: music, writing?'

'Does breeding count? I tend to do that very well.' Nikki laughed, rubbing at her belly.

I blushed. 'I suppose so.'

'Oh, how depressing, Sarah. I don't even have a hobby.' Nikki whined like a bored child. In many ways she reminded me of a delinquent, rebellious teenager, so different to her icy older brother and sister.

'We'll think of something.'

'Don't bother, once the baby comes I won't have time to shower, let alone dabble in pottery. Isn't it utterly depressing how we lose such a huge part of ourselves when we're trying to keep these little screaming human beings alive?'

'I hardly think I'm an authority on the subject. I mean, I get weekends off.'

Nikki clutched her heart. 'Oh, that sounds divine – a whole weekend.' She scooted up in her seat. 'I'm going to have to live vicariously through you. What have you got planned? Tell me in the most intricate detail, don't leave anything out.'

'Well,' I winced, 'first, I think I might sleep in.'

'Mary, Mother of God, tell me more.'

'Are you sure? I don't want to rub it in.'

Nikki laughed. 'Sarah, my love, any time you're having a down day, feeling alone, homesick, as though the sleep deprivation might tip you over the edge, I want you to think of the woman in Brooklyn dreaming of being you, even if it's just for an hour.' Nikki glanced at her watch.

'Ah, crap, an hour that's already over. I better get going. There will be rioting on the streets of Brooklyn if I'm not back before they close the door to the city.'

My heart sank. 'Are you sure? I was just about to check in on Grace.'

'Well, in that case I definitely better go; one cuddle from her and I won't want to leave.'

I followed Nikki to the front door, helping her with her bag. Although I knew it was probably a huge mistake, I just couldn't let her leave without at least posing the question.

'Nikki, can I ask you something?' I said, leaning against the edge of the door.

'Let me guess, you want to know the best Thai takeaway around here?'

I did, but I didn't want to confuse my purpose. 'Ah, not exactly.'

'I have three minutes, so ask away,' she said, looking at her watch again, which surprised me since she didn't strike me as the most punctual of people.

I felt nervous in spite of my determination. I looked directly at the glowing, smiling Nikki, the closest thing I had to an actual friend in this city. If I was going to ask anyone it had to be her – there was no one else.

'Will Ben be okay with looking after Grace on the weekend? I mean, if I'm out?'

And when I saw her smile fall from her face and darkness set in her eyes, I wished I had never asked. I'd been so adamant about not overstepping my boundaries – maybe questioning her brother's parenting ability was a bridge too far.

Nikki sighed. 'He's going to have to be, Sarah, he's been apart from reality for far too long, and now's the time he has to step up, whether he likes it or not. Just promise me one thing.'

'What's that?'

'Let him do it. No matter how much every instinct tells you to step in and do the right thing, unless it's a life-or-death situation, just leave it with him.'

I breathed out a laugh, thinking those were the exact words Ben had uttered to me about contacting him during business hours. And I had done as he'd asked, just gotten on with it, battled through the uncertainty. Nikki's tough love did make me feel better, if not totally anxiety-free, but she was right; I had to let Ben step up to the mark. And for that reason, come Saturday, I would be anywhere but here.

Chapter Twelve

On Friday I received a succinct message:

Village tonight. B

I had resigned myself to the fact that it was going to be Grace and me alone again. The rest of the week had rolled on quite nicely. No more unexpected visitors, and even Penny Worthington hadn't made good on her threat to visit; she was probably reacquainting herself with her prodigal son. I wondered if Ben knew about Alistair's return. But then I wondered a lot of things, like did Ben even like beef stroganoff, which I was cooking for dinner tonight? I had pretty much been flying blind all week. Not that I had minded, there was a certain comfort in just hanging out with Grace; we were settling into a new routine: afternoon strolls to the park, followed by bathtime and storytime. I was even becoming accustomed to what her cries meant, and her sleep patterns.

I started to prepare for Ben's homecoming by peeling extra vegetables. It intrigued me that he didn't refer to the townhouse as home; did Lafayette Street mean more to him? Were Grace and I just his dirty little secret from the corporate world? As for Grace's mum, she was still a mystery. Not even Nikki, the one person I thought might have some answers, had offered a clue. But after our conversation in the hotel bar I knew better than to go there again.

'Dad's coming home tonight, Grace,' I said, aligning the remote controls and fluffing the cushions on the couch as she twisted and kicked on her little rug on the floor. I blew out a breath as I looked around the lounge to see if everything was as Ben had left it.

'I wish I was as carefree as you are, Grace,' I said. I lay next to her on the rug, my head resting on my palm as I placed my finger in her hand for her to grab and squeeze. 'If you sleep more than three hours through the night for your dad, you and I will be having some serious words, you hear me?'

Grace's eyes moved to my face at the sound of my voice.

'Yes, I'm talking to you.'

A gummy smile formed, and her kicking and gurgling increased with excitement.

'This is not a laughing matter, Gracie Worthington, I am very serious indeed,' I said, tickling her belly and making her squirm until the oven timer buzzed, the reminder to check dinner. Grace flinched from the sound, her smiley, happy face dropping into misery as she thought about whether she wanted to cry or not. She decided she did.

'Oh, Gracie,' I sighed, sitting up and bringing her to my shoulder, rubbing her back soothingly as she cried and drooled on my top. 'Your dad is going to have so much fun with you.'

~

I don't know what had me thinking Ben would get home late, that we would all be in bed, a note on the bench telling him dinner was in the oven. Maybe it's what I wished would happen? So when I heard the front door open while it was daylight, well, I wasn't entirely prepared. His footsteps came up the hall and, as I mashed the potatoes, each step made my heart beat faster, and my mashing became more frenzied, the steam of the potatoes curling the wisps of hair that framed my face. My cheeks felt flushed and I suddenly panicked about having seasoned dinner enough. Shit, had I put salt in the potatoes at all? Was this dinner too rich, maybe Ben was a kale and couscous man with an intolerance to dairy? Surely this was a life-or-death question. This meal could be a disaster.

I was just about ready to throw the masher in the sink and break down uncontrollably in a pile of potato when Ben rounded the corner carrying a plastic bag. He stopped dead in his tracks.

'Oh, you cooked,' he said, looking as if the thought left a sour taste in his mouth.

I remembered all the times my mother went off at us kids for not appreciating the meals she had slaved over. I gripped the masher with white-knuckled intensity, trying to remain cool, not an easy feat when standing over a saucepan of hot potatoes. My eyes went to the plastic bag Ben was holding as he placed it on the bench.

'I bought Chinese for dinner. I can see communication is going to have to get better between us,' he said in a way that made me feel like this was somehow my fault. Was he serious? Mr Don't-contact-me-unless-it's-a-life-or-death-situation was speaking about communication? I wanted to bludgeon him with my masher.

I opted for a language he would recognise: passive-aggression. If Penny Worthington had taught me one thing in my short time here, it was that being passive-aggressive was by far the most infuriating way to communicate.

'That's okay. The stroganoff has been slow cooking for four hours, but I'm sure it will keep for tomorrow,' I said, casually washing the masher in the sink.

Ben didn't move, but out of the corner of my eye I could see him staring at me, probably equally pissed that his thoughtful gesture was not being recognised. After all, I thought bitterly, he had hunted and gathered for his family, surely that deserved a medal? It took every fibre of my being to reel in my snarkiness when I turned to him. I plastered a calm smile across my face as if it was no bother at all and placed the lid on the pot of potatoes.

'Well, it smells . . . nice,' he managed, in a way that sounded foreign to him, like he had to search for the word required to give a compliment. Yeah, he hadn't exactly pulled it off.

'Thanks,' I said.

'Listen, Chinese tastes better the next day if you want to—'

'No, it's okay, this will keep.'

'So will this, it's no trouble to—'

'I know, it's no trouble either.' Ugh. God, this was painful.

He had been in the door less than five minutes and we were already dancing around each other awkwardly, trying to balance contempt and civility over something as simple as dinner. For the first time I wished Grace would cry out, break the awkwardness and take me away from this situation. There was something very clear, though: Ben was not the kind of man who backed down or negotiated. He ignored my insistence and placed the takeaway in the fridge as if the argument was non-negotiable – we were having what I had cooked and that was that. Now I felt anxious, hoping that it was something worth eating after all. The weekend was going to be a nightmare.

As if escaping any more arguing, Ben did the one thing that seemed most unnatural to him: he walked over to where Grace lay on her blanket, delighting in the mobile that danced above her. Instead of getting down to her level, he stood there, looking at her, a lightness in his eyes, a smile tugging at his mouth. I wanted him to pick her up, for him to prove me wrong. Show me he was capable of some form of emotion, that he wasn't a robot, functioning solely in the business world. I wanted to storm over there, pick up Grace and shove her into his chest, tell him to bloody man-up.

How on earth was he going to manage this weekend on his own? Had he ever been alone with his daughter? Did he even know how to change a nappy? What the ratio was for formula, or how long to heat it?

Okay, Sarah, stop! I was already crossing the line and the weekend hadn't arrived yet.

As if sensing my concern, Ben looked at me. 'She seems so happy, I don't want to disturb her,' he said.

If being disturbed meant the warmth of her dad's arms then I was sure it was worth the risk.

'Might as well get in one last cuddle before I dish up.' I tried to keep it light by saying something my mum might. And much to my amazement, it worked. Even as anxiety showed on his stern face, he approached Grace, lifting her as if she were the world's most precious thing. The distant, abrasive man was gone; here stood a dad, looking into the eyes of his daughter, a surprise dimple appearing in the corner of his left cheek. I had never seen him like this, so overwhelmed with love for the squirming bundle in his arms. This was what it was all about, this was instinct, this was natural. I had worried needlessly, thinking he wouldn't be able to cope. Of course he could, there was nothing more protective and reassuring than a father's love. It was going to be okay.

And then of course the worst thing happened. Grace's face screwed up as she began to scream. Ben looked at me, his confidence shattered, as if he he had somehow caused her misery. And as much as I knew I shouldn't, I went to his side.

Before I could offer him reassurance that this was nothing to do with anything he had done, he handed her over and walked away.

'I'm going to take a shower.'

What I would have given for Grace to have continued screaming the house down, but she stopped crying and settled as soon as she was in my arms. This was not good.

Grace's teary eyes landed on me and she was okay, squirming and happy now the strange man had gone. My heart sank. As much as I wanted to insist that Ben stick it out and talk to Grace, soothe her, he had shut down and it broke my heart. Here was this beautiful little girl with no mother in sight and a dad without a clue who wanted – *needed* – to be loved. My arms could not be her sole comfort, it just wasn't right.

It might have been the Worthington way for children to be seen and not heard, raised by staff members and nannies, but in my world it took a village to raise a child, and if that meant that I would have to help bridge the gap then I would do it for her.

Somehow.

Chapter Thirteen

I served Ben's dinner and knocked on his bedroom door to tell him it was ready, but he never came down. And much as I had imagined the night might go, I took his plate from the table, wrapped it in foil and left a note for him with a recommendation on how to heat it. I took Grace to the bathroom for her nightly lavender-scented bath, hoping against hope that it would make her drowsy, so drowsy she might sleep eight solid hours. One could dream, right?

Rubbing her dry with the aid of baby powder and a few songs out of my nursery-rhyme archives, Grace was either bored by me, or she was actually tired, her little bow shaped mouth expelling a yawn. I wasn't willing to let myself get too excited about the latter possibility. I glanced over at the nursing chair where *Charlotte's Web* lay exactly as I had left it. It was too much to hope that Ben might appear to sit with Grace and pick up where he had left off.

I laid Grace down, crept to the door and waited with my heart in my mouth to see if she would settle. It seemed that fatigue was on my side for once. Sarah – 1, Grace – 0.

Never knowing how long any victory would last, I decided to ready myself for an early bedtime too. Pulling my long hair free from my bun and allowing it to tumble over my shoulders felt incredible. My back was killing me. I stretched out the pain caused by having to carry a little baby up and down flights of stairs. I was going to need an extra-long hot shower tonight, but before I could give into the joys of such a thing I heard the unmistakable sound of movement from below, the clinking of cutlery in the kitchen, the closing of a microwave door. I winced at the beeps, hoping that I had thought to switch the baby monitor off in the lounge and that the noise wouldn't wake Grace. But that wasn't the thought that had me coming to an abrupt halt on the stairs, a line creasing my brow. Oh no, it was something else entirely as the unmistakable aroma hit me. Chinese food.

'You've got to be kidding me,' I said under my breath, walking down the stairs. This time I didn't worry about stepping as delicately as before; if anything, I wanted my presence to be known as I swung around the bottom banister and padded toward the kitchen. Never once did Ben pause, not even when I came into view. There he was, hair damp from the shower, dressed as casually as I had ever seen him, in jeans and a simple grey tee. As he retrieved his reheated Chinese food from the microwave, he seemed more like a uni student ready to dive into some tucker than a successful businessman about to have dinner in his multi-million-dollar townhouse. If he felt guilty about not eating my home-cooked meal made with love and questionable seasoning, he didn't act like it.

'Did Grace go down all right?' he asked, and I wondered if he cared about the answer or if he was just making small talk as he plucked a succulent prawn from his plate with his chopsticks.

His words jogged my memory, and I went over to the lounge monitor to turn it off. I wanted to say something smart about dinner, but then another part of me didn't want to feed his power by having him think I cared too much about it. So he fancied Chinese tonight – I just had to let it go.

'She was tired, a little grizzly,' I said, thinking maybe that would alleviate any thought he had of having upset her. While I had his attention I thought it best to tackle the things that kept me up at night, in addition to Grace.

'So are you right with her? I mean, for tomorrow?' It was a simple enough question, one that I never would have expected to cause such a glare.

'You mean, will I be able to cope on your day off?' he asked, his words laced with sarcasm.

'No, I mean . . .' What did I mean? Wasn't that exactly what I was getting at? I wanted him to reassure me that I was okay to enjoy my day off. I know that it was written in the working hours of my contract, but I wanted to hear him say it, to do as the Liebenbergs would have done: ask me what I had planned for the weekend and tell me to enjoy myself. But I wasn't in Kansas any more, and Ben Worthington was a far cry from the Liebenbergs. The sooner I started to realise the difference, the better.

'Well, if you need me for anything, you have my cell number,' I said, moving past him to grab a bottle of water from the fridge. It was only then that I realised I had his full attention, noticing how his eyes quickly snapped upwards; he had been looking at my hair.

'What? Is there something —'

'No, I just haven't seen you with it down before.'

'Oh, yeah, well, I'm sure Grace would love to get her little fists into my hair and yank every piece out if she could. Hours of fun.'

A hint of a smile touched Ben's lips and I wasn't sure if it was the thought of my hair getting pulled out that was so amusing or if it was the mention of his daughter.

'Yeah, well, goodni—'

'Going somewhere tomorrow?' he asked.

My mouth closed, and I frowned. I felt silly telling him my plans because, turning them over in my mind, they seemed clichéd. I could just imagine the eye roll that would result from saying I was heading to Tiffany's. Screw it. The Worthingtons' secrecy made me want to be nothing but an open book. I lifted my chin as I unscrewed the lid to my bottle of water and took a long swig.

'Actually, I'm going to Tiffany's.'

'For breakfast?' he said. It wasn't quite an eye roll but there was an undercurrent of smartarse in his words.

'Nah, I was thinking more of a brunch thing, I might have a bit of a lie-in,' I said, thinking, there, I had done it. I loved my sleep and seeing as I would be off the clock, I fully intended to claim some of it back. If I was expected to somehow function during the week, maybe I could do a weekend catch-up. It seemed reasonable to my mind.

'Well, sounds like you have it all figured out then,' he said as he shovelled more rice into his mouth.

'Yes. Yes, I do.'

A silence fell between us. I excused myself with a nod, and was at the door before he spoke again.

'Just one thing,' he said, and dread swept over me. What did he want? For me to be back by a curfew?

I turned, trying not to look as though I was worried about what he had to say next.

As if sensing my unease, Ben drew out the silence a little longer as he chewed thoughtfully. 'Don't forget to let your hair down,' he said.

I couldn't help but blink with surprise. Was he being . . . playful? This was different, but I took it for what it was: the approval I was looking for. A newfound hope made me smile in return.

'Yeah, maybe I will.'

Chapter Fourteen

'm not sure why I'd believed that, come the stroke of midnight on a Friday night, I'd be handing over the reins and baby monitor to Ben. Because that hadn't happened, and now at 2:11 am Grace was crying so loud neither of us would need a baby monitor. I groaned. Rubbing the sleep from my eyes and peeling the doona aside, I cursed myself for not clarifying the night-shift duty. Half-asleep, I navigated to the doorway, bumping into the dresser and cursing as I did every time I walked into it at some ungodly hour of the morning. I tried to wake up a little more to make sure I got down the staircase without breaking my neck. I arrived at exactly the same time as Ben, equally sleepy and dazed, his hair a mess. He scratched at his bare chest, and his light blue pyjama pants rested low on his narrow hips.

Seeing him half-dressed like that, I was suddenly awake. My eyes roamed over the impressive indentations along his stomach, a toned, smoothed-out landscape I couldn't help but want to reach out and explore.

'It's okay, I got this,' he croaked as he zigzagged toward Grace's room.

I suddenly found myself grabbing his arm. 'Wait.'

He stopped, his eyes narrowing at my hand on his arm, which felt like granite under my fingers. He opened his mouth to speak but I placed my finger to my lips, signalling for silence.

'She's gone back to sleep,' I whispered. We'd hit a spot of luck: for the first time in, well, forever, Grace had managed to settle herself.

Ben tilted his head as though he didn't entirely believe me.

'I swear if she sleeps for you on the weekend, I will be so annoyed.' I half-laughed.

'Doesn't Grace sleep?'

It was then I realised that, of course, he wouldn't know, he had been here only one night, and before me he'd probably never truly been here. Why would he know his daughter's sleeping habits? He was simply a parent who got to breeze in in the daylight hours and enjoy the best of what their children had to give – the smiles and the cuddles – before handing them back for a nappy change and to wipe the drool away. Welcome to reality, buddy!

I was suddenly less anxious about the weekend and began to look forward to it. A few days of reality might have Ben eating my home-cooked meals and being a little more appreciative.

'No, Ben, Grace doesn't sleep. Well, not for long, anyway.'

He seemed troubled by this. 'Is there something wrong with her?'

'No, there is nothing wrong with her,' I said, turning to the stairs.

'Maybe it's hereditary. I don't sleep much either.'

'You'll be the perfect night-time companion for her then,' I said, smirking at him, but by the stony expression on his face, he wasn't amused. 'Look, she's a baby – a baby who has to settle into her surrounds. I'm new in her life too. Grace will adjust in time.'

And then I said something so stupid I could have kicked myself. 'Just yell out if you need anything.' *No, no, noooo, Sarah, shut up! Don't cross the line!*

But I couldn't help it, I could tell he was worried and anxious; it was the first real sign of vulnerability he'd shown and I couldn't help but feel sorry for him. Besides, if he was anxious, Grace would be too. She'd pick up on how he was feeling and it would not make for a happy family.

Something flared in Ben's eyes and his mood seemed to darken. He squared his shoulders, becoming the confident, no-nonsense businessman once again. 'Thanks, but I think I can handle my own child,' he said coolly.

Right. I wanted to tell him where to go. Instead I nodded. 'No worries,' I said, as light and carefree as I could manage. 'Goodnight, Ben.'

And good luck!

Chapter Fifteen

had an amazing, deep, dreamless sleep, right?

Wrong. So, so wrong.

Not only did Grace's cries wake me, but I was ever aware and pained by the knowledge she was having a restless night, and I could hear Ben pacing, trying to comfort her. I had gotten out of my bed several times to lurk on the stairway and it took every ounce of my willpower not to interfere. Even though it was the night from hell for all of us, Grace finally settled at 6 am, and Ben survived his first night as a single parent.

So I wasn't exactly replenished, but I was nevertheless high-spirited. Forgoing the sleep-in, I was showered and dressed by 8 am and headed down the stairs expecting a quiet household.

The aroma of freshly plunged coffee hit me first, then the sound of the radio playing jazz from the lounge. It was an incredibly civilised way to greet a New York City weekend, but when I entered the room, an unexpected sight greeted me. The same topless, pyjama-bottom-clad Ben was on the couch reading *The New York Times* with a happy, inquisitive Grace propped on his lap. He was intently focusing on the print through black-framed reading glasses, his hair in disarray, a light stubble dusting his jawline. My God, if he wasn't the sexiest thing I had ever seen in my life. Aside from the scene being picture perfect enough for a designer catalogue, I couldn't help but smile at the cushion fortress on either side of his lap, a preventative measure should Grace tumble over, not that that could happen with his strong, muscular arms caging her in protectively. It was then I knew Grace would be fine, that I could go out and enjoy my day without having to worry about their wellbeing. Hell, Ben even had leftover beef stroganoff prepared for his lunch, all the washing was done and the house was clean – what was there to worry about?

'The coffee has just been plunged if you want some,' he said without once taking his eyes from the paper. It was a welcome distraction from my instinct to go straight to Grace. I had to snap out of that headspace. The sooner I got out of here, the better.

I grinned as I poured my coffee, watching Ben's ongoing battle to prevent Grace reaching for the newspaper, no doubt wanting nothing more than to tear it and shove it in her mouth,.

I glanced at the paperwork on the bench: the instructions for the baby formula. The steriliser was plugged in and brewing a batch of clean bottles. If I was going to do something out of the kindness of my heart I could maybe have offered to watch Grace while he took a shower and got dressed, but I shut the thought down. I would give Ben the baby-transporting advice if he wanted to get things done and that would be it. I really had to go!

Finishing my coffee, I rinsed out the cup and placed it on the sink. I could get something to eat while I was out and about, otherwise I would end up making something here and cooking breakfast for Ben as well. I had to be all about tough love on the weekends, I *had* to be.

'I see you have your hair down.'

Ben was in the same position. Either he had amazing peripheral vision or he had managed to sneak a peek when I was in the kitchen, but then I realised the more likely option as I met his eyes in the mirror over the mantel.

'It suits you,' he said matter-of-factly before looking down to his paper.

Although the comment sounded like he was reading an Ikea flat pack instruction sheet, it felt strange to hear something nice come out of his mouth.

I grabbed the BabyBjorn carrier and walked over to the lounge, placing it on the coffee table in front of him. Ben looked over his paper. Despite how damn sexy he looked from this angle, all I could do was smile at Gracie, who was as happy and bubbly as ever.

'I don't know where you get your energy from, Miss Gracie.' I tucked a strand of hair behind my ear.

'Youth.' Ben scoffed. 'What's this?' He folded his paper and looked at the BabyBjorn with interest.

'This right here is going to be your best friend,' I said, tapping it.

He looked confused.

'It's my secret weapon, I pretty much wouldn't get anything done without it. She might have a bit of a cry but at least she'll be in sight and you can talk to her. But if you set the day up with everything you need down here, then you shouldn't have to do too much lugging. I learnt that pretty early on,' I said, thinking back to the first day and how ducking upstairs with a screaming baby for a nappy change was not smart time management.

Ben nodded as if impressed. 'Well, thanks for the tip.'

'You're welcome,' I said, thinking my good deed was done for the day. As much as I was trying to be Miss Independent off the clock, I couldn't help myself. 'Well, I'll have my cell on me if you have any burning questions,' I said, backing away. I waved to Grace.

'Sarah, wait,' Ben called and I froze, my heart dropping at the sound of my name. I felt awful knowing that I would either have to be rude and say no – tough love – or buckle and help out, resenting him all the more for it.

I turned around. Ben came to stand beside me, awkwardly juggling Grace in his arms and accentuating all the ripped muscles in his tall, toned frame. I had to get a grip, this was a kind of cabin fever I didn't want to experience.

'Since you showed me your secret weapon, I guess I better reveal mine,' he said.

It was hard enough to concentrate with him half naked next to me, so the idea of him showing me his 'secret weapon' had me blinking in confusion. 'S-sorry?'

Manoeuvring Grace into a firmer hold, he grinned. 'Follow me.'

Standing on the stoop of a colonial townhouse in New York City with a baby and a half-naked man, I didn't think my life could get any more bizarre. But when I saw driver Dave parked out front in his shiny black Rolls Royce, I turned to Ben. I hadn't thought this was how my weekend would begin.

'Dave will take you anywhere you want to go in the city.'

Was he for real? I had planned to stroll through the streets, jump on the subway, get lost, ask for directions, stumble across some eateries en route to Fifth Avenue, do what any tourist might in the Big Apple. This was not the most typical way to immerse yourself in New York – not that I was in any way complaining.

'This hardly seems like a fair trade for a baby carrier,' I said.

Grace squirmed in Ben's arms, whacking him in the face with her little fist as he pulled his head away and squinted. 'Don't be so sure about that.'

Chapter Sixteen

Carrying my little Tiffany-blue bag of heaven, I bid Dave goodbye and bounded up the townhouse steps, skipping every other one, elated by the pleasure I had immersed myself in. It felt wrong, to have a chauffeur-driven car pull up in front of Tiffany & Co., only for me to emerge in jeans, sandals and a simple white tee. I was more California gal than New York chic. I'd never felt more like an imposter in my life, but as soon as I laid eyes on the iconic landmark of Tiffany's – *the* Tiffany's – starry-eyed wonder and giddy excitement settled over me. I crossed the pavement to stand in front of the window just as Holly Golightly had done all those decades before. I had vowed that I would not be leaving New York without a little Tiffany-blue box tied with a white bow, even if all I could afford was a paper clip. I'd approached the entrance and been greeted by a smiling doorman, who opened the door for me and said, 'Welcome to Tiffany.' I was in heaven.

The first day of the first weekend of my new life couldn't get much better.

Now, at the top of the townhouse stairs, my spirits were high enough to withstand the idea of spending the evening with Ben Worthington; I was excited to talk about my day with someone who could do more than gurgle and drool. As I unlocked the door, the last thing I expected was a mouth-watering scent drifting from the kitchen. Was Ben *cooking dinner*?

If he had managed to do a night shift, look after Grace and cook dinner on his first dad duty day, and still manage to look as good as he usually did, I was going to be annoyed. And I wouldn't be wholly convinced that he wasn't Superman. Maybe my first week of fatigue and settling into Grace's routine was something I was being overly sensitive about. I straightened my spine, feeling a new determination about my role; if Ben Worthington could pull it off then I would be just fine.

As I rounded the corner into the kitchen I went from newfound optimism to a record-scratching halt.

I wasn't one to forget a face. Especially a scowly, weathered, wrinkled one. Ruth from the Lafayette apartment turned from the simmering pot on the stove, regarding me with an unenthusiastic up-and-down glance. I felt like I was a teenager sprung sneaking in past curfew.

I tried not to feel alarmed as my insides churned. I put my things on the bench and lifted my handbag strap over my head. 'Where's Ben?' Maybe he had gone to the park with Grace? Or was giving her a bath or just generally being Father of the Year with her somewhere?

'Mr Worthington —' Ruth looked at me pointedly '— had to go to work to attend to a business matter.'

'And Grace?' I asked, looking around the childless room.

'I have put her down for a sleep.'

Was she mad? If Grace slept now she'd be awake all night – was this woman trying to kill us? And then I remembered tonight was not my problem, and if Ben couldn't manage to last one day with his daughter without calling in reinforcements, then it would serve him right. I could feel something brewing inside me – frustration, disappointment, disbelief that he could so easily tap out of his responsibilities. I had gone from giddily excited at the prospect of talking to him about my day, to not wanting to see him at all.

Would Grace ever get to know her father? Was this the way her life would be, destined to be brought up by the help? My family was so different. No drivers or nannies, but plenty of time spent together. The Liebenbergs had been a huge professional and cultural shock too, but at least they filled their house with love. There was no mistaking their affection for their children or one another. But not here: this house was modern and cold. All the glittering beauty of this world where money was never an issue, and none of it mattered. My New York experience was lacking something: substance.

I had to get away from these people. Which meant retiring to my room for the rest of the evening. It wouldn't be entirely terrible, sliding the door across to listen to the strangely calming sounds of the city, and at this point I needed to be calm. I grabbed my things from the bench with a sigh. I didn't know exactly what I'd expected to come home to. Ben with messy bed hair, the kitchen a bit trashed with the remnants of bottle preparations, a small smile on his lips as he juggled his whining daughter? And he would half-laugh and say, 'I don't know how you do it.' I would have taken comfort from that. Finding an immaculate, unlived-in house with the militant Ruth preparing dinner was not what I expected. I didn't even know if what bubbled on the stove for dinner included a ration for me.

'Okay, well, I'm just going to my room,' I announced as I left Ruth in the kitchen tasting her sauce. Like she even cared where I was or where I was heading.

The small peacekeeping smile I had offered her slipped away as I went up the stairs with heavy steps. I continued past the forbidden third floor of Ben Worthington's lair, which, regardless of my curiosity, I always made sure to stay clear of. On Grace's floor, I found myself slowing down, not just because I was out of breath but because I had automatically entered stealth mode, ready to tiptoe across the floor and hover near the doorway.

Not for you, Sarah, not today.

And the reminder pushed me to the next set of stairs, my heart almost thundering with the fear of hearing something from Grace's room, anything, because I knew that my instinct would be to go to her, to comfort her, and saving her from having to spend any more time in cranky Ruth's arms. With that thought carrying my weary self to my room, I realised that my feet were not the only things weighing me down, my heart was heavy too.

How could he just leave his daughter? How could holding her, loving her, be such a difficult thing to do? Would he ever know how lucky he was? Ben wasn't enjoying his child, he was simply surviving her. And as I sat on the edge of my bed in my terribly plush New York City room with my Tiffany bag by my side and an evening all to myself, I still couldn't shake that incredibly sad feeling. More than anything, though, I was disappointed. I almost felt like an annoyed wife waiting for her husband to come home from the pub.

It was then I realised how ridiculous I was being; maybe he did have a work emergency, and it had been thoughtful of him to call Ruth so he wouldn't disrupt my weekend off. I tried to convince myself but the situation felt a little off. Or maybe it was the hunger pains twisting my stomach, the ones I was trying to ignore as I lounged on the roof terrace, sketching out the exterior of the Tiffany building in black and white, which I was copying from the picture on my phone. I would add a woman out front, not one in jeans and a tee but someone elegant, weighed down with shopping bags from Fifth Avenue and about to enter for the final purchase of the day. I hadn't worked on character sketches since high school, when I was asked by the art teachers to make individual caricatures of all the Year Twelve students for the yearbook. I hated being pressured into it – I'm not interested in that kind of art. I'm all about abstract, and I'd wanted to be a tortured artist talking about art as a visual language of shape, form, colour. The yearbook was a smash hit, more so than anything I had ever done before. The buzz of recognition lasted longer than any good grade I'd received for the work I'd done in art class, but I denied the feeling, because I felt like I was a traitor to my true artist self. Tucked away on the terrace, taking joy from doing something that came easily to me, my art almost felt like a dirty little secret once more.

By the time the sun was dimming in the sky I had reached the colouring-in stage, the picture coming to life in a way that excited me. I stopped when I found myself getting annoyed at not having the right shade of Tiffany blue for the woman's bag. Then I remembered I had my own Tiffany-blue bag and felt decidedly smug. I dragged it over, reaching in for the blue box tied with a white ribbon. It seemed such a shame to untie the original bow, but I did. Taking out the drawstring bag, I gently tipped the contents into my palm. The little heart-shaped silver earrings fell into my hands. New, shiny, and engraved with the classic 'Please return to Tiffany & Co. New York'. I stood, skipping into my room to the mirror, pulling my hair back from my

ears and pushing the studs through. I gathered my hair
and turned my head from side to side, admiring the way
the light made the earrings glint. This was the answer to
happiness. In the future, I'd just prescribe myself a dose of
Tiffany for any sleep-deprived state of hopelessness. Sure,
my allowance was going to be blown and the purchases
would have to be minuscule, but there was something
therapeutic about the place.

There was a creaking on the stairs outside my room,
so fleeting I thought I might have misheard, but when
a shadow lingered underneath the door there was no
mistaking someone was there. It made me unexpectedly
nervous: was Ben home? Coming to check how my day had
been, maybe? To explain why he had been called out to
work? But that was a ridiculous thought. Ben Worthington
didn't explain himself and especially not to me.

I hated the way I had to collect myself to face whoever
was on the other side of the door. I hated that weaker part
of me. Putting on my best casual 'Oh, hey there' expression, I whipped open the door.

'Oh, hi, Ruth,' I said.

The cranky woman held a tray of food. I was surprised
that she'd served me but also amazed that she hadn't so
much as spilled a drop on the tray after navigating those
stairs. She didn't even seem out of breath. Was she for real?

'Dinner is ready,' Ruth said curtly, shoving the tray
into my hands.

'Th-thanks,' I managed, juggling the tray and, much to my annoyance, spilling some of the delicious sauce over the edge of the plate onto the tray.

Ruth pursed her lips together, looking at me like I was the most incompetent human being on the planet. 'Don't thank me, thank Mr Worthington.'

'Oh, is he home?' I asked, hating the way my voice sounded so eager.

'He is downstairs with Grace,' she said, turning to leave.

'Ah, Ruth?'

She paused at the top of the staircase.

'Do you think it would be all right if I ate my dinner downstairs?' *Instead of up here like a leper*, I wanted to add. If I was going to fit in, be an integral part of this household, then I would have to make an effort to get rid of this ridiculous intimidation I felt when I was around Ben Worthington. This was his house after all, and I would be the one who would have to adjust if I was going to stay.

Ruth looked seriously pissed off. More so than usual, like she had wanted me to be locked away out of sight, or maybe she was just annoyed that she had gone to the trouble of carrying the tray all this way. She doubled back to me in a huff, grabbing the edge of my tray.

'Fine,' she bit out, trying to take the tray from me.

'No, look, it's okay, I can carry it,' I insisted.

Ruth scoffed. 'You can't even stand still and not make a mess, give it to me.'

'No, Ruth, I've got this.' I pulled back, making the cutlery tinkle.

Ruth's eyes were ablaze as she held onto the tray. 'Give it to me,' she barked, drawing it to her chest.

'No!' I yelled, hauling it closer to me. Back and forth we heaved until the inevitable happened. The tray went flying, and the shit hit the fan, or rather, the ragout hit the cream Westminster carpet.

It looked like a crime scene. A reddish, orangey-tinged crime scene that trailed down the staircase in a splattered effect that any abstract artist might have appreciated. But it just made me feel terrible, even more so when my eyes landed on a particular gooey chunk that had landed on an Italian leather shoe on the landing below.

Ben stood there holding Grace, his narrowed eyes following the sprawling mess to where Ruth and I stood frozen, mouths agape like two naughty teenagers.

Chapter Seventeen

It didn't take long for the panicked blame game to start.

'You stupid girl,' Ruth cried. 'I told you to let go, how many times did I tell you? Now look what you've done.'

'What I've done?' I said incredulously. 'I told you I had it, but you wouldn't listen. I was going to bring it down myself, I was trying to do you a favour.'

Ruth scoffed. 'I wouldn't trust you with organising a lucky dip let alone carrying a tray down the stairs. Why do you think I was the one called in today to look after Grace?'

'Ruth!' Ben's voice held a warning. His gaze burned hot – it was enough to make me want to recoil. 'That's enough,' he said. 'Take Grace downstairs.'

He had directed Ruth in a way that didn't invite negotiation. It was also a clear means to dismiss her and leave him alone to deal with me. Never had I thought that I would want Ruth to stay but I did now, desperately, as I watched her pick her way down the stairs past the mess. She took Grace from Ben, giving me a parting glare. I read victory in that look. Should I just resign now? Or hand over my weekly allowance for the next six years in order to pay for the damage?

Ben's expression was stony as he folded his arms and casually leant against the wall. I braced myself for the lecture, so when he said, 'Nice earrings,' I nearly swallowed my tongue. Was he serious?

The lighthearted observation didn't make me feel any more at ease. Maybe he was being smart, giving me a none-too-subtle hint that my Tiffany expeditions were over now? There was a gleam in his eyes, but I couldn't tell if it was an indication that he wasn't mad, or if it was the calm before the storm.

'How was your day?' he asked. Why was he making small talk while standing on a staircase deeply soaked with tomato ragout? Shouldn't he be yelling at me to get some paper towels or something?

'It was a good day,' I admitted, and it had been. Damn near perfect until now.

Ben sighed, pushing off the wall. 'Well, there's no need to cry over spilt . . . whatever the hell this is.'

'Ragout,' I said. I didn't want to admit that I had been looking forward to this. Ruth mightn't have a soul, but she sure could cook.

'Right, okay,' he said. 'Well, I'm sure there's more where that came from, come on.' He tilted his head down the stairs, and I followed, stepping as delicately as I could manage around the slush. Without thinking, I grabbed

Ben's hand, which he held out for me to take as I skipped and jumped down the last couple of steps to relative safety. Except now I was in the rather dangerous position of holding Ben's hand, so warm and large. I bet if we placed our hands palm to palm he would be able to bend the tops of his fingers easily over mine. I wanted to test the theory, but that would be inappropriate, as was me holding his hand. I pulled away and could feel my cheeks burning as red as the stained carpet.

'I think I should probably clean this up first,' I said, thinking how much worse it looked from this angle.

'Ruth can clean it before she goes.' He seemed unfazed. His home was a pristine showcase and I was taken aback that he didn't want heads to roll.

'Ah, that's probably a bad idea,' I said, following him to the next set of stairs. Didn't Ruth hate me enough as it was?

Ben stopped on the edge of the top step, almost causing me to slam into him. He turned to look at me, a glimmer of something in his eyes. 'Well, like she said, Ruth doesn't trust you to run a lucky dip – how can she trust you to clean that mess?'

Was this his way of punishing Ruth? My shoulders slumped. 'She is going to hate me.'

Ben laughed, a deep-bellied laugh that made me frown as he turned to the stairs. 'I think it's safe to say she already does.'

Ruth cleaned without complaint, which only made me more uncomfortable. I made a mental note to no longer eat food provided by Ruth, at the risk of being poisoned.

Now that my clothes were infused with the smell of dinner, I had lost my appetite. Honestly, I couldn't think of anything worse than another plate, even when Ben assured me there was plenty.

'Um, if it's all right with you, I might just make myself a cheese toastie,' I said, smiling at Grace in her bouncer as I tried to pry a giggle out of her. She was playing hard to get.

'A sandwich?' Ben repeated with horror.

'I'll have you know that it's not just any sandwich; in fact, I don't want to boast, but I make a world-famous grilled cheese.'

'Really?'

'It's known from Australia to Slovenia.' That was true – the Liebenbergs loved my cheese toasties.

Ben's brows rose as he nodded, apparently impressed as he dished out a plate of dinner. 'Cheese between white toast. Sounds mouthwatering,' he said.

'Oh, it's so much more than that.'

'Right,' he said, placing the plate on the bench.

'It's pretty intense, and usually served on the side of my world-famous minestrone soup, but that's a whole other story.'

Ben grabbed another plate, filling it. He was facing away from me but I could see the pinch of his cheek that said he was smiling. It seemed strange that we were bonding over this topic, but aside from Grace, there wasn't much else to talk about.

Ben turned, putting the plate in front of me, then pointing at it. 'Eat,' he said, in that no-nonsense style of his that probably had all his business associates quivering.

I barely flinched at his attempt to lay down the law. For the first time, I didn't feel intimidated by him, and I didn't know whether it was because he had stood up for me against Ruth or because he insisted I eat, even though I'm sure Ruth had no intention of feeding me.

Ben picked up his plate and, without knowing what else to do, I picked up mine and followed him to the glass dining table where only two places were set, opposite one another. At the Liebenbergs' I was used to eating with the children at their dinnertime, so this was a bit of a first for me. I glanced at Gracie, who seemed too fascinated with trying to stick her foot in her mouth to notice what was going on. She seemed in a particularly happy mood, no doubt that late sleep had given her plenty of beans.

I suddenly didn't feel so bad about Ruth on her hands and knees upstairs, scrubbing the carpet. It's what she deserved for making me think that the reason she had been called was because I couldn't be trusted. I took my seat, thinking – or hoping – that wasn't the case, that my first week had showed Ben I was capable of looking after his daughter. And then strange things began running through my head.

Maybe this is him wanting to have a chat with me. Soften the blow over dinner. Oh God —

The sound of a cork being pulled from a bottle of red drew my attention, and before I could register what was going on, Ben was pouring me a glass. My eyes returned to Gracie and Ben smiled.

'Relax, you're off the clock, remember?' he said, placing a glass next to my plate.

'Yeah, but you're not,' I blurted.

He looked up from filling his own glass. 'Just one with dinner.' He said it in such a convincing way, I believed him.

'True,' I said, watching him take a sip. 'I mean, it's not like you're breastfeeding or anything.'

Ben choked and spat out a dribble of red, clasping a hand over his mouth, before having a coughing fit, his eyes watering.

I rescued the glass he put down in haste, moving it from the table that trembled with each cough.

'Are you okay?' I asked, trying not to laugh, because there wasn't anything funny about seeing someone gasp for breath.

Ben nodded. 'Fine,' he rasped, wiping down the front of his blue shirt that now had a smattering of red wine. With ragout on his shoes and red wine on his shirt, he was a hot mess. One night in with me and his dry cleaning bill had skyrocketed.

'I'm sorry. I will not say "breast" mid-sip ever again.'

Ben regained his composure. 'Let's toast to that,' he said, taking his glass, clinking it with mine and giving me a sheepish smile. I masked my own smile, bringing my glass to my lips just as Ruth entered the dining area carrying a mop and bucket, her eyes darting between us. Sharing a joke with Ben, I felt awkward once again. It didn't matter how Ruth had treated me, here I was, reflected in the eyes of an outsider, no doubt being wildly inappropriate with her boss.

If only Penny Worthington could see me now.

I put down my glass, silently swearing off another drop.

'How did you go?' Ben asked Ruth, unaware of – or ignoring – the laser beams that were shooting out of her eyeballs.

'It will need to be professionally cleaned, but I don't know if that will make any difference.'

I thought of how my mother would have reacted: she would have been devastated by an unmovable stain in the carpet, but in Ben's world it wasn't a big deal.

'I'll call the carpet layers tomorrow and get them to replace it.'

Oh, to have money.

'Anything else, Mr Worthington?' Ruth asked, like a robot programmed for obedience against her will.

'No, that's all, Ruth, you can go now.'

'Will you need me tomorrow?' she asked, glancing ever so briefly at me.

'No, Ruth, that'll be all.'

She nodded before turning to head out.

'But, Ruth . . .'

She paused, looking expectantly at him. 'Yes, Mr Worthington?'

He casually shifted the base of his wine glass under his fingertips, his eyes focused intently on the way it turned. 'If you are going to walk through the front door of this house, know this: Sarah is the appointed caretaker here and I would remind you to give her nothing but the utmost respect. Am I clear?' His eyes lifted from the glass. It was a look that said, 'Don't fuck with me, and don't ever bring your dirty looks or attitude here again.'

My heart would have felt all warm and fuzzy had the tension not been so thick and I hadn't wanted to slide under the table, mortified. I decided to opt for a sip – make that a big bloody gulp – of wine.

The silence was broken by Ruth. 'Yes, Mr Worthington.'

'I'll walk you out,' he said, pushing his chair back. I thought Ruth might object, but she remained quiet, waiting for him before turning down the hall. I wanted to say goodbye to her but realised now wasn't the time.

And now that I was alone with the wine and the food, I wished I'd just taken the tray and stayed in my room. I was faced with a meal I didn't want and an expensive glass of red I couldn't bring myself to tip down the sink.

There was nothing for it – I skulled the wine.

I winced then cleared my throat, eyes watering, taking in the impossibly large pile of food before me. I couldn't eat it. Ugh, why didn't Ben have a dog? A hungry Rottweiler under the table would be perfect. I had limited time to think of a good enough reason to excuse myself. Headache? Nausea? Menstrual cramps? Definitely not.

'What am I doing, Grace?' I looked at Grace, who was staring at me and kick-kick-kicking her legs.

'You're no help,' I said, thinking maybe I was being ridiculous, that I should just have dinner, get to know Ben a little; this was a prime opportunity. I didn't know how many one-on-one dinners there would be, considering his work seemed so demanding, so I'd better take the chance while I could.

I refilled my glass with wine, thinking myself mature and worldly, turning again to the plate of food. I ran my fork through the stew, letting the steam rise. Breathing in the aroma of spices made my mouth water. Who was I kidding? I would never turn down a feed, even if seeing it plastered all over the stairs didn't do wonders for my appetite.

I was about to take a sneaky taste when light, quick footsteps came down the hall and, much to my surprise, Ruth appeared. I froze, fork suspended in front of my lips, as I watched her walk to the kitchen stool to unhook the coat she'd forgotten.

'Lucky you remembered,' I said, trying to seem like there were no hard feelings, but when Ruth turned to me, pulling on her coat, I could tell that the feeling was most certainly not mutual. I was nervous with her being within reach of sharp objects.

'He might let you into his bed, but he will never let you into his heart.'

I lowered my fork. 'Excuse me?' I said.

'I've seen your kind before. He'll find out soon enough.' She almost spat out the words, looking at me in disgust.

'And what kind is that exactly?'

She buttoned her coat and swung her bag over her shoulder. 'Gold digger,' she sneered, looking me right in the eye, making sure I understood her.

'He hired me!' I said, astonished. I couldn't help it – was this what she really thought of me? And then I realised how I sat at the table set for two, sipping red wine; all that was missing were some candles and some Barry White crooning in the background. Was this crossing the line? Ruth seemed to think so.

Ruth strode off down the hall, to where Ben no doubt held the door for her. Her words were spinning in my head.

He might let you into his bed but he will never let you into his heart.

Is that what this was all about? Did he plan to wine and dine me tonight? Was Ben Worthington a smooth-operating playboy with an illegitimate child he was burdened with from a past lover? My stomach lurched, and it wasn't just the red that had done it.

I heard the front door close, and without needing any advice from a squirming Grace in her bouncer – or from anyone for that matter – I grabbed my dinner plate, marched to the kitchen and dumped the food in the bin, happy never to see it, or Ruth, ever again. I rinsed and shoved the plate into the dishwasher just as Ben reappeared. I didn't give him a chance to speak; without meeting his eyes, I handed him my serviette.

'Goodnight,' I said, going down the hall to the stairs, aware of him watching me the whole way.

Chapter Eighteen

I must admit, I had been called far worse things in my life than a gold digger. Besides, the notion was so ridiculous I should have laughed. And yet I didn't; I couldn't find anything amusing about it. Ruth's accusation bothered me, and I tossed and turned in my bed, smelling the faintest odour of damp carpet chemicals. Why was I wasting my last opportunity for an uninterrupted sleep by letting Ruth's words keep me awake? And I was still bloody starving! Lying on my back, staring at the ceiling, I debated going all the way downstairs to get something to eat. Grace hadn't stirred in hours and as far as I could tell the house was still, so if I was going to do it, I would have to do it now.

I ripped back the covers, pulled on my fluffy bed socks and pressed my ear against the door, listening intently before turning the handle and stepping out into the—

'Oh shit,' I whispered, feeling the damp of the carpet seep through my socks. Even now Ruth was torturing me.

I humphed, skimming my way along the wall to avoid the wet patch. By now I was an expert at moving from floor to floor in silence, stalking through the night like a jungle cat. I could almost feel my heartbeat spike when I reached Ben's floor, but it was unlit and quiet like always. I had never explored this floor but it gave me the feeling that no one was home, no one lived here. Or maybe that was because I never, ever lingered on the third floor out of fear of finding out that someone very much did.

Halfway down to the second floor, I came to a standstill, grabbing the railing and craning my head over the banister. There were lights and voices coming from the front parlour. Someone was most definitely here. At first I thought maybe Ruth had come back to stir up more trouble, or worse, Penny had dropped by. But I doubted it was Penny – it was the middle of the night and she was probably strapped into her coffin right about now. I lingered on the stairs, torn between my instinct to retreat to my room and my curiosity about who the voice belonged to. The female voice talking to Ben.

I slowly stepped down, hoping that the shadows would help me stay hidden as I came closer to the parlour.

Ben stood with his arms encircled around a woman: slender and blonde and . . . crying. He rubbed at her shoulders in a soothing caress as he made comforting sounds in her ear. Oh my god. I felt something inside of me twang unexpectedly, shocking me as much as the scene before me.

Even though her back was to me I could tell she was from money. Her long tan coat was beautifully cut and made from lush fabric, her heels were black and high, and there was a Louis Vuitton purse hooked in the crook of the arm wrapped around Ben. She held on for dear life as her sobs filtered up the stairs.

Who was she?

And then as she drew away, looking at Ben's sad eyes as he wiped tears from her dampened cheeks, it suddenly occurred to me. Was this Grace's mother? My stomach plummeted with the thought.

I wanted her to turn around so I could see her face, but then I was afraid to stay watching because – for some reason that really troubled me – the thought of him kissing her made my insides twist. I did not want to stay to see it. Whoever she was, she had come to see Ben in the middle of the night. And then with horror, I realised that if he chose to lead her up the stairs, I would be blocking their path.

I cautiously made my way back up until I heard movement from below. I made the safety of the corner of the staircase in the nick of time, tentatively peering around to see the blonde striding to the door.

'I have to go,' she said, barely keeping her emotions in check as Ben rushed after her, forcing the door closed as she tried to open it.

'Holly, wait!'

It was then she turned to him, her face flushed, her eyes big and bloodshot from crying. She was plain; pretty enough but not overly beautiful. It was a surprise that someone like Ben would be into her, I thought rather bitterly, before scolding myself for judging, and for caring.

'I have to go,' she said quietly.

Ben sighed. I could see the resignation in his broad shoulders as he looked at her, it was almost like he knew he couldn't stop her. He grabbed her hand and gave it a firm squeeze.

'Promise me something.' His voice was etched with a meaning that dare not be denied.

'What?'

'Don't go back to him.'

A small, sad smile touched the edge of her mouth. 'Why, because it would break your heart?'

Ben shook his head, reaching for the door and opening it for her. 'It's already broken.'

~

I wasn't sure what to do.

Leaning against the front door below me, palms flat against the glossed wood, stood a defeated man. I wanted to go to him as much as I wanted to run from him. I had come closer to learning something about this man's life, but rather than it being a story shared over a civilised dinner, I had witnessed it in the shadows, witnessed something that raised more questions than answers.

'Do you want a grilled cheese sandwich?' His voice trailed up the stairs.

Fuck! My heart stopped, my mind returning to the present. Oh God, how long had he known I was there, being a total creeper?

I took a deep breath before stepping onto the landing, suddenly wishing my oversized T-shirt with *I ♥ NY* on it was longer. He turned to me, his eyes stormy and his arms folded. I wanted to shrink into the shadows, lock myself away for what was left of the weekend and pretend this had never happened. I could have slinked up the stairs with a thousand apologies, but I had already slunk away once tonight and there were only so many times you could play the coward card. So this time, even with every fibre of my body screaming against it, I went down, closing the distance between me and the wolf that waited at the bottom the stairs. If he asked, I would totally deny that I had seen or heard anything.

I stopped on the fourth last step, giving myself a height advantage. I enjoyed having the tables turned, him having to look up at me with those penetrating grey-blue eyes. There was a wry smile on his face as his gaze swept over my attire. I fought against the urge to stretch the hem of my tee down over my thighs.

He breathed out a laugh, shaking his head. He didn't ask if I'd been eavesdropping, or if I was hungry. He just left me standing there as he walked down the hall to the kitchen. I lingered, wondering what I should do and then, before I knew it, I was heading for the kitchen too. It was unlit; the only thing illuminated was Ben, who stood in the doorway of the fridge as he peered inside. He was lit up like a god and I found myself lured to him like a moth to flame. I stood beside him, peering into the fridge, giving its contents as much serious attention as he did. The cool air caused my skin to prickle and I rubbed my arms against the cold. The movement caught Ben's attention and he looked at me as if seeing me for the first time. I thought he might break the silence with some quip about grilled cheese, or drop his gaze again to my daggy apparel, but there was nothing, not an ounce of humour on his stern face. I shivered – maybe it was the cold blasting from the fridge? No, it was those eyes. Eyes that seemed haunted by something I wanted to discover so much. *So many secrets, Ben Worthington.*

I didn't expect him to tell me. I all but sighed in relief when he let the fridge door close. I knew he was looking at me though, I could feel his eyes on me. A part of me wanted him to turn the light on, but then a whole other part of me took comfort in the shadows. I thought I could handle the strangeness of the situation, forget about the mystery that shrouded this man, ignore the depths of his questioning stares. And then the unexpected happened. He spoke.

'I'm not cheating on my wife, if that's what you're thinking.'

I was stunned by what he'd said. This was the smallest amount of information he had ever parted with, but perhaps held the most meaning. I was relieved that I hadn't asked, and then I wished that I could see his face, read in his eyes the anger, the sorrow. And almost as if he had read my mind, the glossy marble slab was lit by the pendant lights above. I had to blink to adjust my eyes. Then I saw Ben, leaning against the counter, his arms folded and a faraway expression on his face that made my heart ache. I knew there was a story here. Caught between wanting to know more and frightened by the change in a man who was usually so stoic, I didn't question him, didn't dare bring him out of his memory. I moved slightly, feeling the coldness of the stainless steel fridge at my back. I knew that it was not advised to disturb a sleep walker, but what if someone was revisiting a memory, one that seemed so painful that lines of fatigue etched across their face?

I wanted to go to him, comfort him and reassure him that everything would be okay, even if I wasn't certain it would be. That he didn't have to tell me anything but if he wanted to, I would listen. I wanted to say all the right things, and more than that, I wanted to touch him, let him feel the consolation of my hand. Maybe I wouldn't need to say anything at all, maybe I could show him just by touching his shoulder, by rubbing my hand across his shoulder blades in a soothing way or placing my hand over his. Turning on the light was the worst thing Ben could have done, but not nearly as bad as what happened next. Like some out-of-body experience where I could hear the words escaping from my mouth but was unable to stop them, I broke all the rules.

I asked the biggest question of all.

'Where is your wife?' My voice was low, shaky. Ben's eyes looked into mine, harsher and darker than I had ever seen them before. I almost shied away from them. He was clearly distraught, and how I wished I could take back my words.

'Caroline,' he said.

I swallowed. 'Caroline,' I repeated. I swear my heart stopped. *Caroline*.

Knowing her name made it real, and I wished almost immediately that Ben would take it back, that I could wipe it from my memory, because as much as I'd thought I'd wanted to know, now I realised I didn't; ignorance really was bliss and I didn't want what was an already complicated existence to be muddied further.

'Caroline . . . she . . .' For the first time, Ben seemed unsure about what to say. 'She died, Sarah. My wife is dead.' He turned away from me and gripped the edge of the counter so hard I thought the marble might shatter.

I exhaled a breath I hadn't realised I'd been holding, my horrified eyes boring into Ben's slumped shoulders. I had never hated myself more. *Oh God, why did I have to ask, why couldn't I just keep my mouth shut?* I had suspected a broken home, a wayward wife, but not this, never *this*.

I could see the rise and fall of Ben's shoulders as he took deep, measured breaths. Before, I had fantasised about going to him, comforting him, but this time I didn't think,

I just did. I placed my palm on his shoulder, rubbing the soft fabric.

'Ben,' I whispered, hot tears welling in my eyes as I wished that the arrogant man would return. 'I'm so sorry, I shouldn't have asked.'

Ben shook his head. 'It should never have been a secret.'

I could feel the warmth of him, and I wasn't sure if my touch was helping him but it was helping me, calming me, as I concentrated on the slow movements of my hand over his shirt.

'Grace was born,' he said, and I gripped his forearm.

'It's okay, you don't have to.'

'But I want to.' He straightened and turned to me. His eyes were squeezed shut as if he was summoning the patience to continue, his jaw clenched. He wasn't sad, it was something else; an emotion I couldn't quite put my finger on. I stepped away a little, waiting for him to tell me about her, about Caroline.

He stilled himself as he began. 'Grace was a few weeks old when Caroline had the accident. Car accident,' he added. There was a faraway look in his eyes again as he remembered. 'We were just starting to get our lives back together. Our relationship was on the rocks – with the fighting, the arguing, there didn't seem to be anything worth salvaging, but then there was Grace: a beautiful surprise.'

A suggestion of a smile appeared as his finger absent-mindedly traced the marble of the countertop. 'You see,

Caroline never wanted to have children, but when she found out she was pregnant, it changed everything. It took what was broken, and seemingly irreparable, in our relationship and it pieced it all together. There was purpose in our lives, a reason for trying.' He glanced at me and I saw the rawness in him had resurfaced. I found myself being drawn into him once more.

'And it's all broken again, and Grace is the memory of a piece of my life I don't want to remember.' His voice broke a little but his words were heavy like thunder. 'And as much as I try, I can't forget, and I so desperately want to forget.' He swallowed, shaking his head, torturing himself with an inner turmoil that made me want to just fall into him, plead for him to forgive me for judging him. It was no wonder he hadn't bonded with Grace, had kept his distance from her, from this house. He was haunted by a time and a life he hoped for and now it was gone.

'Ben, I am so sorry.' I was sorry: sorry I'd asked; sorry I knew. I was beyond sorry to see this vulnerable side to him. I stepped closer, taking his hand and squeezing it, my heart spiking as the gesture freed him from the memory that pained him. He had wanted to forget, but he was tortured by it, so palpable I could feel it through his fingertips as I ran mine over the back of his hand, along the roughened ridges of his knuckles. I turned his palm as I traced his jagged heart line, marvelling at how strong it was.

Ben closed his hand around mine, stilling my fingers. I caught myself, realising how intimate the action was, how inappropriate, even if I was intending to comfort him. I looked into his serious, ever-watchful eyes.

'I don't want to forget Grace, that's not what I mean, I just want to forget the past. I'm trying, I am, but no matter what I do I just . . .' His words fell away and his hand squeezed mine, as if with pure frustration at the inadequacy of his words.

I placed my hand on the side of his face. 'I know you love Grace, I know it. And it's going to take time and that's okay. You might not forget, but you'll learn to live with it, I promise you that.'

He was thinking so deeply, looking at his hand holding mine, that I stood frozen, my hip digging into the cool marble counter. I didn't feel cold, far from it. I felt flushed, my cheeks aflame at the way he was examining my fingers, making me have to concentrate on breathing. In and out; I had to put conscious thought into the action as long as he kept his hand where it was.

He looked at me, and it wasn't out of anger, or sadness, or anything that I could define. He was seeing me in a new way, a silent question in his gaze as it dropped to my mouth. Beyond my control, my eyes copied his, but I couldn't be sure if he was thinking what I was thinking: what would it be like to kiss those lips? To taste his tongue in my mouth? To have his hands on me? And it was wrong, so wrong to think, to feel that way. I had wanted to comfort him, but glimpsing the softer side of Ben Worthington made me want to do so much more. It was wrong but I wanted him to forget, to take away the anguish, even if for just one night. I wanted to be the one to help make him feel better, consequences be damned.

Blocking out every rational voice inside my head, I moved to him and I kissed him once, softly.

He didn't kiss me back. I felt the firm lines of his shoulders and his confused eyes watch as I pulled away a little and then kissed him again, slowly enough for him to protest, to tell me to stop, but he didn't. I pulled away again, my heart spiking with the knowledge that, from the heat in his eyes, he wasn't trapped by memories of the past, he was in the here and now. I saw it in the way he watched my lips press together as if savouring the taste of him, and by the third time my mouth pressed against his, I felt his body melt. His arms circled my waist and he kissed me back, capturing my breaths with his kiss. He pressed into me, firm and fevered, as I opened myself to him, my hands twisting into the fabric of his shirt as his tongue teased me. His breath was warm and he tasted of wine and mint. I could hardly believe this was happening; as much as I was allowing myself to get lost in the throes of the moment there was one thing that my mind couldn't stop repeating.

You're kissing Ben Worthington. You're *kissing Ben Worthington*!

Chapter Nineteen

was an awful human being. I let the thought run fleetingly through my mind as Ben moved me around, edging me against the counter. I yelped when he lifted me onto it as if I weighed nothing. Once again I was above him, a vantage point of power, and I liked it. I offered a cocky smirk to tell him as much, but he hooked his finger in the neck of my T-shirt and pulled me down to meet his mouth. Oh, I was going to hell.

This time he kissed me slower but deeper, hands cupping the sides of my face before they lowered, grabbing the backs of my knees and dragging me to the edge of the counter and against him. I instinctively wrapped my legs around his hips, the heat from his hardness pressing into the thin scrap of my panties. Ben's hands moved slowly up my thighs, under the edge of my tee, and gripped my hips. My hands rested on his shoulders, feeling the power in the way his body moved and the taut muscles of his back. I didn't know what to do; being face to face like this seemed so intimate – probably because we were touching and moving in the most intimate of ways. Seeing the change in my face as he ground against me and the pressure built between my thighs, Ben took my mouth again, capturing the whimper I had no control over. He felt good. His mouth, his breath, the smell of him so close, wedged between my thighs, pushing against me as if he wanted more, needed more. And then when he moved my hand and guided it lower, pressing against the firm outline in his pants, I swallowed. Dear God, I would follow him anywhere.

I wasn't sure when reality sidled in; maybe it was when his tongue delved into my mouth again, or when his hand tugged my T-shirt up and I watched him take my nipple into his mouth, swirling and sucking it. Maybe it was then, watching the top of his thick hair, unruly from my fingers running through it, pressing him against me, encouraging him to keep going, that the words ran through my mind: *He's just using you. He let her go and you were there. He'll let you into his bed but never his heart.*

I knew Ben was using me, unleashing something within him that needed to alleviate whatever pent-up emotions his desperation to forget had created, and then my mind started playing tricks.

So what if he wants to use you, use your body, fuck you into next week, what's wrong with that? A moment of pleasure doesn't have to mean anything. How long has it been, Sarah? Hmm? Exactly. You will never land a man like this ever again, so if he wants to use you, then you use him right back!

That little devil on my shoulder made total sense, and it was all I needed to have the confidence to take it further. I sat up straight. Looking directly into his eyes, I reached for his belt, working to unloop the leather then undoing his button and gliding down his zip. Surprise flashed across Ben's face, but if he wanted me to slow down, he never let on.

'Touch me,' I breathed, and it was all he needed, as his fingers delved past the sheer, now damp, fabric of my panties to press deep inside me.

'Ben.' I said his name like a plea, gasping, not knowing if I wanted more, or for him to stop. All my nerve endings were on the brink of explosion so when he took his hand away, I cried out in protest. It was short lived as he hooked his fingers into the elastic of my panties, drawing them down my thighs, his eyes so hungry, knowing the barrier was gone. He then did something I wasn't expecting: he pulled me up, taking my mouth once again, kissing me slowly, tenderly, like a lover. If this was how he made me feel while using me, then I was okay with that; he made me feel so desired – not just for my body, but for me. Even if it was a lie to get what he wanted, I wanted it too.

Then Grace's cries were broadcast through the baby monitor.

We froze, our only movements the barely controlled rhythm of our heart beats, the only sound the pant of our heavy breaths.

No, no, no, no, no – Grace, please go back to sleep!

'It's okay,' I said. 'She might settle.' I kissed the side of his jaw, working my way to his mouth.

He kissed me, but his focus was solely on the green light on the monitor. We were so close, and I knew that once we started, there would be no going back. I just needed this, needed him inside me, to fuck me. And just as he readied himself once more to push inside me, he stopped.

'Ben, please . . .' I begged.

But he stepped away, leaving me lying on the bench, feeling suddenly cold and exposed. I sat up, pulling my T-shirt down, watching him buckle and zip himself up.

'What the fuck are we doing?'

'Ben. She's okay, we'll check on her,' I said quietly.

'I'll check on her. Jesus, you're supposed to be the one reacting to her cries.' He went to the sink to wash his hands.

I straightened, angered by his harsh words. 'I do, all the time.'

'Well, that's why I pay you,' he said quietly, but I heard him.

I slid off the bench, straightening my panties, feeling the fury swirl in the pit of my stomach. 'That's right, you do pay me to look after *your* child,' I snapped, thinking I had gone too far, but if my words hit a nerve, Ben didn't show it. He dried his hands on a paper towel and left the kitchen.

My legs felt weak, and I was flushed and flustered, a little sexual frustration and a whole lot of deep-seated anger. How dare he imply I didn't care about Grace, that I was incompetent in looking after a daughter he hardly even saw through the week? One day of caring for her and he was suddenly Father of the Year? If he had decided to use me then he had gone the right way about it. I had never felt so stupid, so utterly ashamed. I had crossed the biggest line of all, breached professionalism and all sanity. I was suddenly thankful for Grace's cries, for stopping us from doing something we would no doubt regret in the morning – if not instantly.

I washed my hands, splashing the cool water against my cheeks in a bid to calm down. I could hear Ben speaking softly and reassuringly to Grace through the baby monitor as she still cried. And like a robot, I went to the fridge, grabbed a bottle and took it to the microwave, heating the formula. I carried the bottle upstairs, feeling numb. I tried to convince myself that I wasn't a bad person, just a severely misguided one. Sleep would clear my mind, give me time to know what to do in the morning.

I crossed the landing toward Grace's opened door. Ben was sitting in his chair nursing her, rocking her. His head lifted as I stepped inside. I held out the baby bottle to him before he could say a word. His confused eyes lowered to the bottle and only then did the harsh edges of his face soften a little. I could see his resolve thaw in the frame of his shoulders as he took the bottle from my hand.

'Listen, Sarah I —'

'Goodnight, Ben.' I turned to the door, making sure I held my head high. This time saying goodnight wasn't about being a coward, or running away. It was about not wanting to hear his reasons or excuses. I didn't need his patronising speech; if I had a job come morning, I would lay down the law and gain some semblance of power back because, above all else, I knew it would be the only way to repair my damaged ego.

Chapter Twenty

'Listen, Ben, about last night . . .'

'Whoa, what was the alcohol percentage in that wine, Ben? I don't remember a thing!'

'Ben, I think sleep deprivation can do strange things to the mind.'

'Ben, I think we need to disinfect the kitchen benchtop.'

'Ben, we have unfinished business.' Okay, no, that sounded bad – way too suggestive.

Try as I might, nothing seemed to sound right, no matter how many times I rehearsed in the bathroom mirror. I had never wished for a weekend to be over so much in my life; at least if it had been a Monday, Ben would be off to work and I wouldn't have to worry about how I was never going to be able to look him in the face again. A memory of him kissing and licking my nipple rushed into my mind and I buried my face in my hands. Oh god, how the hell had this happened? Oh, that's right;

I wanted him to forget about his dead wife. Jesus, Sarah, who are you?

After all my failed ideas to fix this situation, there was only one way to tackle it, and that was with a blank mind and no expectations. I had crossed a line last night, we both knew it, and more than anything else, Ben Worthington was a businessman. And now the deal to care for his most prized possession had been compromised. Despite his early inner turmoil and reluctance to show any emotion or spend time with her, he was getting better; I could see the change in him, even over the last few days. So if there was going to be a complication in his life that might jeopardise his relationship with Grace in any way, I knew he would cut ties if he had to. I was likely to go downstairs and find a cheque sitting on the kitchen bench and a car waiting to take me to the airport.

By the time I left my room, I had all but convinced myself that was exactly what was going to happen, and had psyched myself up for it. So when I turned the corner into the kitchen to find Penny Worthington sitting at the kitchen counter opposite Ben, all my preparations and expectations fell away. Maybe Penny had the place rigged up with nanny cams and had seen what happened last night. Maybe she was here to fire me.

'Good morning, Sarah, or should I say afternoon?' she quipped. It was barely ten am. Not that I had gotten much sleep, and I knew Ben hadn't either. Even if I hadn't heard Grace's cries throughout the night, the way he nursed his coffee, the circles under his eyes and the light dusting of stubble were dead giveaways. The only person who looked like a million dollars was the fossil-like Penny. With her bright grey eyes, her pearl necklace and impressively coiffed hairstyle, Penny looked like she'd just stepped out of a salon.

'Sarah, Grace needs changing; can you be a love and see to it?' Penny passed a squirming, unsettled Grace over with pursed lips, as if she found babies disgusting. Yeah, they sure could be, but Penny's reaction said more about her lack of maternal instinct than it did about Grace's dirty nappy. Maybe I had been too harsh on Ben's parenting abilities, considering his role model.

Ben sighed. 'Mom, it's Sarah's day off.'

'Oh, she won't mind.' She waved away his words. 'I'm sure she's more than happy to dispose of the smell,' she said, speaking as if I wasn't even present. And unlike Penny's cringeworthy handling of her granddaughter, I held Grace close, caring little if she smelled. It wouldn't be the first or last time I would have to deal with it – as long as I wasn't about to be fired.

'Don't do it near the bench though, Sarah – not very sanitary near a food preparation area.'

The minute the words were out her mouth, Ben and I locked eyes. My horror was evident, but then something unexpected happened: Ben looked on the verge of laughing, as he eyed me knowingly and scratched at his stubble. If only she knew.

That shared moment told me we would be all right. There would be no packing of bags today, and right now I only had one thing to focus on: changing a stinky but adorable baby.

So it was my day off; that didn't mean I couldn't make silly faces and tickle Grace when she was in such a happy mood, smiling and gurgling and whacking me with her arms in excitement. It was also the perfect ruse to listen in on Penny and Ben's conversation.

'What do you mean, you're not coming?' Her words were high-pitched and hoity.

'I'm just not.'

'Why?'

'You know why.'

'Oh, honestly, Benjamin, when is this family ever going to come together? It will be around my death bed, that's when!'

'Well, can't say I can promise, Mother,' he said, sipping his coffee.

'You know, sometimes I think how much easier my life would have been without children.'

'How can we forget? It's something you remind us of every day,' Ben replied. His tolerance for his own mother seemed paper thin, and it was no wonder considering the way she spoke.

Try as I might, there was no endearing quality I could find in Penny Worthington; she was reminiscent of the third floor: vacant. Her eyes were cold, and her manner indifferent. It was a miracle Ben could find any humour in anything, ever. And again I wondered how Nikki managed to be such a happy-go-lucky free spirit.

'Well, I am sick and tired of it, Benjamin. You're the eldest, you sort it out,' she said firmly, then stood and grabbed for her designer handbag.

Ben dumped his cup into the sink with a sigh.

Penny turned to us, smiling in that disingenuous way of hers. 'Sarah, goodbye. Grace,' she said, offering a little wave. Honestly, for a socialite, her people skills sucked. Every grandmother should have a bone-crushing goodbye hug for their grandchild, but not Penny. Wouldn't want to get drool on the Dior.

As the front door closed, I picked Grace up, lifting her to the sky and then down to my eye level, making her squeal. I pulled a series of over-the-top faces. Laughing because Grace was, I propped her in my lap, reaching for one of her chew rings, which she eagerly shoved in her mouth, a stream of saliva spilling onto my hand. I didn't care, I could only laugh as I swept her thick, soft hair aside. I loved how babies had that particular smell about them – well, post-change anyway.

It was then my attention shifted to where Ben was standing, watching with interest. My smile faltered slightly, thinking I had overstepped the mark again, playing with Grace on my day off. I wasn't exactly sure what the rules were for such a thing, but then I wasn't sure of much around this house.

Ben walked from behind the counter to join us in the lounge. He leant on the back of the sofa. 'Ever been to Central Park?' he asked.

I shook my head. 'It's on my list.'

Ben thought, then nodded. 'Well, get ready, because you're about to cross it off.'

~

From the outside, the three of us looked like any normal family on a Sunday stroll. Ben pushed Grace in her pram, navigating the less-than-perfect terrain of the pavement. Or maybe he was out of practice. I tried to help, but he was adamant that he could do it, so I stood to the side, shielding my eyes from the sun as he fiddled with a brake that was giving him grief. Grace began to cry because we had stopped. I waited, sipping my now lukewarm bottle of water, my eyes taking in the impressive Plaza Hotel. Being a total tourist, I attempted to snap some pics on my phone, but the building was far too big to fit into one photo at such close range, so I turned my attention to the Pulitzer Fountain, tiered with flowing water basins. I was impressed by the bronze statue of Pomona, the Roman goddess of abundance, and I couldn't help but walk around the perimeter of the fountain, taking a seat near one the corners. I remembered a beautiful black-and-white photo I'd seen of Marilyn Monroe seated at this fountain, probably in this very spot.

'You ready?' asked a hot and flustered Ben. He looked impatient and over the expedition already and we hadn't even entered the park yet. Considering what I had been feeling only eight hours beforehand, I welcomed the reappearance of his normal, moody façade. He had proven that, whatever had almost happened last night, nothing was going to change between us. He was as cranky and distant as ever, and although I'm sure there were good intentions behind the trip to the park, he clearly wished he was somewhere else – namely work, as he checked his phone every five minutes. Or maybe he was waiting on a message from Holly, the plain blonde from last night. He had a deep crease etched on his brow as he read something on his screen, before he finally pocketed the phone.

We crossed the road at a busy intersection and entered at the southern end of the park. We wandered the winding pedestrian paths, passing a pond, rocky outcrops, bridges, open fields and skyline views. I cared little if it annoyed Ben, I couldn't contain my happy-snapping pleasures and even got him to play photographer as I stood on the bridge with the Plaza Hotel in the distance. I took my phone from him, smiling at the screen, thrilled that he had taken a good shot. I glanced at him to say thanks, but was surprised to see the amusement that lined his face.

'What?'

'Nothing.' He shook his head, turning to continue to push the pram along, shifting me into motion. 'Come on, I'll take you to Bethesda Terrace.'

'Bethesda Terrace?' I repeated, searching my New York City guide.

'You'll know it when you see it.'

'Probably,' I admitted, having had a binge session of all my favourite New York movies two days before my interview.

'It's one of the most photographed monuments in Central Park. The bronze sculpture is called the Angel of the Waters, it symbolises the purification of New York's water supply in the eighteen hundreds. Below the angel are four cherubs that represent the Victorian sentiments of Purity, Peace, Temperance and Health.'

I walked beside him, tilting my head and squinting at the sun. 'Well, listen to you,' I teased. 'Quite the tour guide.'

'There's not much I don't know about this city.'

'Okay, well, you might know this then. I can see it in my head. A long walkway with a beautiful canopy of trees and bench seating and —'

'The Mall.' He laughed. 'We're going that way.'

'We are?' I said.

'It's one of the main walkways leading to Bethesda Terrace.'

I grinned broadly, thinking how often I had seen the iconic strip on TV, and I was soon to be walking through it.

Watching the squirrels dart around on the expanses of lawn, I wanted to wake Grace up and show them to her, but she seemed so peaceful, and then I realised there would be plenty more opportunities in the future for us to picnic in the park with or without Ben; this city was ours to explore. I just had to not get caught up in the urgency of wanting to see everything in New York in a minute, and start accepting that I wasn't going anywhere in the foreseeable future. This was my new job, my new home, and if I wanted to keep it that way, whatever happened last night could positively not happen again. Even though Ben, all tall and lovely with his navy Ralph Lauren polo and Ray-Bans, looked so incredibly good that I had wicked thoughts and fantasised about it happening again, without interruptions.

No! No, there won't be a next time, Sarah. Jesus, just look at the pretty park surrounds and get your head out of the gutter already.

~

The canopy of elms offered us a shady respite from the bright summer skies. Without a skyscraper in sight, it truly felt like we'd left the city behind. Tempting as it was to grab a bench and people watch for the afternoon, we pressed on down the shady promenade.

'You know, the Mall was specially designed to accommodate the width of carriages so they could drop off their wealthy passengers to enjoy the scenery and mingle with people of lesser status.'

I envisioned Victorian ladies strolling with their parasols and grand men in top hats.

'So I guess, back in the day, a carriage would have dropped you off and you could have socialised with me, the "lesser status",' I joked, but Ben didn't seem to find that particularly funny. If anything, he looked pretty uncomfortable.

He cleared his throat and continued playing tour guide, ignoring my comments. 'When these visitors finally reached Bethesda Terrace, their carriages would be waiting to take them to their next destination,' he finished.

I wanted to add, 'Here endeth the lesson,' but thought better of it.

From what I could tell, the Mall was still a gathering place, although the Victorian grandeur of ladies and gents in their Sunday best was long gone. The Mall was now occupied by skateboarders, rollerbladers and street performers. A long line of artists sketched tourists as we walked through to the Concert Ground.

I smiled. 'You're right, I do know this place.'

Bethesda Terrace sat on two levels, united by two grand staircases and a lesser one that passed under Terrace Drive, providing a passage from the Elkan Naumburg Bandshell, an elaborate amphitheatre. We stopped there for more photo ops, me standing on the stage in the centre with my hands above my head as Ben operated my phone. I was a total embarrassment, but I didn't care. The upper terrace flanked the 72nd Street Cross Drive and the lower terrace provided a podium for viewing the lake. Ben described all the intricate details in the way that only an architect could: mustard-coloured New Brunswick sandstone, with a harder stone for cappings, granite steps and landings, herringbone paving of Roman brick. It had me thinking I was the luckiest tourist in New York.

We stood on the staircase and, in a pinch-myself moment, Ben nudged my arm and offer me a sip of his water, since I had long since finished my own. His eyes may have been shielded by his Ray-Bans, but there was no hiding the smile.

'Go on, you weren't exactly worried about my germs last night,' he teased.

I didn't know how to react. Aside from our shared guilty looks this morning, not one word had been mentioned about last night. The speech I had been dreading – the 'this can never happen again' speech – never came. Nothing until now, and he was making a joke of it? I did not understand Ben Worthington.

I took the bottle of water from him and took a long swig of it, gasping and smacking my lips together in appreciation as I retorted, 'De-licious!'

Chapter Twenty-One

I danced around with Grace in the lounge, because you do anything you can to keep a baby happy, and bouncing up and down, with the occasional jolted drop, seemed to thrill her no end.

'You're going to be a thrillseeker, huh?' I laughed as I whizzed her around and she cackled. 'I think she's going to be a rollercoaster rider, this one,' I called to Ben, who had been in and out of the lounge while I entertained Grace. He walked into the room, staring at his phone, lines creasing his face. While it wasn't out-of-the-ordinary to see Ben like that, something was up. 'What's wrong?'

Ben blinked out of his trance, looking at me with his steely grey eyes. 'You know not to let anyone into the house while I'm away, right?'

I calmed my swinging of Grace to a slower rocking as I looked at him, confused. 'Of course.'

He nodded.

'The only people I know in New York are the well-meaning female members of your family,' I added, praying that if he was concerned about letting anyone into the house, maybe he could stop his mother rocking up on the doorstep. The suggestion I would just let anyone in made me feel annoyed. 'I'm going to give Gracie a bath,' I said coldly.

'You don't have to do that.'

'It's okay, I don't mind.' And I didn't. The less time I had to be near the kitchen with Ben the better. Some memories you just didn't need to recollect. We might both have been able to sweep last night under the rug, but it didn't mean living together would be completely free of awkwardness.

Just one more day and then he would be back at work, I told myself, and it would be me and Gracie in our own little world.

Regardless of the fresh air of the day and the liberal use of lavender bath liquid, Grace was as awake as ever, trying to escape getting dressed, as if she had somewhere better to be.

I laughed. 'Grace, keep still!'

I felt a nudge to my upper arm and did a double-take to the outstretched bottle, this time full of formula rather than water. Even though it was only the back of Ben's hand touching me, it felt like an electric shock, and I had to concentrate on my next breath.

I went to take the bottle but he pulled it away. 'No, it's okay, I've got this,' he said.

I pressed the last of Grace's studs together. 'Okay, well, I'm going out for dinner tonight.' I picked her up and handed her to Ben.

'I thought you didn't have any friends in New York?'

I frowned. 'I don't. You don't need to have friends to go out for dinner.'

Ben's mouth twitched as he tried not to smile.

'What?' I asked, getting annoyed. I may be rather tragic without any friends, but if I was going to have my last night of freedom for an entire week, I was going to search for a meal and save myself from another awkward dinner for two.

He shook his head. 'Wow.'

'Wow, what?'

'You really don't want to be alone with me in that kitchen.'

My mouth gaped and I felt heat flood my cheeks, not knowing how to respond.

'No.' I half-laughed, sounding so not convincing.

'You sure about that?'

'Yes, of course.'

'Because, you know that last night . . .'

Oh god, here we go, here came the speech, the one that I had been successfully avoiding all day and was more than happy to avoid for the rest of my life.

'Did you want me to bring you something back?' I blurted clumsily.

Ben's mouth shut abruptly as if his train of thought had been derailed. 'Oh, um, no thanks.'

'Okay, well, just text if you change your mind,' I said cheerily as I left him with Grace in the nursery, my fake smile falling as I turned away, breathing a sigh of relief at another bullet dodged.

One more day. One more day and he would be back at work.

~

I had no agenda, so when I stumbled across a line outside of Momouns on St Mark's Place I decided to be adventurous. And if it was a cheap meal on the go (as I overheard the woman next to me tell her friend), then all the better. I was proud of my adjustment to the bustling life of the city. I had gone from small country town girl to true New Yorker; well, kind of . . . actually, not really. A visit to Tiffany's and a trip to Central Park does not a New Yorker make.

Edging my way in, I received a friendly hello from a man I assumed was the owner.

I had done some research by taking note of what people around me were having, so I skim-read the boards and then said, 'Can I have one chicken kebab and one shawarma, please.'

Once I got my hands on the mouthwatering morsels, I walked out of the shop and found a place to perch in the dying rays of the day. Both the kebab and the shawarma were equally amazing. The flavour and seasoning were perfection, and Momouns' signature hot sauce provided an appropriate kick. I wanted to fist pump, I was so happy.

But of course, all good things must come to an end. As I sat in the afterglow of my dinner, my phone started to ring. I knew only one person had this number, and, sure enough, Ben's name flashed on the screen. Panic ran through me.

'If this is a late dinner request, I hope you like Middle Eastern?' I tried for humour.

'I told you I didn't want anything,' Ben said, annoyed.

Well, this was going well.

'Okay,' I said, waiting for him to come to the point. Surely if he needed something there would be a magical app he could touch instead of resorting to calling me? He never called me, ever. He wasn't trying to carry on the 'talk', was he?

'Are you going to be late tonight?' he asked, speaking as abruptly as I had heard him speak to his business associates.

I frowned. 'Well, after I finish my dinner, I'm going clubbing till sun up, might even do a good ol' walk of shame.'

There was silence, as if he was trying to work out if I was joking or not. And then I realised that probably wasn't the smartest thing to say. I was not some young girl who randomly hooked up with people in kitchens or at clubs and I didn't want Ben to think otherwise.

'I've got work in the morning,' he pointed out, and I rolled my eyes.

'I know, and I won't be late.'

I had planned on heading back after dinner – I was only a ten-minute walk away – but now I wanted to stay out a little longer. Well, until the sun went fully down anyway. After all, I was a single woman – I had to have a life outside of being an au pair, there had to be a balance.

'Well, just be quiet when you come in, I've just put Grace down so . . .'

Okay, now I was annoyed. I wasn't an airhead. One weekend of partial caring for Grace and he was suddenly dishing out advice.

'Will do!' I said, trying to keep my annoyance in check as I began to wrap this awkward, wooden conversation up. But before I had the chance to hang up and truly escape unscathed, Ben continued speaking.

'Sorry, what did you say?' I asked.

'I said, when you get back, come to the third floor, there are a few things I want to talk about.'

The 'talk'. On the forbidden third floor, of all places. I closed my eyes, gritting my teeth. This could not be happening. Maybe I would go clubbing.

'Okay,' I said, trying to sound like it was no big deal when all I could think of was maybe faking food poisoning, or a case of sunstroke from our outing today.

'Well, see you in a bit,' I said, and just as I hung up the phone, a momentary lapse of concentration saw the remnants of my dinner falling off my lap. They landed on the grubby New York City pavement where the three-second rule absolutely did not apply.

'No!' I cried out at the disaster at my feet.

Okay, now I was pissed off.

~

I took my time by admiring the lights of the Washington Arch while indulging in a peppermint ice cream, but even with the serenity of such a place, my mind was troubled the whole way home. I walked into Ben's townhouse to find the lower floor in muted lamplight, just as it had been last night; it gave me a certain chill regardless of the warm, welcoming feel. I had turned the ten-minute walk into an hour-long one to delay the inevitable, but now had to drag myself up the stairs to the mysterious third floor.

He had told me not to make a noise when I came in and yet I could hear music: Pink Floyd's 'Comfortably Numb'. Along with the brighter light that glowed on the third-floor landing, the first time I had seen it that way, the music made the usually quiet, soulless house feel very much alive.

I crept onto the landing, then stood slightly to the side to watch Ben. He stood before a library, but not your typical library: this was a wall of records. Unaware of my presence, he was singing under his breath, wearing the thick-rimmed glasses that made him look less businessman and more sexy nerd, reading the back of a record cover. This particular look on him made certain parts of me react. All I wanted to do was to fog up his glasses in the naughtiest of ways.

The third floor didn't reflect any other part of the house. It was open and broody with copper light fittings and navy-and-ochre furnishings; sexy and masculine, like him. A leather chair with a matching leather ottoman sat with a floor lamp directly behind it and a pile of records on a side table. One glimpse into Ben's room and I had learnt more about him than I had in a whole week. I had obviously stumbled across Ben's favourite pastime.

'Good thing there's a vinyl revival happening,' I said, causing Ben to look at me in the doorway.

'Nothing to revive. It never went anywhere for me,' he said. He put the cover down, and turned his full focus on me, which only made me more reluctant to enter. If being in the kitchen was awkward, being in Ben's room, near his luxurious king-size leather bed, was damn well unnerving. I walked in the opposite direction of the bed, even though I wanted to dive on it like a big kid.

The third floor resembled more of an apartment than a bedroom. A beautiful marbled bathroom opened into the main room – no modesty barriers like doors or walls here – as did the enormous walk-in wardrobe, which was bigger than my childhood bedroom.

I nodded in appreciation. 'Nice man cave,' I said, thinking how much it differed from any man cave I had known. I thought of my dad's shed at home where he kept his old vinyl records, next to the collection of road signs he had pilfered over the years working for the local shire council. Yeah, opposite ends of the spectrum.

Ben watched me with interest, his hands in the pockets of his jeans. 'It's just a room.'

'Oh, it's a little more than that,' I said. 'Still, I'm a bit relieved – at least there's no sex dungeon on the mysterious third floor.' I could honestly have kicked myself; when I'm nervous I tend to make jokes: inappropriate, unfunny jokes of the most tragic kind. Now Ben was thinking that *I* was thinking that's what was on the third floor, like he was some kind of sexual deviant. I prayed the ground would open up. Then I saw a slow smile spread across his face.

'Nah, the sex dungeon is on the lower level.'

His words made me feel slightly less embarrassed. 'Oh, you mean the "media" room?'

'Yeah.' He laughed. 'That's the one.'

Were we talking about this now? I would have given anything for a subject change, until of course it happened.

'Take a seat.' Ben gestured to the chair opposite him, near the empty fireplace. It wouldn't be difficult to imagine how amazing this room would be in the wintertime. Leather chairs next to the open fire, sumptuous rug, a tray full of liquor and crystal tumblers; it was a classy, sexy room.

Ben reclined casually in his big wing-backed chair, his elbows resting on the arms. 'Did you have a good day?' he asked.

I realised I hadn't thanked him for, or acknowledged, today's expedition, and I felt bad. I had been too busy trying to get my head around the reality that I was spending my day with Ben at all, and in Central Park of all places. As far as a Sunday goes, it was not the usual outing.

'I did, thank you.' *Ugh, you are so lame, Sarah!*

Ben nodded as if pleased by the response.

A silence grew between us, made even worse by the music coming to an end. The only sound seemed to be that of my heart, and the breaths I attempted to keep even as Ben's cool eyes looked into mine. I swallowed, trying to think of ways to continue the conversation so we could put it to bed as quickly as possible. I glanced at his bed. Okay, bad analogy; now was not the time to think about Ben Worthington and his bed.

So instead of letting Ben watch me squirm and going another day waiting to talk about the elephant in the room, I squared my shoulders. 'About last night,' I said, trying to keep my voice even.

Aside from the slight lift of his brows, Ben's face remained unchanged. 'Good,' he said. 'What are your thoughts?'

'Oh, um . . .' I stammered. Thoughts? I couldn't tell him those, they contradicted what my good sense wanted me to say. I couldn't tell him how I had been on the brink of a screaming orgasm just before his daughter interrupted the hottest sexual encounter of my existence. I couldn't tell him that I regretted nothing and if it was okay with him, I'd like to pick up from where we'd left off and finish the job right, if not multiple times. So I lied, I lied so hard.

'Well, clearly it was a mistake.'

'Right,' he said.

Which felt like a slap in the face; I had to stifle the pang that created inside me, and quickly moved on with 'my thoughts'.

'And it can never happen again,' I said with an edge of certainty that I was proud of.

He didn't reply. I was about to apologise for stepping over a line but stopped myself, wondering what I had to be sorry for – he'd kissed me back!

I tried to not let myself get too excited about that, I knew it was just a reaction to the emotions and memories I'd caused with my questions, but I couldn't help myself. If we were being candid, I needed for him to know that I had a pretty good idea why he'd kissed me.

'Who's Holly?' I asked, and as soon as the words were airborne I wanted to take them back.

Ben froze over like an Arctic chill had run through the room and I broke away from his severe stare. I could tell he was angry at me for asking, and again I was ready to apologise, until he said, 'A friend,' which gave me an answer, but didn't exactly clear anything up. I didn't press for more.

Ben stood and walked to the door of his room. He grabbed it and looked at me. It wasn't the most subtle of hints.

I got up, trying my best not to scramble as I went to the door, lifting my chin a little to present an illusion of confidence. I was more than ready to leave the third floor, leave and never linger there again.

Just as I reached the doorway, Ben's voice stopped me in my tracks.

'I'm going to be away all week for work.'

I don't know why I was so shocked by this – he worked, travelled, of course he did – but there was something about the sheer convenience of him 'working away' that left me sceptical, at best.

For all the time I had felt weak for avoiding the inevitable conversation about last night, it was clear now that I wasn't the only coward. Far from it.

'Anything else?' I asked coolly.

'I'm leaving early, can you look out for Grace tonight?'

'Of course.'

Ben nodded; it seemed his favourite acknowledgement.

I don't know why, but I didn't move straightaway, and I wasn't sure if it was because I was looking into the deep, cloudy depths of his eyes, or because I hoped he might say something comforting, something funny. Something to make me change my mind about resenting him, but he didn't. He just looked at me in the same heated way he had last night right before he kissed me.

My heart thundered against my chest and I could feel my breath catch in my throat at the familiarity of the look, so when he said, 'Goodnight, Sarah,' I blinked out of my trance and moved onto the landing, trying to pretend like my heart hadn't sunk to my feet.

'Goodnight, Ben.'

Chapter Twenty-Two

With space came clarity, and I was grateful for that. Ben didn't report in all week and with no life-or-death situations, I didn't contact him. To most this would be a dream situation: New York City at my feet, any facilities I could dream of at a touch of my finger and an absentee boss who pretty much let me get on with things. There was just one slight problem. Grace didn't want to sleep – ever. And come the week's end I was beyond exhausted and beginning to doubt everything I did. Was she too hot? Too cold? Did I like the mattress in her cot, should I trust that brand? My trips into the city were limited by the fact that most days I couldn't spare time for a shower or to get Grace ready to leave the house. I felt like I was a failure – failing Grace, failing myself – and as the week drew on I became even more jaded and angry at Ben. Of course Penny called and threatened a visit, but I always made up some engagement that made our lives sound well-adjusted and balanced. In truth most of the time all I could do for a break was to draw on the roof terrace, until Grace began to cry again, something that made my own tears well in dismay.

I couldn't do this. I just couldn't.

On Thursday afternoon, I was ready to break my streak and dial Ben's work number. I had to tell him that I was tired and defeated and I couldn't do it any more. Just as my finger hovered over the call button, the doorbell rang, causing Grace to scream louder.

I scurried down the hall, praying that the doorbell wouldn't ring again. I didn't care if it was Penny nor if I looked like shit, nor that the living room was a mess and Grace was screaming down the place. I was over the avoidance, I was over pretending that I had my shit together when I clearly didn't. I wasn't getting paid enough to be a full-time single parent, and I certainly wasn't living the New York dream; if anything, I was living a New York nightmare.

I unlocked the door and swung it open, finding Nikki Fitzgerald standing before me. Seeing her, I couldn't hold the tears at bay any more, and Nikki's bright, cheery demeanour slipped from her pretty face.

'What's wrong?' she asked, stepping forward and grabbing my arms as I began to cry.

'I'm just so happy to see you,' I said.

Nikki smiled. 'Yes, well, I do have that effect on people.' Grace's screams drew Nikki's attention down the hall. 'Trouble in paradise?'

'How did you guess?' I said, closing the door.

'If I know that cry, I would say that stubborn Worthington gene is kicking in.'

'Please tell me there's a cure.'

'What? For being a Worthington?'

I just looked at her, praying she was about to part with words of wisdom.

'I'm afraid not, lovely, she's a Worthington to the bone.'

'That's what I was afraid of,' I said, as I followed Nikki down the hall and closer to the screams. 'She won't sleep. What's wrong with her? What's wrong with me?'

'Firstly, there is nothing wrong with you. You are doing a great job, and a difficult job. There is also almost certainly nothing wrong with Gracie,' she said when we got to the living room. She held the baby over her shoulder, rubbing her soothingly on the back, instantly calming her tears. I was grateful as well as hating her a little for having the mightiest touch. When it came to babies, Nikki was an authority on the subject, and I would take everything she said as gospel.

'Next: there are lots of reasons why a baby won't sleep. Some of the most obvious are: they're hungry; they're distracted by something in the room; they're uncomfortable – too hot, too cold or in pain. If you've ruled out all of those—'

'And I have.'

'Well, the most common reason is that they are often overtired and don't know how to go to sleep.'

'But how do you teach them?' I asked, dismayed.

'The biggest challenge with using various techniques when your baby won't sleep is *consistency*. The truth is, you have to be strong in these situations. You have to be entirely consistent as much as you possibly can. That means bath, feeding, bed at the same time each day, no matter how much she fusses. Babies will pick up on the slightest change and hope that next time, they will be able to get you to feed them more quickly or get you to pick them up. They are pretty clever!'

I thought on what Nikki was saying and my shoulders sank. Grace's care was going to be a combination of job-sharing between me and Ben. I had handed Grace over to him come the weekend and he had handed her to me on Sunday night; throw in a day with Ruth and there was no consistency at all. It was a light-bulb moment and I was too afraid to hope that there could be something to be done about this.

'You have to soldier on, Sarah, try to help Grace learn how to settle on her own, otherwise you will always have to feed or cuddle her to sleep. Commit to being consistent for three days. If you can think of it as just three days, it doesn't feel as daunting, and after three days, babies will usually have started to learn new habits. Really consolidating the habits can take around two weeks, but three days is a brilliant start.'

I grimaced. 'But what about weekends?'

'You're Grace's main carer, you have to set the routine, the standards, and Ben will have to follow them. For once in his life he has to conform, because if you don't work as a team, poor Grace will be all over the place and will wear you down. By the looks of it, she's already succeeded.'

'Oh, please don't tell Ben, I'm just a little tired, that's all. I don't want him thinking I'm incapable of doing my job.' I had visions of a family crisis meeting, all the Worthingtons in attendance as they evaluated my performance criteria.

Nikki smiled. 'Oh, honey, your secret is safe with me, but don't think I won't be giving Ben a little piece of my mind when I see him,' she said, handing Grace over. She mercifully didn't cry, simply looked into my widened eyes.

I felt panic spike inside me. 'W-why would you do that?'

'Because you should not have to be shouldering this all on your own, Sarah. Being a full-time carer to Grace is not part of your job description.'

'Oh, I don't mind.' I shrugged. I might be on the verge of a nervous breakdown but at least without Ben here there was no awkwardness, no weird sexual tension.

'It's not right, and I know you're tired and you probably hate admitting that, but you are only human.'

'Well, I feel so much better, thanks to you.'

Nikki still seem enraged, though, even after I'd expressed my gratitude. 'Sarah, it's not right.' She looked at me pointedly. 'Why should he get to be at Lafayette

Street, entertaining friends and getting a full night's sleep all week when you're here on your own with Grace?'

'B-but I thought he had to go away for work?'

'I don't think Lower Manhattan counts, do you?'

I felt a knot twisting in the pit of my stomach, as anger swirled my insides. He was in New York? At Lafayette Street? Wining and dining friends, probably hanging out with Holly, while I was in the Village raising his daughter on my own? Oh hell, no.

Nikki must have sensed my anger, even poor Grace was picking up on it as she began to squirm and whimper.

'Listen, Sarah, don't worry, he probably just had to put in some groundwork for a project. I'll talk to him, you just start with your routine and leave Ben to me, okay?'

I smiled weakly at Nikki. 'I'll be fine, my priority is Grace.'

A silence fell between us – we both knew what the other was thinking: *If only Grace were Ben's priority, too.*

~

It took some convincing to make Nikki promise she wouldn't say anything to Ben. I assured her there were more important things to handle right now and, first and foremost, that was to settle Grace into a routine.

Things were about to change around here, and one of them was the means of communication. If Ben Worthington was going to hide out in his little penthouse thinking that it was a matter of out of sight, out of mind until the weekend, well, I had news for him. If I had been entrusted to look after Grace, his most prized possession, then it was up to me to enforce the routine that would roll over to the weekend. A schedule for Ben, Ruth, Penny – anyone who came into this house would have to abide by these rules. I felt like an idiot not having thought of it in the first place. Poor Grace had been dragged from pillar to post, with no semblance of routine. It was no wonder she couldn't settle.

'Well, Gracie girl, things are about to change,' I said to her, sitting at the kitchen bench with the laptop open. I opened a blank email and with great pride and a whole lot of power I set about writing a detailed plan. One that Nikki and I had discussed, and which I would start immediately. The first three days of consistency would bleed into the weekend, which was not ideal, but I was more than willing to sacrifice a weekend to ensure that Grace's routine was being adhered to. Short-term pain, long-term gain.

My email was professional, direct and fully thought out. I even attached some links to reading material to support my routine. Without alluding to my close call with an epic meltdown, I was honest about it having been a difficult week. But when I reread those words, I decided to delete that admission. Now was not the time to show weakness in any form. I had to be strong and steadfast, I had to be an authority. I wanted to add in a bit of a tongue-in-cheek dig, a 'hope it's sunny wherever you are in the world', but decided against it. I settled on a brazen read-receipt request to let me know if and when Ben had read my email.

I clicked send, straightening on my stool, feeling empowered by my email. I shut the laptop down and stepped away from it.

'Ball's in his court, Gracie.'

~

Email sent at 2.05 pm.

Email read at 2.38 pm.

Current time: 6.01 pm. Still no response.

Unbelievable.

Chapter Twenty-Three

I'd decided that, notwithstanding the sleep deprivation and the fear of screwing up Grace's childhood and doing irreparable damage to her psyche, the most difficult aspect of my job was dealing with Ben, whose selfishness knew no bounds.

I raged on through the night, and come Friday morning with no reply or any word that he was going to be home on the weekend, I took drastic measures.

I showered, dressed and got Grace ready for a morning stroll, which was something I had built into her routine. As part of my desperate amount of googling for information on a sleepless baby, I'd read that it was helpful to have your baby associate light and activity with the day and darkness and inactivity with night and the key was exposure to morning light: it suppressed melatonin, a hormone that regulates the sleep–wake cycle so that it peaks at the right time – apparently. After another sleepless night, I was willing to try anything. And, to be honest, my intended destination of Lafayette Street also made my steps a little more determined.

'Come on, Gracie, let's go pay Daddy a little visit.'

I don't know what I planned to say and I tried not to let myself feel like a total bunny boiler by showing up on his doorstep, but I needed to have some answer as to why he'd virtually abandoned his daughter. At the very least he needed to get his shit together and let me know when he would be home.

I thought I'd managed to cobble together a little speech to give him but, as soon as I came to a stop at the entrance of his Lafayette Street apartment, I froze. My ability to think, to move, to speak fled as I looked at the imposing red-brick building. What was I doing here? If a phone call or an email was only acceptable under life-and-death circumstances then what would an unannounced drop in do?

Oh God, help me.

I was wrestling between turning and going home or stepping up to the door. There'd be no turning back once I made that move. I took a deep breath, pushing myself into the foyer, hoping against hope that he wasn't going to be in. That would most certainly be a sign that this was a bad idea and I should just go home.

I would have given anything for a sign as the suit that brushed past me in the foyer turned.

'Sarah?'

I paused, turning toward my name. 'Alistair?'

So God must have a great sense of humour. He decided to give me a sign in the shape of Alistair Worthington, Ben's younger, smiling brother.

'What are you doing here?' he said in surprise.

'Oh, Gracie and I just thought we'd pop in to see her dad.'

Alistair's eyes shifted down as if seeing the pram for the first time, his smile dimming a little.

'Gracie?' he repeated, moving forward, tilting his head, a look of warmth and adoration in his eyes. He smiled brilliantly. If only Ben were more like his little brother. 'Wow, she's out like a light.'

'I know, right? I can't believe Grace has chosen to sleep now, of all times. She never sleeps.'

'Never?'

'Ever. I wish I was exaggerating.' I laughed.

He grimaced. 'Ah, well, it's a family trait, I'm afraid. I wish I could tell you that she'll grow out of it.'

'Please don't tell me that.'

'Would you feel better if I lied to you?'

'Yes, please.'

'She will totally grow out of it; she'll be sleeping eight hours before you know it.'

'I would settle for two.'

'Well, lucky she's cute.'

'Yeah, when she's asleep.'

Alistair burst out laughing, before quietening for fear of waking her up. For the second time in as many meetings, Alistair was the unexpected delight of my day. I had been so worked up marching toward my doom, until I was greeted with a smile and the grey-blue eyes of a Worthington, except this pair were kind – they even had a little sparkle in them. They were by far the most attractive part of him.

I had to pull myself away from those eyes and remember why I had come all this way.

'Well, we better head up and see the lord of the manor,' I said, readjusting my grip on the pram.

'I'll save you the trip – he's not in.'

'Oh.' Now this was the sign I was looking for.

Alistair shrugged. 'Something about heading over to Brooklyn to check on some building project he's contracting, apparently.'

'I wonder if he'll drop in to see Nikki?' I said, mainly to myself. Perhaps it wasn't too late to tell Nikki to go ahead and give him a piece of her mind, knock some sense into him.

'There's no way he would get away with being in Brooklyn and not dropping in for a visit. If Nikki found out, it wouldn't be worth his life.'

I laughed, knowing that what he was saying was true.

'Well, it was nice seeing you. No doubt I'll bump into you again,' I said, moving the pram around to head outside. Alistair quickstepped around us, beating the doorman to open the door.

'Hey, listen, are you busy right now? Do you want to have lunch or something? My plans are pretty much shot with Ben not being around, so I have some time up my sleeve.'

'Oh, um.' I tried to think of an excuse: laundry to do, washing my hair . . . I don't know what made me want to say no, but when I couldn't think of a valid reason, I changed my mind. Just because some people choose to hide away from the world doesn't mean I had to.

I smiled. 'Well, Gracie and I were just going to grab something to eat and hang out in Washington Square Park if you want to come?'

Alistair nodded, and for a second I could see the resemblance to Ben. My heart skipped a beat.

'An excellent choice,' he said.

~

Alistair Worthington was a breath of fresh air and, just like Nikki, I questioned his parentage as I watched him dote and fuss over Grace, who excitedly whacked him in the face with her rattle.

'Ah, that's gonna bruise.' He chuckled, nursing his eye socket.

'Grace, that is no way to greet your uncle.'

He squinted. 'She packs a mean punch, that's for sure.'

'She's also partial to face gouging and hair pulling,' I said, taking Grace from his knee to rescue him.

He laughed, shaking his head. 'Such a brute.'

'Does this iron will of hers come from your mother's or father's side?'

Alistair blew out a breath, crossing his arms and relaxing on the bench as he idly watched the spray of the fountain before us. 'Hard to say. The old man's as stubborn as a mule, and, well, you've met my mother.'

I nodded, perhaps a little too vigorously.

'You'd like my dad. He's a tough old bastard but he's a charming one as well. Makes up for the fact he wasn't the world's greatest dad.'

There was something refreshing about Alistair's candidness, maybe because his brother was such a closed book. With Alistair, there were no hushed secrets or things left unsaid. I had found out more about his family in one afternoon than I had in almost a fortnight working for Ben. I had so wanted to ask Alistair about Ben specifically, but I kept the conversation to him and his life, which was far from boring. His tales of European summers, a life of rebelling against his family and causing havoc to the Worthington reputation had me more than convinced that I had found myself a new BFF.

'So, what sent you away? And what has you coming back?' I asked, placing Grace into her pram and pulling up the sun visor.

Alistair looked at me sideways, squinting against the sun's rays. 'Wow, so many questions.'

'Oh, sorry, I'm being nosy, just tell me to mind my own business, that's what everyone else does.'

He shifted forward on his seat, fully focused on me and, God, if he didn't look like Ben more than ever now that he'd turned serious. He leant his elbows on his knees. 'Who tells you to mind your own business?'

'Oh, no, well, not in so many words, just not to ask any questions, you know? Which I can understand,' I lied.

Alistair scoffed, leaning back again. 'Yep! Welcome to the Worthingtons,' he said before looking at his watch. 'Damn it, speaking of Worthingtons.'

'Coffee date with Penny?'

'Not exactly – whisky and men's business with Father.' He sighed, standing and blocking the sun so I didn't have to shield my eyes. 'Don't tell me she's asleep again, I'm starting to get a complex.'

'Ha! I know, right? For one who never sleeps. Seriously, what are you doing tonight?'

Alistair looked at me with a spark of interest that had me blushing at how suggestive my words must have sounded.

I cleared my throat. 'I mean, you're obviously the baby whisperer,' I said quickly.

'Either that or the most boring person she's ever met.'

'I doubt that.'

And there was that smile again, broad and bright and almost something I had to shield my eyes from.

'Hey, Sarah, you know that you can ask me as many questions as you want. I'll never tell you to mind your own business.'

My smile mirrored his. 'Good to know.'

Alistair nodded. 'Well, I better get going, it's been great hanging with you girls,' he said, backing away with his hands in the pockets of his pants. 'By the way, I still haven't caught up with Ben, but we have a family dinner coming up. Do you think you can keep the secret of me being in town?'

'You think he doesn't know? As if your mum or sister haven't said anything.'

He laughed, shaking his head. 'I would have thought you of all people would know how good Worthingtons are at keeping secrets.'

'Wow. So. True.'

'Deal?'

'Your secret is safe with me.'

Alistair bowed. 'Much obliged, see you around, Miss Williams.'

Alistair turned to exit through the Washington Arch, and then I realised.

'Hey, Alistair, you never answered my questions.'

He turned to me with interest.

'What drew you away and what made you come back?'

He thought, a knowing smile curving his mouth. 'That's easy,' he said, 'because the answer is the same for both.'

I folded my arms and waiting, ever so intrigued.

Alistair smiled, that same glorious smile, as he winked before continuing to walk. 'Her name is Holly.'

The smile fell from my face and my blood ran cold.

Holly?

Oh my God.

Chapter Twenty-Four

was shocked. Surely he couldn't do that to his own brother?

If Alistair had left because of Holly, did that mean that he knew about her and Ben? Was Holly why Ben and Caroline's relationship had been on the rocks – had Ben had an affair? No wonder no one wanted me to ask questions, not even Nikki. The idea that I had almost become another notch in Ben's bedpost made me feel ill.

I glanced down at Grace in her pram as I walked back to the townhouse, thinking if it wasn't for her I would be writing a letter of resignation and packing my bags. Tears welled and I felt a new sense of hopelessness. But as I looked at her sleeping, my heart ached, and I realised I couldn't possibly leave. Despite the sleepless nights, the tears, the screams, the drool, the poop and the hair pulling, I had gone and fallen in love with her. And I was the only stable thing she had in her life right now.

I cautiously bumped Grace up the steps, pausing at the top to hold my breath as she squirmed and frowned in her sleep. I blew out a sigh of relief, having managed not to wake her. I rolled her down the hall into the lounge, enjoying the peace a little longer as I took my bag from my shoulder and put it on the couch. I wiped a light sheen of sweat from my face then went to the fridge for a bottle of water. I twisted the lid and gulped big mouthfuls before I realised where I was standing. The memories flared in my mind. Damn him! Why couldn't he be a crap kisser?

I quickly moved to the opposite side of the bench, opening the laptop to record Grace's sleep and daily routine to monitor her patterns. But before I even had a chance to click onto the Word doc my eyes caught on something above the little envelope at the bottom of the screen: a small red circle with a white number one inside.

I swallowed, not letting myself truly freak out until I clicked on the envelope . . .

'Oh, fuck.'

Ben had replied.

A part of me hoped that it was an email telling me I was fired, but I knew I wouldn't be that lucky. I psyched myself up to open it, the cursor hovering over his name, my blood pulsing loud in my ears like the countdown to launch time, and before I could chicken out, I clicked.

There was no way this man could possibly infuriate me any more than he already had. His response to my thoroughly thought-out, articulate, fifteen-hundred-word email?

On my way home. – B

'You've got to be kidding me.'

I checked the time the email was sent: twenty minutes ago. I had no real idea of how long it took to travel from Brooklyn, especially in a chauffeur-driven Rolls Royce. But, as I looked around the room, I did know that it looked like a bomb had gone off.

I started to clean like a woman possessed. It was always important to me, no matter who I worked for, that they come home to a clean and organised home; I wanted to seem like this superhuman force who could do it all, even if I felt anything but. A part of me wanted to say screw it and give Ben a dose of reality – he deserved it, I thought bitterly – and then I stilled, wondering if that was born from the disappointment of him avoiding his daughter or that he was a massive love rat who'd betrayed his own brother. How was I ever going to continue working for a man like him?

I was about to find out.

The front door slammed and Ben's footsteps sounded in the hall. I attacked the bench even more vigorously. Maybe if I seemed busy I wouldn't have to interact with him too much.

'Get ready,' he said.

No hello? No how has your day been, your week even? 'Sorry?'

'We've been invited to dinner with a colleague of mine.'

I twisted the dishcloth in my hand, looking at him in confusion.

Ben sighed, unfastening the single button of his jacket. 'They all want to meet Grace.' He said it in a way that almost sounded bored. So . . . what? She was good enough to use as a showpiece?

'Did you get my email?' I asked.

'Yes,' he said, going over to Grace in her bouncer. 'She doesn't live in this thing, does she?' he said.

'Of course not!'

Ben glanced at me, not seeming to appreciate my tone, but I didn't care – I didn't appreciate the accusation. I should have left the house messy after all, show him a bit of reality.

I walked over to Grace, pushing past him to unclip her from her seat. I nursed her over my shoulder. 'We've actually had a productive day, haven't we, Grace? We had lunch in Washington Park.'

There was no response as he tried, and failed, to ready Grace's baby bag.

'In fact, we dropped in to your office, but you weren't there.'

'Where?'

I rolled my eyes, adjusting my hold on Grace. 'To your work, but you were in Brooklyn.'

'Who told you that?'

My mouth gaped, almost spilling the truth. *Your brother told me.*

'So you weren't in Brooklyn?'

'Why would I go to Brooklyn?' He seemed to find the thought unsavoury.

I wanted to tell him what Alistair had told me, but I had promised to keep his secret for a little longer. Then I wondered if maybe someone was preventing Alistair from getting to Ben. I thought of the snarly Ruth answering the door at the Lafayette Street apartment and suddenly had no doubt who was behind the misinformation.

'Well, I suppose I should have just called in every day, seeing as that's where you've been all week.' I tried not to sound snarky, but I couldn't help it. I wanted him to know I knew. And that he was weak for hiding out and taking the easy option.

He never said a word, simply averted his attention to Grace, his eyes shiny with a new lightness as he cocked his head and smiled at her, touching her cheek. Just as quickly as the emotion came to him, he shut it down, turning to me, his expression serious, and he was every bit the devil I had pegged him for. I wanted as little to do with him as possible.

'Get ready,' he repeated.

I left the room knowing that I couldn't bite my tongue forever, and if this night was going to be as awful as I predicted, then come morning, I would be handing in my resignation letter. That thought was the only thing that kept me moving up the stairs.

Chapter Twenty-Five

Grant and Melissa Peterson lived on the Upper East Side. They embodied everything that was fine and good. They had lovely wine glasses and an impressive art collection. They were bubbly and welcoming and cooed appropriately over Grace and made even the lowly au pair feel welcome. I wondered if maybe Alistair had been invited? Or Nikki? My thoughts were interrupted by Grace being torn from my arms by an overexcited Melissa.

She laughed. 'Oh, Grant, doesn't it make you want another one?'

Grant's eyes glazed over and if this was a cartoon, he would have been loosening his collar and sweating bullets. But this was reality, so he just laughed nervously and took a long sip of his champagne flute.

'How many children do you have?' I asked.

'Oh, just Evie, she's four, and in desperate need of a brother or sister.' Melissa smiled, dropping a less than subtle hint as she glanced at her husband, who had chosen to have a deep and meaningful discussion with Ben. She rolled her eyes. 'Men and their business talk. You would think they'd just want to leave it at the office.'

Melissa spoke to me as if I was a fellow frustrated wife, sharing the same shortcomings of our partners. And as much as I had dreaded the dinner party invite and how out of place I would feel, I recognised a similar loneliness in her. She was fair, with flame-red hair and a nervous disposition, and she looked at her husband with wide, watery eyes in a pathetic bid for approval. I could see she was eager for another baby – I had seen it before, in other women. She just wanted something to love. The tall, dark and sexy Grant Peterson seemed like he would always rather talk business, not babies.

It was so fascinating to people-watch, to make a judgement within the first few minutes of meeting someone. I wondered what people would make of me, standing next to Ben. What would people who weren't in the know think, looking across the room at us? There's no way they would see us as a couple: Ben was brooding, stiff and uncomfortable; in a room full of people, he spoke only to Grant, and was genuinely annoyed when people intervened to shake his hand and offer small talk. I couldn't help but enjoy watching him squirm. I smirked when a highly botoxed New York socialite with little notion of personal space advanced on him. 'Benjamin, darling, how are you?' she all but purred.

I had been so wrong. This dinner party was nothing to cringe about, this was the best entertainment I'd had all week, and I planned to enjoy every minute of it, even if I only had juice in my decadent champagne flute.

Then a shadow in my peripheral vision closed in. I knew it was Ben, I had seen him untangle the socialite's flailing arms from around his neck as he excused himself from the group. I lazily cast my gaze around the room, acting as if I wasn't bothered by his approach.

'Don't worry, it's non-alcoholic,' I said, looking at him like I was bored.

'Good to know, but that's not what I was going to ask.'

'Oh, what were you going to ask then?' I said, watching him expectantly. I knew I was giving off attitude, being less than professional, but I was finding it difficult to care. Maybe if he was at least present for his daughter I would dislike him less. To me, there was nothing endearing about him, apart from those eyes that made my train of thought fuzzy, and those lips that I knew were soft and lush and – man, I needed a drink. I was parched.

Just as I was about to put my glass down on an empty tray and pick up another, a hand snared my wrist.

'Oh, Sarah, there you are. Listen, come upstairs, will you, I hear dinner and drinks are waiting to be served.'

Earlier, when I had wanted so badly to see a familiar face, I certainly hadn't meant it to be Penny Worthington's.

'Um . . .' I looked pleadingly at Ben, but he seemed amused by the sudden intrusion. Bloody coward.

'Come, there's someone I want you to meet.'

'Melissa has Grace so I—'

'Well, she's in good hands then.'

I threw Ben a parting frown; smirking, he saluted me with his champagne as Penny pulled me away through the crowd. Bastard.

～

Louisa Tourky was an English rose. Blonde hair, peaches-and-cream complexion, big round eyes and a knowing smile. The way she tucked her hair behind her ear and blinked – once, twice – made the simple act almost erotic. She made me feel like a bag lady.

'Louisa, this is Sarah Williams. She's Australian,' announced Penny Worthington by way of introduction. It was as though she thought making sure people knew I was Australian would explain everything, especially my faults. 'Perhaps Louisa can give you a few pointers, Sarah. Grant says that Louisa is the cream of the crop as an au pair.' Penny turned to offer a barely there smile. It was a none-too-subtle dig at me. Oh, how I hated her.

As soon as Penny had descended the stairs, Louisa crossed the room, peering out to the landing and stepping back to shut the door behind her.

'Ding-dong, the witch is gone,' she sing-songed. 'Want a smoke?' She cracked a window, her long blonde hair swishing over her shoulder as she looked at me with a mischievous smile. I liked her instantly.

'Ah, no, thanks, I don't smoke.'

'Well, working for the Worthingtons, that's probably a good thing.' Louisa clicked her lighter and inhaled until the cigarette was aglow.

I wondered what she knew about them. 'How long have you worked for the Petersons?'

She blew her smoke out of the window. 'Oh, I don't know, eighteen months?'

Eighteen months. I could only assume that she must have liked her position, and then I thought of the prospect of being employed by the Worthingtons for that long and I just couldn't see it. I couldn't see any longevity in it because, try as I might, I never actually felt that this world was a part of my reality.

Even though Penny had pretty much dragged me here, I was enjoying the calm in the charming wood-panel-and-leather library with Louisa. It was quiet and cosy, away from the elite and their children. Louisa had extinguished her cigarette and was sauntering across the room with a sense of ownership; she'd obviously hung out in this room often, which surprised me as she didn't strike me as the bookish type. She reached for the crystal decanter of whisky on the drink cart.

'Want one?' she asked, smirking at me as she tipped the rich liquid into the sparkling crystal tumbler.

'Ah . . . no tha—'

'Let me guess, you don't drink whisky either, tut-tut-tut, such a saint you are, the Worthingtons struck gold with you,' she teased, bringing the tumbler to her lips.

I felt like I was in high school all over again, like Louisa was double daring me to do something stupid, and as far as I was concerned, drinking on the job when you were supposed to be caring for children was right up there.

'Ugh, here, hold this, I gotta go pee,' she said. I thought how incredibly American she sounded, even with her posh English accent. Louisa shoved the drink into my hand and I had to rebalance so as not to spill a drop on the rug. I wondered, come time for me to go home, would my friends notice any change of accent? Would they notice any change in me at all? Probably not, I was always just Sarah. My moral compass was also painfully strong and true – I don't think I could ever be in danger of being controversial. I always did the right thing: working hard and enjoying the simple pleasures in life, not that Tiffany's was exactly simple.

An image of Ben's lips surfaced, and I remembered how they felt on my body, and I suddenly didn't feel so saintly after all.

I looked at the tumbler in my hand, and it had me thinking, remembering. How did I feel when I broke the rules? Did I feel any different? Guilt-ridden perhaps? Elated, empowered? Maybe I even walked around with an air of confidence just like Louisa did; I mean, sure, this was her domain and she probably felt at ease here. But even in my own environment, each day was about waiting, and worrying whether Ben would be back or if he was going to disappear . . . and what if I kissed him again?

What would happen, what would he do? All the questions running through my mind were starting to wear me down. Oh, how I wished I were more like Louisa, a free spirit – maybe that was what worked, what got you noticed? Penny Worthington certainly seemed like a fan. And right then, as I stared down into the whisky, I thought, Fuck it! I lifted the glass to my mouth and knocked back the rich, fiery contents so quick it took my breath away.

It was right about the time I got my senses together, recoiling from the disgusting yet no doubt expensive whisky, that a movement in the corner of my vision brought my attention to the open doorway. Ben stood there, his hand resting on the handle as his eyes moved from my face down to the empty tumbler. He stepped into the room, shutting the door behind him with such a loud thud it made me jump. He folded his arms and pressed his back against the door.

'Let me guess, that's non-alcoholic too?'

I placed the empty tumbler on the drink cart. 'What are you doing, lingering in the servants' quarters?'

'Servants' quarters?'

'Well, this is where your mother dragged me to meet Louisa.'

'Ah, Louisa.' He said her name like he was recalling an interesting memory.

'She's just ducked out.'

'Well, that explains why I can't find Grant.'

'What?'

'Oh, nothing,' he said, but his mind seemed far away. 'Listen, we won't stay long, we should get Grace home and settled.'

My mouth opened, ready to argue the point, until I realised. He was being . . . thoughtful.

'Have some dinner and then come downstairs.' He smiled and I hated the way my insides twisted.

'You sure about that?'

There was something in the way he gazed at me; his eyes were a cool blue, but they burned with intent. I hadn't seen him all week, and yet, being near him brought back all my mixed-up emotions. I tried to hate him; in spite of everything I had learnt, I thought seeing him again would be easy. But then he looked at me in a way that made my thoughts blurry and my skin hot.

'You won't have to ask me twice to get out of here,' he said, pushing away from the door and opening it just as Louisa was about to enter.

'Oh, hi, Mr Worthington.' Louisa smiled, and blinked once-twice in that alluring way of hers.

'Louisa, how's young Evie going?'

'Tucked in bed like a little angel.'

He nodded. 'As Grace will be . . . soon.' He lifted his eyes to me, as if to accentuate the time frame.

'Did you want me to come get her?' I asked.

'I don't like your chances of prying her from Melissa's grasp; let her have her moment. I think she's using Grace's smile to entice Grant into extending the family.'

Ben directed his words mainly to Louisa, whose smile weakened. 'Ladies.' He nodded, walking through the door.

Louisa closed the door. 'Ugh, Susan, you are so lucky.'

'Sarah.'

'Oh, right, Sarah,' she said distractedly as she walked across the room and threw herself into the oversized chair near the fireplace. 'So lucky,' she repeated, reaching for her drink, only to frown when she saw it was empty.

'Um, how do you figure that?' I half-laughed, wanting to divert her attention. I took a seat opposite her on a Chesterfield lounge. Today more than ever I had come to the conclusion that my job was somewhat of a disaster. The more I learnt about the Worthingtons' secrets, the more I was convinced that I couldn't stay.

'Because you don't have a neurotic, insecure wife wanting to bone Ben all the time.'

Was she talking about Melissa? 'She wants a baby pretty bad, then?'

'Seriously, she just needs to get a hobby or something, because the more she's around, the more she makes my life miserable, I swear to God.'

I could feel myself bonding with Louisa. Even though she was doing all the talking, it was nice to hear from someone who also had battles with her employers. It made me feel like I wasn't alone.

'Yeah, well, I have Penny Worthington,' I said, trying to offer some common ground.

'Pfft, Penny's a doddle. I would take her any day, she loves me,' she said, shrugging.

Well, why didn't she love me? I thought I was totally lovable.

There was a knock on the door.

'Come in,' called Louisa.

The door opened, revealing a man with a trolley and a smile.

'Oh, thank god, I'm starving! Just put it over there, please.' Louisa directed the man like she was lady of the house. I couldn't get past the knowledge we really were in the servants' quarters, being fed here while the beautiful people lingered below. While I hadn't thought I'd be sitting at a long, white linen–clad dining table rubbing elbows with everyone, being tucked away out of sight seemed rather shitty.

'Guess there's not enough chairs for us au pairs at the dinner table then,' I quipped, as the man unveiled meals that looked impossibly small and posh. I'd have to ask driver Dave if he knew of a nearby Macca's on the trip home.

'Well, blame Melissa for that. This would have been her idea, hey, Manuel?'

Manuel smiled and shrugged, obviously not wanting to get involved as he bowed and bid us goodnight, quickly exiting with the empty trolley.

'She seems so nice,' I said, mainly to myself.

Louisa scoffed. 'She's a bloody psycho.'

It was awkward hearing Louisa speak so candidly about the family she was working for. As much as I knew Ben was impossible most of the time, to openly bag him would be . . . wrong.

Louisa brought her plate to her chair, sitting down to tuck into her tiny meal. 'So tell me all. What's it like working for the Ice Man?'

I laughed. 'Ice Man?' I repeated, bringing my plate to the couch and grabbing a cushion to rest it on, just as Louisa had.

'Oh, hell yeah, those eyes – cold as fucking ice.'

Now I understood. I had been on the receiving end of those stares and they did cause a shiver down your spine. It also managed to evoke a heated response in me, but I chose to block that out.

'Which is ironic, seeing as he's so bloody hot.' She laughed.

Something inside me twisted, hearing her speak of Ben that way. She gave me a devilish little smile, licking sauce off her knife.

'So . . . have you fucked him?'

I nearly choked on my food, coughing and spluttering as I grabbed for my water.

Louisa looked at me with interest. 'You have.'

I shook my head vigorously, mainly because I was working on just trying to breathe. 'No!' I croaked.

'Well, sucked him off, then?'

Oh my God! 'No!' I shouted.

'Hmm, you sound pretty defensive,' she mused, popping in another sliver of veal and chewing thoughtfully. 'But I think I believe you.' The admission didn't alter the fact that my reaction had made me look prudish, or guilty, even though I hadn't done *that* with Ben.

'Such a shame. You haven't got anything standing in your way.'

'Being an au pair's not a dating service,' I said. I couldn't believe the nerve of this woman; I didn't even know her.

'I'm not talking about marriage proposals, I'm just talking a little fun.'

I had thought that I'd found a kindred spirit, a new friend in New York. But the longer I spent with Louisa, the less I liked her. These people entrusted this woman with their daughter, and they had done so for almost two years? And then it occurred to me.

I put my plate aside, having lost my appetite after nearly needing the Heimlich manoeuvre. Although Louisa was turning my stomach, I wouldn't let this opportunity slip away.

'Louisa, can I ask a question?'

She shrugged. 'I'm an open book.' So typical that she assumed it was about her.

'Did you know Ben's wife?'

'I knew her,' she said, nodding.

'It's so incredibly sad.'

'Yeah, I know, like way to tear a family apart, right?'

I don't know if it was the blank look that gave me away, but it didn't take Louisa long to catch on that I didn't exactly get what she was saying.

'You know, because of how it happened.'

I shrugged. 'All I know is that Grace was a few weeks old, and that Caroline died in a car accident.'

Louisa shook her head. 'Fucking Worthingtons.'

At any other moment I might have found her words comforting, a means to bond over a common character assessment of the Worthingtons, but all it made me do was shift with unease. 'W-what else is there to know?'

Louisa scoffed. 'You sure you don't want a drink? You might need one after this.'

Chapter Twenty-Six

'What?'

Louisa became solemn as she put her own plate aside. She wiped her hands on the serviette and sat forward, giving me her full attention.

'Caroline wasn't driving the day she died.'

I could feel my blood run cold; Ben's tortured face appeared in my mind and my heart ached. 'Oh my God, you don't mean . . .'

Louisa nodded, leaning further forward. She lowered her voice. 'Alistair Worthington was driving.'

'*Alistair?*'

Louisa fell back in her chair, waving my words away. 'Oh, you probably don't know who that is, but let me tell you, it caused a major rift in the family.'

I went to speak, to clarify that I did know who Alistair was, that I had met him, but thought better of it.

'Alistair is the estranged little brother of the family, the wild, rebellious black sheep, if you will,' she said.

'How awful. Surely it was an accident? I mean, he wasn't at fault, right?'

'Regardless of fault, Ben was meant to pick Caroline up that day, but instead she ran into Alistair and he offered to take her home. And the rest, as they say, is history. A very sad one. You know, Ben's never been able to forgive Alistair and, well, Alistair hasn't been able to forgive himself. So he hightailed it overseas, and no one in the Worthington family dares speak about it.'

I couldn't believe what I was hearing – poor Alistair. His request that I not tell Ben he was here made sense now. I felt something spike inside me, a great empathy for the man who would have to live with such trauma for the rest of his life.

I shook my head. 'Ben doesn't seem to know how to bond with Grace, he really struggles, and I think before I came along he didn't have much to do with her. Is that right?'

Louisa nodded. 'He's always working, day and night. And when Caroline died he just became even more obsessed with work and, I guess, avoiding reality. Like, he just doesn't want to deal with the baby.' Louisa shrugged. 'Grant says he's grieving and needs time.'

I so desperately wanted to ask about who Holly was, but didn't dare go there. Louisa didn't seem one to keep a secret, and mentioning Holly could open a can of worms. The situation was far more complicated than I could have ever imagined.

Poor Alistair. Poor sweet Grace.

My sadness soon morphed into anger, but it was a new kind. I was angry at the Worthingtons – Penny, Emily, even Nikki – for not being honest with me. It was one thing for Ben to not want me to know, but surely someone could have told me, prepared me?

I blinked back the moistness in my eyes, straightening in my seat and trying to keep my emotions in check in front of Louisa, who looked at me intently with her big doe eyes.

'What was she like?' I asked. I wanted to know but I didn't want to know, if that makes any sense. Not that anything made sense anymore. There was not one picture, no trace of her whatsoever at the townhouse – it was like Caroline never existed. I knew people dealt with grief in different ways, but I just couldn't process it.

Something crossed Louisa's face, something I couldn't quite read, as she suddenly found a stray thread in her shirt particularly fascinating. 'Yeah, she was nice.'

I wanted her to say more, but I wouldn't push. It was more information than I would have ever garnered on my own from Ben or his family, so I was grateful to her for that. Louisa wasn't going to be my new best buddy or anything, but at least she'd told me the truth, even though her sudden change in demeanour made me think she was holding something back. Maybe I was just being paranoid.

With the mood in the room altered and our half-eaten dinner gone cold, I was ready to call it a night and head downstairs to give Ben the sign to escape. I could only hope he had finished his meal and was ready to go. Now that I had unearthed such a huge secret, I had no idea how to act or feel. I'd gone from not wanting to look at him to not knowing how to look at him.

'Wait a sec, I better go check on Evie,' Louisa said, uncrossing her legs and launching out of her seat as if fire burned underneath her.

Before I could say goodbye, and thank her for the information, she was gone. I sighed, throwing myself against the chair, mentally drained and desperate to get home.

Just because I knew the truth didn't mean I would be letting anyone else know. If the Worthingtons had worked so intently to keep the secret from me, then I would happily play along. Right now I wanted to hug Grace to me tightly and never let her go.

This job was as it had always been: all about Grace. More so now than ever.

~

I didn't know if I was lost in my thoughts or just a poor judge of time, but Louisa seemed to be taking far too long to return. Perhaps sweet little sleeping Evie wasn't so sweet or sleepy at all. I decided to leave the library, and made my way down the long, dim hall to try to see if I could say goodbye to Louisa before I headed downstairs. I crept along, a true expert at being quiet in any house. It was a talent I had perfected. If Louisa was having difficulty with Evie I didn't want to disturb them.

I approached a door that was undoubtedly Evie's, coloured letters spelling her name across its surface. I smiled, thinking I would do the exact same thing to Grace's room one day. I put my head closer to the door to listen for crying or voices. There was a soft glow coming from the bedroom and I peered through the doorway, half expecting to see Louisa comforting Evie with a bedtime story, or perhaps lying by her side until she settled. So when I found only the tiny bump in the bed of a deeply sleeping Evie, I frowned. Louisa was nowhere in sight.

I backed away from the door. She'd probably gone down to the party, forgetting about me and our depressing conversation. I was a bit annoyed, thinking I had been left there all that time while Louisa was probably arm-in-arm with Penny, her number-one fan. Oh, well, I had tried to do the right thing but now it was time to go. Just as I was about to head down the hall, I heard a crash, followed by a muted giggle. I stopped dead. Even though the noise had come from the opposite direction of where I had to go, it got the better of me. I doubled back and crept down the hall.

A strip of light from the bathroom at the end of the hall lit a streak across the carpet – the door was not fully closed. A shadow flickered across the strip of light; there was definitely someone in there. If it was Louisa, I could say goodbye after all. I owed her as much after she'd shared such valuable knowledge. I stood to the side of the door and peered in through the gap to see if I could see her, hoping I wouldn't catch her on the toilet.

I could see her all right. I could see way too much of her. Her hands gripped the vanity and her skirt was hitched over her hips, her top and bra peeled down in front. The only thing preserving her breasts' modesty was the hands that gripped them – hands that belonged to Grant Peterson. He slammed into her from behind, groaning and cursing under his breath. He was looking down, his trousers around his ankles as he moved his grip from her breasts to her hips for better leverage, pushing her higher onto her toes as he moved faster.

Holy shit!

I ran down the hall, caring little about making a noise that might wake Evie – or alert the whole house, for that matter. I just wanted to get the hell out of there. And if I never came back or saw the likes of Louisa again it would be too soon. I swung around the banister to hit the stairs and slammed into something bony.

'Oh, you stupid girl, watch where you're going,' spat Penny Worthington, her eyes ablaze as she rubbed her arm. 'Honestly, Sarah, a bit of decorum wouldn't go astray.'

I breathed out a laugh, not in the mood for her bullshit tonight, nor any other night. 'Don't speak to me like that,' I said, perhaps a bit too loudly. I glanced past Penny to where Ben lingered, leaning against the bottom banister, watching us. The expression on his face was nothing compared to the way Penny looked at me now. I suppose no one spoke to Penny Worthington like that – no one.

'I had hoped you might learn something from Louisa,' she said icily, still rubbing at her arm.

It took all my strength not to roll my eyes. 'I certainly did.'

'Oh, good, well, there is hope for you yet,' she said, patting me on the shoulder in the most patronising way. 'Now, where is lovely Louisa? I have to ask her something before she retires for the night.'

In spite of the shock of what I had just stumbled across – Louisa and Grant Peterson, her boss, the father of her client, a married man – I couldn't bring myself to throw her under the bus. I stood in Penny's way, blocking her.

'Um, I think she's just dealing with Evie, she was pretty restless tonight, probably best not to disturb her.'

Penny smiled. 'Such a tireless employee,' she said with a sparkle in her dead eyes.

'Yeah, really dedicated,' I said under my breath, standing my ground until I was certain that Penny was going to move in the direction I wanted. It took a stare that would most likely melt the flesh from my face, but she moved, although not without a sigh.

I shook my head and followed her down the stairs. I locked eyes with an ever-watchful Ben, and I mentally slapped myself for the public spectacle with his mother. Sprung in the study with a tumbler of whisky, now this? *Nice one, Sarah.*

As much as I dreaded each step that drew me closer to Ben, I lifted my chin and remained calm as I stood before him. Nothing to see here. Or upstairs, for that matter.

'What did she say to you?'

'Nothing, why?' I shrugged.

Ben folded his arms as he studied me intently. 'You're blushing.'

An image of Louisa and Grant zipped through my mind and I swear I could feel myself turning a deeper shade of scarlet. I cleared my throat and tried to forget what I'd seen. 'You know how you said I wouldn't have to ask you twice?'

He nodded.

'Well, trust me, we have to go.'

'I just thought I'd say goodbye to Grant and —'

I grabbed his arm. 'Right. Now.'

Chapter Twenty-Seven

I f Ben had seemed shocked by the confession of what I had seen, he didn't show it. In fact, I was rather disappointed by his reaction when I told him I had caught Louisa and Grant together. I would have expected outrage, disgust, an ounce of surprise, but there was nothing. Just brooding silence that lasted our whole way home. I tried not to let the tension build in my mind.

Don't judge, Sarah. This is how he deals with things, he bottles up his emotions, remember?

Already my newfound knowledge stopped me from thinking the worst of Ben, who I spied on through the reflection of my passenger window. I wondered if he was thinking about what we had almost done, and what a mistake it had been. I felt like a hypocrite, judging Louisa for something I had almost done myself. But it was different: Ben wasn't married, he was a widower.

Yeah, Sarah, that's so much better.

Oh, how I hated the little voice inside my head, the one that pointed out all the things I didn't want to think about. I suddenly felt sick.

Pushing the disasters of the night to the back of my mind, I had a small victory in putting Grace down to sleep with little difficulty. Of all the nights I needed a distraction, Grace wasn't going to be the one to give it to me. I sighed, brushing her hair from her face, and my heart swelled as I looked down at the beautiful sleeping figure.

'You can keep me up all night, every night, if you want, I'm not going anywhere,' I whispered, kissing the tips of my fingers and touching her gently on the cheek. If anything, the news about Caroline only made me more adamant to ride out the fatigue, to not give up on Grace, to be there for her and Ben in this mixed-up family, even on the days it was bloody awful. The Liebenbergs had put me forward to help out with this situation. And that was exactly what I was going to do, in a calm, patient, understanding way. I felt uplifted as I descended the stairs, my confidence high.

'Did you have a good night?'

I peered across the foyer to where his voice had come from, and sure enough, there he was at the window in the parlour. He was sitting in the dark, his elbows resting on his knees, folding his tie in his hands. He'd obviously been waiting for me. It took me a moment to realise what he was talking about. My blank expression must have told him as much.

'Well, aside from the live-sex show and wanting to push my mother down the stairs,' he continued.

I was taken aback by his tone. I had partly regretted my actions tonight, but there was another part of me that stood by my abruptness with Penny: I'd prevented her from seeing said live-sex show. He should be bloody thanking me that I'd averted a heart attack.

'Apart from that,' I said, not denying it.

'I know she's not the easiest person to get along with but I do think you should make more of an effort with her,' he said, lazily pushing himself back into his chair.

I could feel my blood boiling. He was one to talk about making an effort with family. 'Well, family connections are very important, especially for Grace,' I said.

'Mother did mention tonight that you seemed reluctant for her to come visit.'

Was he serious? Was I on the stand here? Rage burned in the pit of my stomach. Since when was he Team Penny?

'Ah, she cancelled on me.' *To secretly have lunch with your estranged brother.*

'So you do want her to come and see you?' he asked, looking at me expectantly.

I thought about it, and as much as I told myself I would try to become more patient, to not forget what Ben had endured and not take his manner personally – after all, this wasn't about me or Penny, this was about Grace – I couldn't help my anger; it wasn't just his questioning, it was something else altogether.

'I just want your mum to see me.' I raised my voice. 'I want this family to see me, not lock me away to raise a child and not even be able to eat in the same room as any of you like it's the eighteen hundreds.' The floodgates were beginning to open.

'Louisa wasn't at the table either,' Ben said matter-of-factly, as if that explained everything.

His words only served to make me angrier. 'And that makes it okay?'

'Is that what this is really about?' he said, standing and walking into the light of the foyer. He leant against an alcove, crossing his arms over his chest and looking down at me. 'Do you always need to be the centre of attention?'

I would have snapped had there not been a mischievous glimmer in his eyes, like he was trying to bait me, something I couldn't have seen without the glow lighting his face.

I took a deep breath, calming my anger as I spoke quietly. 'I just want to be respected.'

Ben went to say something, but thought better of it. He closed the distance between us, and I could feel the heat of him next to me. My stomach gave a strange flutter as he examined my face almost like a caress. Why did this man have to be so damn sexy, so distracting? Every inhalation of his cologne made it tough for me to concentrate.

'I respect you,' he said, and I could feel my heart tighten. I was lost. Ben said the words I wanted to hear, and I could feel my frosty resolve begin to thaw. But of course he had to spoil it by continuing to talk, his face shuttering once more, a troubled expression etched across his brow. 'But what happened tonight at the Petersons' —'

'Oh, you mean a married man fucking the nanny?'

'That's none of our business.'

'Did you know about it?' It was the million-dollar question; he hadn't seemed surprised when I'd told him and that bothered me.

His silence told me all I needed to know.

'You're angry at me because my actions prevented your mother from witnessing them in the act? How long have you known? God, you probably swill whisky and smoke cigars in your boys' club, comparing notes.'

'I think you've read one too many historical romance novels,' Ben scoffed.

'Well, tell me it's not like that, tell me you don't laugh about the little piece you have stashed in your townhouse, the one you nearly did in the kitchen,' I blurted.

Ben's eyes were ablaze; never before had I seen him so angry as he stepped closer to me.

'I'm not Grant Peterson,' he said with a harsh edge to his voice. 'Why do you think I have you in this house, away from that world? I can't help that I'm a Worthington, or that I was born into money. So much of that life is ugly and I don't want Grace exposed to it. If that means you feel isolated or lonely here, so be it.'

I could feel my heart racing, looking into the eyes of a man who held so many secrets, so much pain, so much anger. He wanted to build a new world, a new life for himself, I understood that. Some secrets deserved to be locked away, and until the day Ben told me about them himself, I would let him keep them. All I could do with the little knowledge I had was to be there for him, and for Grace, in this world that was new to all of us.

The tension in my shoulders began to melt. I didn't even know why we were arguing. I knew Ben wasn't Grant, but the insecurity I felt touched a nerve. I didn't want to be a plaything like Louisa, I didn't want to be tucked away two years from now, all jaded, like her. I just wanted – hell, I don't even know what I wanted any more. And when my heart whispered what it truly wanted, I shut it down, because what my heart wanted was the stuff of fairytales. Ben was not the man for me, he was a man I was enthralled with the idea of. The reality was oh so different.

I met Ben's gaze dead on. 'You're right. It's not about me, or you . . . it's about Grace. And if you want to build a new world for her, then you are probably going to have to make sure that you're in it.'

It was the first time I had spoken of his absence, and as soon as I did, I saw something unmistakable blaze in his eyes. It scared me. It was enough for me to know I had overstepped the mark in a big way, enough to have me walk away from him, leaving him with those words. I was trembling, knowing that those heated, angry eyes were watching my every step as I ascended the stairs. I feared, hoped, he might stop me going to my room but he didn't, and I don't know if I was relieved, or if I felt even worse.

Chapter Twenty-Eight

I sat as I had done before: on edge; straight back, hands clasped, forced smile. There was no other way to be sitting in Penny Worthington's parlour, opposite the woman herself. Who was laughing at me. She was actually laughing at me, stomach-clutching, eye-watering laughter. I couldn't believe it.

She sighed, catching her breath. 'Oh, Sarah, you do amuse me.'

My smile faltered, confusion lining my face, as I thought about what I'd said. It wasn't funny, at least I didn't think it was.

'I just wanted to apologise for the way I spoke to you last night,' I repeated. Nope, not funny. 'And I don't want you to ever feel like you are not welcome to come and visit with Grace at any time.' I could feel the bile burning my throat as visions of daily visits from Penny sped through my mind. But I'd rolled Ben's words over in my mind all night, and by morning I had convinced myself to make more of an effort with Grace's grandmother. Lord knew it was complicated enough when it came to the Worthington family.

Penny scoffed, waving my words away. 'Oh, my dear, don't think I don't know why you were so adamant about stopping me on those stairs last night.'

'Sorry, what?' I asked, leaning forward in my chair a little.

Penny poured more hot water into her teacup with a knowing smile. 'Sarah, people have been having affairs with nannies, gardeners, pool boys since the dawn of time. It's almost a tradition.'

I stared at her. Surely she was joking? Were these people real? Did this sort of thing really happen?

'Um, I just thought that . . .' I stammered.

'Don't get me wrong – I will be forever in debt to you for preventing me from seeing any more of Grant Peterson than I need to.'

'Oh God.'

'Exactly, and let me tell you something: if the rumours are correct —' Penny wriggled her pinky finger as she daintily held her cup of tea, '— it's no wonder Melissa was having an affair with her tennis instructor in the Hamptons this past summer.'

I spat my tea across the glossy coffee table that divided us, coughing and earning a sour look from Penny. 'Really?' I wheezed, wiping tea from my chin.

'Oh, yes, it's almost like a ridiculous competition between them. Do you know how many au pairs they've had in four years?'

I shook my head, not wanting to know.

'Five – that's a new record.' She nodded, as if almost impressed.

'Poor Evie.' These people who didn't deserve to have children, to live in this world surrounded by nice things, infuriated me. I had gone from feeling sorry for Melissa to being disgusted by her and her husband.

'Oh, don't you worry about Evie, I don't think there will be another au pair coming on board. Melissa has vowed to be a full-time parent, no more nannies or tennis lessons.'

I shook my head, barely believing what I was hearing. It felt like Penny was updating me on a plot of *The Bold and the Beautiful*. It made my little existence with Grace and Ben in Greenwich Village seem dull in comparison.

'I suppose at least I can say that I am grateful to you, Sarah.'

Had I misheard Penny Worthington? Did she just say something nice again? 'You are?'

'Oh, very much so. I never have to worry about Ben being attracted to you, he assured me of that himself. What did he say to me last night? "Not in a million years", and by my calculations I will be long gone from this earth by then.' She laughed. 'More tea?'

'Um, no, thanks . . . I'm fine.' If anything, I was too busy ripping the butter knife out of my heart that Penny had wedged there. Last night? He had said that last night? Probably around the dinner table as they chortled about the help.

'Sarah, are you all right? You're terribly pale – you look dreadful.'

Way to kick a girl when she's down. The worrying thing was, when it came to Penny Worthington, I don't think that she was deliberately being awful, it was just . . . her. And if that wasn't bloody terrifying, I didn't know what was.

'Yeah, I think I might go home and lie down for a bit, I don't feel too well. Ben's out with Grace, so I'll just have a nap.'

'Oh yes, he's gone across to Brooklyn to see Nikki, and the Irishman.'

I couldn't help but find that a little amusing. I didn't know how long Nikki had been with her husband – obviously at least long enough for five children – and Penny was still referring to him as the Irishman. No one was safe from offence.

'Well, I'd see you out but . . .'

'No, it's okay . . . finish your tea, I can see myself out.'

Penny made herself comfy, like she had no intention of moving from her white-walled parlour. Personally I couldn't wait to get out, the room felt like a Scotchgarded igloo.

'I'll call around next week and visit Grace,' were her parting words.

'Great,' I said, hoping that the look on my face came across more as a smile than a grimace.

I couldn't get through the foyer quick enough, wrestling with my bag and glasses, trying to keep my shit together by getting my shit together. I had come to Penny's to mend a fence and, while I suppose I was kind of successful, it had resulted in me feeling worse. Penny's words haunted me: *I don't have to worry about Ben being attracted to you, he told me himself last night.*

'Whoa! Look out, where's the fire?'

I stopped so abruptly my sandals squeaked on the floor. I turned to see Alistair Worthington's beaming smile as he descended the stairs.

'People are going to start talking about us,' he joked, and ordinarily I would have found it funny but, based on what Penny had just matter-of-factly told me, he was probably absolutely right. All I wanted to do was head back to the Village and sleep the weekend away.

'So where are you off to then?' he asked.

'Just home, quiet weekend.'

'Home?' He looked horrified. 'You're in New York City, why would you want to do that?'

'Oh, I'm really tired,' I said, my voice breaking at the final word, stupid tears pooling in my eyes, betraying me. Something in Alistair's cheery disposition made me feel even more hopeless.

'Hey, what's wrong?' he said, grabbing my arm and urging me to look at him.

I shook my head, trying to convince him that there was nothing wrong but, as the tears came, there was no use denying it.

'Okay, come on,' he said, glancing behind him and ushering me out the door. 'You're coming with me.'

'Where?' I blubbered.

Alistair directed me to the waiting car, where Dave looked at me with alarm.

'Are you okay, Miss Williams?'

'She's fine, Dave. Not a word, yeah?'

Dave nodded; no doubt he was used to the code of silence when it came to the Worthingtons' comings and goings.

Alistair got into the back seat next to me, and passed me a tissue to wipe my eyes. 'The Blarney Rock on West 33rd Street,' Alistair told Dave, looking at me warily as I blew my nose. 'And make it snappy.'

I sat in an old Irish pub in the heart of Manhattan with Alistair Worthington on a Saturday afternoon, and in a few hours my cares washed away as quickly as the beer was going down. The rules were simple: there was to be no talk about Ben or family, and although I could see the curiosity in Alistair's eyes, he didn't press any further, which I was grateful for. Even with our lighthearted banter – my life in Australia, sports, painting, his life in Chicago, the city he considered his second home – my attempts to try to forget Ben became more difficult any time Alistair smiled, or creased his brow.

Even as I looked over the drinks menu, my eyes settled on something that reminded me of Ben – the 'Dark and Stormy': a long drink consisting of Gosling's Black Seal Rum and Gosling's Ginger Beer.

'I'll have one of those please.' I pointed to the menu.

Alistair peered over my shoulder and grimaced. 'Are you sure that's a good idea?'

'Time to mix it up.'

Alistair didn't seem as convinced, but knew better than to argue with a woman. 'One Dark and Stormy coming up.' He nodded at the barman.

I felt free, my spirits were lifted, I had even laughed with strangers in the bar, feasted on a bowl of nachos and collectively screamed with joy over a Rangers touchdown on the big screen, giving out high fives. I had never felt more like a New Yorker – I was one of them, just your average Joe, enjoying a Saturday arvo in the local, until Dave weaved his way through the crowd.

'Dave, my main man, have a nacho,' Alistair yelled above the chaos, slapping him on the shoulder.

Dave smiled. 'I'm sorry to interrupt, but I've received word that I'm to pick Mr Worthington and Miss Grace up from Brooklyn, so if you want a lift back . . .'

'Ah, I see, spoiler alert.' Alistair laughed. 'No trouble, Dave.' He downed his last mouthful of beer and turned to me. 'You ready?'

'Aw, I don't wanna,' I pouted, sliding off my stool and

realising the ground had moved since last time I was acquainted with it. I giggled. 'Oops.'

Alistair caught me. 'Yep, definitely time for home,' he said, slinking my arm around his shoulder and helping me zig-zag out of the bar.

'Aw, you're the nice one,' I slurred. 'Not the nasty one.'

Alistair chuckled. 'Thought we weren't going to talk about that,' he said, following Dave out of the bar. The cool air of the alley was welcome against my hot skin.

'I didn't mention any names,' I insisted.

Dave opened the door and helped Alistair pile me into the car. 'Watch your head,' he said, and before I knew it, I had faceplanted onto the leather seat, Alistair attempting to stay out of the way of my flailing legs as he moved me along.

'Don't look at my undies,' I mumbled, my eyes closed.

Alistair laughed. 'I'll try not to.'

'Good,' I said, sitting up, my eyes drooping, head bobbing, and before I knew it I was falling, falling, falling, until I felt Alistair's thigh against my cheek. It was the comfiest thigh ever, and just as I drifted off into an alcohol-inspired state of unconsciousness, I was soothed by the gentle strokes of fingers through my hair, pushing the strands away from my face, and what felt like a blanket being pulled over me. I stirred, and saw the silken interior of Alistair's jacket.

Once I realised the car was moving and I was safely on my way back to the Village, I allowed sleep to claim me.

'Come on, Sarah, you're going to have to help me here.' I heard the strain in Alistair's voice, mainly because my head rested right next to his cheek, and I could feel his laboured breaths against my face. 'Trust your room to be on the top floor,' he groaned, readjusting me in his arms before he navigated the final flight of stairs.

'I told you the couch was fine,' I mumbled.

'Oh yeah, Ben would love that as a welcome home.'

I glowered at Alistair's profile. 'I told you not to say his name.' Hearing it was the equivalent of fingernails running down a chalkboard.

'Oh well, here you go.' Alistair twisted the handle and kicked the door open, dumping me on top of my bed. He bent over, hands to his kness, to catch his breath, then he straightened and stretched his back out.

I grabbed my pillow, hugging it close to me and snuggling into my mattress. 'My hero,' I said, smacking my lips together.

My bedroom door opened, and I looked up to see Alistair lingering in the doorway, getting ready to leave. 'Thanks for making me forget,' I said.

Alistair smiled. 'Any time, although you never did manage to tell me what we were drinking to forget.'

My dopey smile slipped from my face as rolled onto my back, my blurry eyes focusing on the ceiling. 'It doesn't matter,' I said before turning away from Alistair's eyes, so much like Ben's. 'None of it matters.' I drifted off to sleep, only to be haunted by Penny Worthington's voice.

Not in a million years.

Chapter Twenty-Nine

The only thing that dragged me from my sleep was the pounding of my head. I squinted into the dark, realising I hadn't moved a muscle from the position Alistair had left me in. The pounding in my head amplified. No, wait. I twisted myself around, following the sound – it was coming from my door.

'Sarah, you okay?' Ben's muffled voice came through the door. 'Can I come in?'

'Yep,' I blurted without thinking. I sat bolt upright. Oh, bad idea. The room was spinning. I clutched my head as I sank down into my mattress.

The door opened and the light went on, blinding me. I whimpered and covered my eyes.

'Oh, shit, sorry,' he said, turning the light off straight-away. I felt the dip of the mattress as he sat on the edge. 'Jesus, Sarah, are you all right?' He placed his hand on my forehead, then my cheek. 'Mom told me you left her place unwell. I came back as soon as I heard.'

I was unwell, deeply unwell, but not in the way he thought. 'I'll be all right, just a bit under the weather, nothing that some sleep won't fix.'

'You feel hot,' he said, touching my face again with his large hands. He clearly didn't realise that touching me like that was what was making me hot.

'Have you eaten?' he asked. His voice was all seriousness. I wanted to ask if nachos counted but thought better of it. I just shook my head carefully.

'Do you think you could manage something, just something little?'

His voice rolled over me and my skin prickled. I pulled myself onto my elbows. 'I could probably try something.' I still felt a bit tipsy, and my stomach rumbled at the thought of food, but how long it would stay down was anyone's guess.

Ben grabbed my forearm and squeezed. It was incredible that something so small could evoke such strange sensations in me. 'Good girl,' he said, and the lightness in his voice made me think he had smiled.

'I might just grab a shower before I head down,' I said, my voice gravelly, my lips dry.

'Will you be okay?'

I had visions of Ben giving me a sponge bath and foot massage and as much as I was lapping up this softer, dare I say, caring side of him, I knew I couldn't push my luck.

'I think I can manage.'

I let the hot water fall around my neck and shoulders as I pressed my forehead against the marble wall. I was trying to think of the positive: tackle the hangover now and I wouldn't have to face it tomorrow. I had popped two pills to ward off the headache and as much as I gagged when I brushed my teeth under the shower, I was relieved that, beyond that, I didn't feel like I was going to throw up – I was just hungry.

Engulfed in my robe, I made my way to my room feeling almost human. My bed covers were half strewn over the floor, so I picked them up, pausing as I lifted a layer and spotted something black. I bent over to pick it up and recognized it from touch and then smell: cool, clean and crisp. Alistair's jacket. Expensive purple silk lining, and no doubt tailor made.

I draped it over the back of my chair, making a note to give it to Dave to return. I couldn't recall Alistair asking me to keep quiet about our outing, but after what Louisa had told me, I wouldn't be announcing it.

I flicked through my clothes, thinking of nothing but comfort: my grey, three-quarter length yoga pants and my I ♥ NY T-shirt, the one I hadn't worn since that infamous night. I couldn't help but grin putting it on, thinking about the look on Ben's face. It drooped off my shoulder. It didn't take much for the cheap fabric to get stretched, and when I thought about how it got stretched I could feel my cheeks warm. I readjusted it to sit as best it could. Towel drying my hair, I pulled it into a ponytail, letting it fall over my bare shoulder.

Now I felt more like myself again, I carefully made my way down the stairs, skimming along the walls and concentrating on every single step.

But my grand entrance to the kitchen was wasted – Ben was on the phone, his back turned.

'Yeah, she's fine, just about to eat.' He was looking down at a piece of paper, half distracted from the conversation as he agreed, 'Yes, yes, I will . . . I will.' It was then he turned to me. He quickly pushed the paper into his pocket. It had me thinking that whatever was on it was secret. That was soon forgotten as Ben's eyes raked over my attire. He recognised it, of that I was sure, I could tell by the way his Adam's apple bobbed as he swallowed.

'Listen, I've got to go, I'll speak to you tomorrow. Yes, yes, I will, okay, yep, right, bye . . . bye.' He sighed deeply, and ended the call. 'You must have given Mom quite the fright, this is her second call to check in on you.'

I breathed out a laugh. Yeah, so concerned she couldn't even walk me to the door. Still Penny Worthington being concerned at all was pretty amazing. 'That was thoughtful of her.'

'As was your visit,' Ben said, coming to stand nearer to me, and looking down into my eyes, a certain softness in them making me blush.

'Oh, she told you then.'

'You didn't have to do that.'

'I know.'

'But I'm grateful that you did.'

'I just wanted to make sure that—'

'You hungry?'

'Starved!'

He smiled – small, but it was there. 'Follow me.'

Ben opened the door to the basement level that I had forgotten existed. He flicked a switch, illuminating a lush, indulgent cinema room, with wood-panelled walls, a multi-level seating area filled with leather chairs, and the largest screen I had ever seen in a home. On the ceiling, small recessed lights shone through the black as if to replicate the night sky; in the corner was a fully stocked candy bar with a carnival theme. I could just imagine teenage Grace bringing her friends down here and hosting the most incredible slumber parties.

'Do you want to know the best seat in the house?'

'Okay.'

He pointed to the long, curved modular lounge on the top tier, the one covered in a plush chocolate-coloured material. On the over-stuffed cushions sat a blanket and pillow. He guided me to sit directly in the middle. Without saying a word, he grabbed the blanket and threw it over me, engulfing my giggles, then he grabbed the pillow.

'Up,' he directed and I sat forward so he could place the pillow behind me. I couldn't stop running my palms along the velvety fabric of the lounge, thinking if I had a room like this I would never, ever, leave it. And just before I could get settled, Ben reached down and pulled a lever, flinging my legs up so fast I yelped before breaking into another fit of giggles.

'Sorry.' He laughed. 'I'm trying to be a gracious host and so far I've nearly smothered you with a blanket and given you whiplash; I clearly suck at playing nurse.'

I thought about the reason he was making me comfortable, pampering me, making me put my feet up: it was because he thought I was legitimately sick. Pangs of guilt engulfed me; if by some freak event lightning should pierce its way into this cinema room and strike me down, I swear, I'd deserve it.

'Listen, I am feeling so much better, you don't need to fuss.'

'Sarah.' He said my name like a warning, a non-negotiable command to sit down and not move. He handed me a remote that looked like it was made by NASA. My eyes widened as I held it, looking over it in horror.

'I don't know what to do with that.' I shrugged, handing it back to him, and he laughed.

'Okay, how about some music then?'

With my painkillers taking the edge off my headache, music sounded like a dream. 'Perfect.'

Ben seemed pleased. With a quick nod, he headed for the stairs. It suddenly occurred to me how quiet it was.

'Ben, where's Grace?'

He looked at me. 'When I heard you'd come home sick, I thought it might be best for Grace to stay in Brooklyn, give you a night's sleep. I'm going to get her in the morning.'

Now I felt really bad; one phone call from Penny and not only was I getting the VIP experience but now there was quarantine. Oh boy.

I smiled weakly. 'You didn't have to do that.'

'You'll thank me in the morning after you've had a full night's sleep.' He grinned and made his way up the stairs, just before, as though by some magical force, My Sad Captains started filtering through the surround sound system. I settled down in my blanket cocoon, trying not to admit how amazing this was and how much I was loving this treatment from Ben. I was an awful, awful human being.

I would have confessed in a heartbeat if it wouldn't have incriminated Alistair. Perhaps I should use this night as an opportunity to mend bridges with Ben – the way we had ended last night was a bit of a disaster, and as far as working as a team to get Grace into a routine, well, that wasn't going so great either. I had sabotaged my own plans, and it would serve me right if she didn't sleep a wink for me next week.

I rearranged my blanket and thought how easy it would be to fall asleep in this recliner. Of course, Sarah McLachlan singing about angels as I looked up at the fabricated Milky Way on the ceiling wasn't helping. My eyes became heavy, until the sound of footsteps and the clinking of a tray had me sitting straight once more. I turned expectantly to the doorway, amazed that he'd returned so quickly. He must have ordered takeaway.

Ben entered like a total domestic god, carrying a tray with immense concentration. He looked adorable, a tea towel slung over his left shoulder; all he needed was a little apron and he'd be husband material. It was a side to him I hadn't seen and, I had to say, I liked it.

'If you scoot over there's a side table that flips out from the arm rest.' His eyes darted to the side.

'What?' I said, flipping the arm rest back to find, sure enough, a side table. I looked at him with a huge grin. 'No way.'

'It's the couch that keeps on giving.'

'I'll say, it's like a bloody Transformer,' I said, readying myself for whatever was hidden under the silver dome on the tray. 'I think you've missed your calling in life, Mr Worthington. Ever thought about a career change to the hospitality industry?'

He smiled as he placed the tray in front of me, and it made my stomach flip. 'Well, eat first, praise later. If you like it, I'll consider a career change,' he said, reaching over to grab the dome.

My mouth was watering already, thinking about what he had organised: Indian, Thai, Italian?

'Wait a minute, did you cook this?' I asked.

He nodded, seemingly modest about his efforts before lifting the lid to reveal . . .

'Oh. My. God.' My hand covered my mouth, capturing my gasp.

Ben looked worried. 'Well?'

I tried to find words, feeling stupid as tears threatened. I lowered my hands from my face and took in the grilled cheese sandwich and bowl of minestrone soup. He'd remembered.

I shook my head in disbelief.

'Yeah, well, don't get too excited, the soup is from a can, but the grilled cheese is all me,' he said.

'It's amazing.' I laughed, thinking that there wasn't anything better in the world for lifting my spirits than this.

'Thank you, Ben,' I said, making sure I looked him in the eyes so he knew I meant it.

Ben's mouth twitched as if stifling a smile. 'You Aussies sure are easy to please.'

'Yeah, just an elaborate home cinema with a grilled cheese sandwich and I'm anyone's,' I joked.

Ben's expression changed and suddenly what was meant as a joke took on a whole new meaning. Yep, me and my tragic jokes strike again.

'Well, I've got some work to do, so I'll leave the music on for you?'

'You're not having any?'

He shrugged. 'I ate at Nikki's.'

My heart sank. I don't know what made me think that maybe Ben might sit next to me, watch a movie, chat about our favourite things like we were having a slumber party. But of course that was stupid. And then I felt ungrateful. Ben had shown me more compassion and consideration than I could have hoped for. It made me feel truly awful about all the bitterness I'd held against a man I didn't really know.

'Well, thanks again,' I said, saluting him with my toastie.

'Is there anything else you want?'

His words hung heavily in the air and all I wanted to say was: *Yes, stay.*

I smiled and shrugged. 'Nope, all good.'

And of all the little white lies I had told today, that was by far the biggest one.

Chapter Thirty

The music had stopped. My tray was gone. If it wasn't for the lights above me, I would've thought maybe I had dreamt it all. How long had I been asleep?

Time sure was difficult to gauge in a cinema room, not a problem I was usually faced with. I pulled myself from my blanket cocoon and stretched my arms above my head then tried, rather inelegantly, to collapse the footrest. I knew my lethargy was a combination of my boozy afternoon and napping on possibly the most comfortable couch in existence, but I felt like someone had roofied my grilled cheese.

I went upstairs. The house was dark, but judging by the microwave clock, I had only been out for a few hours, so the night was not entirely lost. I could go to my room and get a good night's sleep.

And that was exactly where I was headed before a shadow caught my eye. I stood at the end of the couch, drinking in Ben's sleeping form, the bow of his lips, the fatigue that lined his face. A frown was visible, as though he was worrying even in his dreams. I had no doubt he would, this man bore the weight of the world on his shoulders, worked so hard, and received nothing but grief from me. Ben was a good man whose life had been turned upside down but who was trying to do his best. My heart ached for him, and I wanted to help him. I could at least help him to sleep soundly, knowing that one aspect of his life – perhaps the most important one – was looked after. I didn't want him to worry about Grace. I could care for her and love her for both of us in the times he couldn't.

I tiptoed around the couch, kneeling quietly next to him, and took the papers from under his hands. I put them on the floor next to him, then gently lifted his glasses from his face, revealing his strong, masculine features. He stirred slightly, and my breath caught in – if he woke and caught me staring at him like a creeper, I'd be mortified. But he didn't wake, his forehead furrowing again as another worry reached him in his dreams. I would have given anything to take it away.

I leant over him for the throw rug on the back of the lounge and paused seeing the corner of a dog-eared piece of paper sticking out of his pocket. The same note he had urgently tucked away when I'd entered the room earlier this evening. My eyes shifted to Ben's face, and back to the paper.

Sarah, no, you can't! He obviously didn't want you to see it – it has nothing to do with you.

I left the throw rug in its place as I sat on my haunches, letting a war rage inside me.

Just go to bed, Sarah. Cover him up and go to bed. Don't spoil a good night.

I knew that everything the voice said was right, that I should just walk away, and yet I found myself reaching for the paper. Ever so carefully, I pulled it by the corner and edged it out of his pocket, inch by inch. I bit my bottom lip as, eventually, the paper came free. I sighed with relief.

Then Ben's hand snaked around my wrist so fast I yelped. I looked into his steely stare.

I tried to think of a logical explanation for why I was taking the piece of paper, but of course there was none. The only thing I was aware of was Ben's painful iron grip around my wrist.

Ben unhurriedly sat up, his knees grazing my belly, his grey eyes looking into mine in a way I had never seen before; I would never have thought such an intense calmness would be more terrifying than his anger. He gradually let my wrist go.

'Read it,' he said, so coolly I felt a shiver run over my skin.

I shook my head. 'I don't want to,' I said, handing it to him.

He pushed my hand back. 'Yes, you do.'

'Ben, please.' I pushed the paper into his chest and went to move but he stilled me with his hand, scrunching the paper into my palm.

'Read. It.'

I could feel the heat of my cheeks as shame engulfed me. This was my punishment and I had to endure while Ben watched. I wished the ground would open.

I unfolded the paper, revealing the writing. My eyes ticked over the words in disbelief.

'It's my email?'

He had printed off my email and written little notes in the margins, what looked like an agenda for the weekend, going as far as to highlight passages. He had taken what I had written seriously, put thought and effort into respecting what would be best for Grace. My heart melted.

'I'm not the best communicator, Sarah, especially with anything to do with Grace, I just – I'm trying.'

I could try to claim it was my humiliation or his admission that made me break down, but I knew in my heart of hearts it was guilt and my own issues with communication, and I had never felt so ill about it.

'I'm sorry.' My chin trembled like a small child's. 'You know why I was sick today?'

Ben looked at me, his eyes cast in shadow, his silence intimidating.

'Because I went to an Irish bar and got drunk on cocktails that reminded me of you, and then if that wasn't bad enough, last night —' I shook my head in disbelief.

Ben shifted, sighing wearily. 'We don't have to talk about last night.'

'It's not that, it's . . .' I tried to find the courage to continue.

Ben tilted his head as if to capture my attention as I lifted my gaze to his.

'What?'

I didn't want to keep the truth at bay any more, and notwithstanding all the secrets in my possession, I would be truthful. I inhaled deeply, my voice shaking as I continued. 'I asked about you, I asked Louisa about Grace's mum and now I know what happened and I'm so, so sorry that I always think the worst of you, and then you're so nice to me and you make me cheese sandwiches and I don't even deserve it.' I wiped my eyes and looked at my hands crumpling the bit of paper because I couldn't bring myself to look at him, knowing that now he knew the truth.

There was a long, painful silence, and I just wanted to disappear. I had done it, ruined any chance of being able to be a part of the new world that Ben was building for Grace. It was over.

Then Ben's hand was sliding over mine, preventing me from crumpling the paper any further. He squeezed my hand a little. It was a tender, unexpected gesture, as was the way he moved, dropping to the floor to sit next to me, forcing me to look at him. His eyes weren't angry, they were sad, looking at me as though he was physically pained by my tears. He brushed them away with his thumb as he shook his head.

'You can say what you like, Sarah Williams, but I'll be damned if you don't deserve a grilled cheese sandwich.' He smiled slowly.

I was confused, afraid to believe that he was making light of all I had confessed.

'Sarah, you survived my mother, my sister, *me*, and despite it all, you still continue to love and care for Grace, even in the times when you probably wanted to walk away. Why?'

'Because I love her.'

'Is that the only reason?'

I thought, trying to find an answer. 'Well, I love this city.'

'And that's what makes you stay?' he asked, folding a wayward strand of hair behind my ear.

I nodded, knowing that I wasn't being completely truthful, but I scarcely thought that telling him that he made me want to stay was appropriate, so I left the most powerful part of my confession unsaid.

He let his hand drop and pressed his back against the couch, sighing deeply and rubbing at his face. 'Goodnight, Sarah.'

I panicked that there was nothing for us to say after what felt like such a tender moment. Was he dismissing me after all I had done, all I confessed?

'Ben, aren't you mad?'

'I'm too tired to be mad any more. Where does it ever get anyone?'

And then before I could stop myself, I let my hand glide over his, squeezing it in the same reassuring way as he had done to me. Something changed, I saw it in the way his eyes shifted to mine. I knew he wasn't mad, not in the slightest, because I had seen that look before, and I knew what it meant. All that was left now was for me to decide.

Do I stay or do I go upstairs?

Chapter Thirty-One

Ben Worthington. A man at times so distant, so controlled, so seemingly shut off from emotion. And then he gradually revealed glimpses of kindness: walking me down the Mall in Central Park; taking care of me; fixing me my favourite dinner. So unexpected were these moments it was hard to imagine they had actually happened, especially when the bad stuff was so much easier to recall. He had lost, I knew that now, and that explained so much about this complicated man. I had struggled to discern his indifferences from his kindnesses, but I had never thought that I would see a change so clear in someone. The change I saw now almost made me want to stay, to close the space between us.

I looked straight into his partly shadowed face, and it took every ounce of strength to remove my hand from his. 'Goodnight, Ben.'

His eyes slowly lifted as I stood; if he was surprised he didn't show it. I had trouble fathoming that a man such as Ben could be vulnerable, but knowing his past, there was no other way to describe him. I wished I could take the pain away, to distract him as I had before. But I couldn't.

I let that thought drive me up the staircase. Every step I took I felt stronger and more grateful for the decision I had made.

I closed the door to my room, pressing my back against it, feeling the safety of its barrier shielding me from all that lay beyond it. I was so certain, so resolved, so proud of how far I had come. I had turned away from those, as my best friend Sammi would put it, come-fuck-me eyes.

If it had been so easy, though, why was I faltering, why was I lingering at my door feeling uncertain, like maybe I didn't want to avoid the mistake? That no matter how good I felt about it, there was something bubbling underneath the surface that kept telling me what I really wanted? Try as I might to convince myself about avoiding temptation, all I could think of was walking back into it. Just for this one night. Break the tension and move on.

Yeah, even I wasn't buying my own bullshit, and yet I pushed from the door and twisted the handle, pulling it open to step out into the hall, ready to descend the stairs at a run.

I stopped dead in my tracks.

There, blocking the stairs, was Ben, and in that stunned silence, it was never more clear: we both wanted the same thing, to hell with the consequences. After all, it was our world now.

And as if reading my mind, he moved. He took determined steps, closing the distance to where I stood. Then he kissed me, pushing me against the wall and pinning me there with the warmth of his body. Nothing romantic, nothing tender or soft, just pure need. He pushed, I pulled, there seemed too much space between us even as he crushed his body against mine. Our clothing was an infuriating barrier, but before I had a chance to remove his jacket with eager hands, we slid to the stairs, caring not for comfort, only for pleasure.

Oh, the pleasure of straddling Ben, cupping his face and thrilling in the power of my position, knowing that the hardness of him between my legs was because of what I was doing to him. It only encouraged me to grind against him as I kissed him so passionately I could feel his fingers clutch my hips before gliding over my arse and pulling me closer to him, urging me on, grinding against the seam of my thin yoga pants. My already stretched top was almost beyond help as Ben pulled the front of it down, groaning as he saw I wasn't wearing a bra, then cupping and squeezing my nipple. I bit down on his lip, causing him to smile and squeeze more firmly. Damn, if he didn't know all the right things to do to me. I pushed away from his mouth, my hands on his heaving chest; he looked at me confused, until I slowly peeled my T-shirt over my head, flicking my ponytail to spill over my shoulder and letting the tee drop next to me on the staircase. Ben ran his eyes over me like a slow caress. I had never felt more wanted, more needed.

There may have been things he was unable to communicate with words, but he knew how to convey his desire as he sat up and did something I wasn't expecting. He pulled the elastic from my ponytail, letting my hair spill over my shoulders. The feel of Ben's hands in my hair caused my skin to prickle as he kissed me once more, this time slower, as if he was committing the taste of me to memory.

I put my arms around his neck, thrilling in the way the material of his jacket brushed against my breasts. As much as I loved the feeling, I edged the jacket off his shoulders. Leaving it crumpled underneath him as I pushed him down, I leant over him, my hair falling around his face like a veil. Looking into his smouldering eyes – I can't believe I had ever thought them cold – the moment was almost romantic. I worked at undoing his belt and reached into his briefs to grip the length of him, using the rapid rise and fall of his laboured breath as a guide. Ben swallowed, looking down at my hand on him before his head tilted back with a moan. I don't know whether it was a plea to stop or to keep going but it made me smile, seeing the usually controlled man become so weakened by my touch.

'This is a hell of way to christen the new carpet.' He laughed, his voice gravelly, strained.

I laughed too, loosening my hold on him and moving forward to kiss him tenderly. Before he could protest me letting go, I pulled away from him.

'You have no idea,' I said, shaking my head. I saw the realisation in his eyes as I lowered myself down, and showed him exactly how we were going to christen the new carpet. I took him into my mouth and sucked. He groaned my name, his hands gripping the dampened strands of hair at my scalp, and I had never felt more alive. I was taking great pleasure in tearing down all the defences this man had built up so well.

Every. Last. One.

~

Ben kicked my door open wider, dumping me on the mattress and, working with strong, assured hands, peeled off my pants and knickers, skimming them over my sensitive skin. He tugged them free and I lay before him, naked but not cold, exposed but not sorry. Ben looked like he was committing every curve, every line to memory as he worked on unbuttoning his shirt in a way that was driving me mad. I knew I should have just ripped those buttons apart when I'd had the chance, but then the shirt was gone, tossed aside, soon followed by his trousers. I didn't have time to take him in as he crawled over me, dividing my legs and opening me to him. He settled between my thighs, arms on either side of me, caging me in. My hands moved to his ribs, making him flinch. I laughed, knowing my hands were colder than any other part of me. He punished me by grinding himself against me and making me gasp; I was so wet for him, I knew he would be able to feel it. The carpet burn on my knees, the taste of him in my mouth. It took every inch of my control to stop him and search through the drawer of my side table, trying to concentrate as Ben kissed my spine. I flung papers and documents everywhere, upending the drawer's contents without care, my passport flying across the room along with some foreign money.

I felt the vibration of Ben's laugh against my back as he nuzzled my neck. 'Going somewhere?' he asked, pressing into my rump, almost diverting me from my mission, until: eureka! I dug into the pocket of my wallet, retrieving the magical silver square from inside. I swear a beacon of light should have shone down on it, I was so happy to see it. God bless Sammi for giving it to me as a bon voyage gift. I had hated her at the time for being such a smartarse, but now I owed her a thank-you card and a basket of fruit.

Without saying a word, Ben took it from my fingers and ripped it open with his teeth; sitting on his haunches he sheathed himself, and that's when I started to feel my heart race. I knew the size of him – I had felt him, tasted him. It had been a long time since I'd been with anyone. I was afraid of what was to come, or worse, that he might come to his senses and stop altogether. I lay on my back looking at him, feeling the pang of nervousness as he lowered himself down to me again, kissing me once, twice, three times while moving my legs apart with his knees. His tongue slipped into my mouth, building the intensity in the place where he would invade me.

Ben teased the most intimate part of me, gliding himself against me but not penetrating, teasing me and loving every moment. I squirmed underneath him, bucking my hips.

'Ben,' I gasped, loving him and hating him all at the same time but, just as he smiled that cocky smile, he hooked my legs over his shoulders. I swallowed, nervous about the position, not knowing how deep or how hard he was likely to go but as soon as he began slowly pushing into me, I forgot to care. I watched him watching where we joined, teasing himself in, inch by inch. I felt so impossibly stretched, there was no way he was going to fit, it just wasn't going to happen, but as he lifted his eyes to mine, my thoughts were calmed by how beautiful he was. I couldn't believe that the man who had once made me feel so small, so intimidated was now tender, watching me manage my breathing – in, out, in, out. My fingers pressed sharply into his sides as he pushed fully inside me. My breath fled and I stiffened, so deep was he, filling me completely. I was barely breathing, thinking it was too much, absolutely too much, and then he moved, pushing his weight against my legs. My hands splayed against the bedhead, bracing myself against his long, luscious strokes. He knew what he was doing, and how to build the most delicious friction; the way he looked down and watched himself move in and out of me was almost enough to send me over the edge.

I bit my lip and pushed my head against the pillow as Ben's thrusts became more fevered, more urgent, the cords of his muscles tightening, a vein in his neck pulsing as he lost himself so totally in me. I wanted to run my tongue along his neck but before I could he let my legs fall and claimed my mouth with his. He kissed me tenderly, such a contrast to how he'd fucked me. His hand dived between my legs, his thumb running expert, maddening circles over the sensitive bud, eliciting guttural moans from me. My hands grabbed at his shoulder blades; I rocked my hips into his and bit his shoulder, clawing at his skin, which only seemed to encourage a new sense of need in him. The press of his forehead against mine was intimate but his attention was on my breasts, watching the way they moved every time he thrust into me.

I cupped his face. 'Look at me,' I pleaded, not knowing why it was important, but it was. I wanted him to see me. He wasn't present in so many aspects of his life, and if I needed it, then so did he. Maybe this would be the only time we would truly see each other, the only time we would sate our bodies and fulfil our urges. The only time we would give in to our need.

Ben pulled back and my heart twisted in fear that it was too much, I had pushed too far and now he was going to run, but he pulled me with him. He sat against my bedhead, gesturing for me to straddle him, just as I had done on the stairs. I lowered myself onto him, gripping his shoulders, gasping as I adjusted to him going deeper than before. Ben's eyes were on me, taking in the twisting of agony and ecstasy in my face.

'I want to watch you when you come,' he said, his voice strained, his words a promise, and to reward him I began to rock, slowly to start, watching his face contort – whether in pain or pleasure, it was tough to say. His grip on my hips was so strong I knew I would have bruises there in the morning, but it only made me me grind down harder, arching my back so he could kiss my breasts. He licked the peaks, then sucked them into his mouth, and when he looked at me I could feel the pleasure building, pooling at my nerve endings as I rode him faster. Moaning about how wet I was, how deep he was, how I wanted to be fucked by him. I could barely recognise the words coming from my mouth, it was like I was possessed by this wanton creature who couldn't get enough – and I couldn't. I felt myself building, and leant forward, my screams muffled in his neck, our skin slick with sweat, our voices hoarse from our groans. I was ready, so ready to let go.

'Ben,' I warned, unable to gather myself enough to do anything but kiss him through the climb, and just as I thought I couldn't take it any more, he looked into my eyes.

'I see you, Sarah, I fucking see you.'

'Oh God,' I breathed, clamping my arms around his neck, feeling it build in him too.

'That's it, fuck me. Harder,' Ben whispered against my mouth, his hips meeting mine, and then I was crying, gasping and rolling on the orgasm that took over my body, a fight between pushing down for more and pulling away because I couldn't take any more. But Ben wasn't finished. He pushed me onto my back, pinning my thighs to the mattress as he thrust into me, bringing himself to the edge. Fucking, cursing, moaning, coming and collapsing on me, still inside as we fought for air, not so easy when I was pinned under the heavy warmth of a man. But feeling him on me, in me, the remnants of our passion teasing our sensitive bodies, our hearts and lungs labouring, was the most perfect moment of my entire life. I would be sore tomorrow – there would be no question that I would feel Ben for days to come. He would probably love that he had made me ache, and knowing it would make me think of him, turn me on. I mentally slapped myself.

I brought my mind to the here and now as Ben pulled out of me to lie on his side, his arm draped across my breasts. I could feel him, damp and hot against my belly, and I was relieved he hadn't worried about putting distance between us. A silence hung in the air, and just as I began to fear that he felt the beginnings of regret, he propped himself on his elbow and looked down at me, grinning. He reached out and brushed his thumb against my kiss-swollen lips, so tender I had to hold back my tears. I had never been so relieved. I didn't want to be one of those girls who cried after sex. He must have read something on my face yet he didn't pull away; he closed in, tilting my head to kiss me, sweetly, until once again I felt him harden against me and he moved closer, deepening our kiss.

Just when I thought it didn't get much better than this, fate had other ideas. It took a little while to recognise the sound, but it was there, loud and insistent. Ben lifted his head, both of us twisting to the sound before realising Ben's phone was ringing out in the hall.

Chapter Thirty-Two

Ben came bursting into the room naked, reaching for his pants. 'Get dressed.'

I sat up, pulling the sheets to my chest. 'What's wrong?'

'We have to go get Grace,' he said frantically, zipping his fly and grabbing his shirt off the floor.

'Oh my God, is she okay?' I moved then, grabbing my own pants, covering my chest.

Ben strode into the hall, picking up and chucking me my T-shirt, breathing out a laugh. 'Grace is fine. Nikki's gone into labour.'

'Oh my God, oh my God,' I said excitedly, struggling to pull my top on, only to glance down at the misshapen, wonky heart. I held it out, shaking my head. 'I can't wear this, here, chuck me that grey top from my desk,' I said, pointing to a pile of folded clothes. Without missing a beat he threw it over.

'Thanks,' I said, pulling it on. I brushed my fingers through my tangled bed hair and headed to the door. 'Come on, let's go.'

But when Ben didn't follow I turned to see what was keeping him. He hadn't moved and was staring at my pile of clothes.

'Ben, what are . . .' My words fell away, my eyes narrowing to the jacket Ben was peeling off my chair. He turned the material over in his hands, studying it with deep interest.

'Why is Alistair's jacket in your room?'

I couldn't believe it. In a flurried, panicked confession, I told him every chance meeting I'd had with Alistair, the whole three times we'd met and how it had been a secret only because Alistair had wanted to surprise Ben. That's when I saw the rage in his eyes. He didn't believe me. Oh God, he didn't think I was somehow seeing Alistair behind his back for a whole other reason, did he?

He turned from me without another word and barrelled down the stairs.

'Ben, wait!' I called after him, following his determined, furious steps. 'It's not what you think.'

'I told you not to let anyone into the house,' he said when we reached the foyer.

My mouth gaped – was that the biggest issue? 'But he's your brother, not just anyone.'

Anger rolled off Ben like I had never witnessed before. His hands balled into fists as he stepped closer, glaring at me, standing a few steps above him. 'Pack your things.'

'What?'

'I can't employ someone I can't trust.'

I stared at him, dumbfounded by how he was reacting. 'You're serious?'

'When it comes to the safety of my daughter I am deadly serious.'

I couldn't believe what I was hearing. His reaction was so absurd, so over the top. Then it hit me, and my shock morphed into something else: a deep, burning fury.

'If fucking me was a mistake, then you can fire me for that, you don't have to invent a reason to ask me to go.'

Something flashed in his eyes, something fleeting, as if he was going to deny it, but then he shut it down. 'I asked you not to let anyone into the house.'

'Okay, so I made a mistake, I'm sorry,' I said, at a loss to understand how this had escalated. Alistair was his brother; when I'd let him into the house, I hadn't known what he'd done. As far as Ben knew, I didn't know.

'There are some things that just can't be undone,' he said, mainly to himself. He looked up. 'I'm going to get Grace.'

'Well, can you just wait a sec—'

'No,' he said, going to the front door. He opened it and paused, turning slightly, but not looking back. 'I'm taking her to Lafayette Street.'

A pain sliced through my chest. He was shutting down again, severing ties and throwing me out. I began to crumble.

I rushed to the door. 'Ben, please, talk to me.'

His jaw clenched as if he was thinking about it, and I wanted so much for him to turn around, to talk to me, but he walked straight out the door without so much as a backward glance, leaving me standing in the foyer of an empty townhouse. Just me, and Alistair's fucking jacket.

Chapter Thirty-Three

I didn't need to ask for directions to find Nikki Fitzgerald in the sprawling private hospital, I had found the next best thing standing at the water cooler. Seamus Fitzgerald was tall, tired and sporting a curly crop of red hair.

'Seamus?' I asked.

He turned to me with curiosity.

'Sorry, my name's Sarah, I'm Grace's au pair.' I paused, remembering that I wasn't any more.

Seamus's face lit up. 'Sarah, yes, of course.' He beamed, taking my hand and shaking it so enthusiastically I thought my shoulder might dislocate. 'Nikki's told me all about you trying to tame the wild beast in her brother. I hope you've been riding him hard.'

I thought of how hard I'd ridden Ben merely days before, and my face flushed.

'Oh, yes, one tries.' I smiled, wanting nothing more than to change the subject. 'Is Nikki okay?'

Seamus puffed out his chest, pride filling him as he smiled broadly. 'Mum and bub are both doing fine.'

All gloom left me as my heart swelled for him. 'Congratulations! Boy or girl?'

'A beautiful girl, just like her mother,' he said, gesturing for me to follow him, to a nearby doorway. 'Well, almost like her mother.' He spoke out of the corner of his mouth as if parting with a secret as he pushed through the door, and I saw exactly what he meant. Nestled in Nikki's arms was a sweet, tiny bundle wrapped in white, sleeping peacefully, with her pink, wrinkly face and a full head of ginger-red hair.

Nikki laughed when she saw me approach. 'I swear if a hairy baby gives you heartburn during pregnancy, then fire-red hair must burn even hotter. It all makes sense now.' She smiled, stroking her daughter's mop lovingly. Then she glanced at her husband, taking his seat beside her.

'She's so beautiful, guys. Have you got a name?'

'Well, we did ask the boys, but we didn't think Dora or Pugsley were a good fit, so we just went with what we wanted.'

I laughed. 'Oh?'

'Sarah, meet Hermione "no middle name" Fitzgerald,' Nikki said.

'Nice to meet you, Hermione,' I said, thinking how incredibly likeable this family was, and how loved they were by all, if the sea of flowers and the odd balloon collection was anything to go by. There was scarcely a spare surface in the room, no mean feat seeing as Hermione wasn't even seventy-two hours old. I wondered which one had been brought by Ben, who by now was long gone. I wanted to ask if he had visited but I didn't want to ruin the mood, until I made the mistake of admiring a beautiful bouquet of orchids.

Dearest Nikki, Seamus, Daniel, Alec, Josh
and Taylor.
With warm wishes and much love to you all on the
safe arrival of beautiful Hermione.
Love always, Aunty Holly xo

The colour drained from my face. I didn't know where Alistair's girlfriend fit in all of this; inappropriately embracing Ben and crying on his shoulder, and apparently still friends with Nikki. My mind was running at a hundred miles an hour; was there more to the fallout between the brothers? Ben had been so angry with Alistair. Was it because Ben was in love with Holly? Had he just used me to try to forget her?

I just wanted to return to the Village, pack my things and leave and never look back, and I was just about to do that when Nikki spoke.

'Sarah, are you all right? You look like you've seen a ghost.' She half-laughed.

I turned to her, my face cast in sadness, because, unlike the Worthingtons, I wasn't an expert at locking away my feelings.

'I'm leaving New York, Nikki, coming here was a mistake.' The biggest mistake of my life.

'Leaving? But why?' Nikki was dismayed.

'Does anyone want a drink of water?' Seamus asked, getting up to make an exit.

'Oh, sit down, Seamus, there is only so much water a man can possibly ingest,' Nikki scolded quietly, careful not to wake the baby. Her attention turned back to me. 'Is it Mother? Ben? Christ, I knew I should have spoken to him earlier, I could just kick myself sometimes.'

'Well, you've had other things on your mind, love,' Seamus said, tilting his head at Hermione.

Nikki wouldn't have it. 'I should have done more. Sarah, I'm so sorry, you deserve a bloody medal. Emily didn't have something to do with this, did she?'

I scoffed. Emily was the least of it. The problem ran far deeper than any judgemental look from Emily or her mother.

'Alistair, actually,' I said, watching with interest as the blood drained from Nikki's face.

Seamus straightened in his chair, his eyes moving from Nikki to me. 'Now I really need a drink,' he said, leaving the room, quite possibly in search of something stronger than what was to be had from the water cooler.

Now I couldn't let it go. As much as I had no intention of bringing my troubles to the hospital, to the happy new parents, Nikki had asked, and I had answered, and now I was more worried than ever.

'Looks like you're the one who's seen a ghost, Nikki.'

Nikki shook her head. 'How much do you know?'

I sat in the seat Seamus had vacated. 'I know Alistair was driving the day Caroline died.'

Nikki nodded sombrely, adjusting Hermione as if to make her more secure.

'Who is Holly?' I couldn't help myself, maybe because I was sitting opposite the big white orchids.

Nikki looked at me for a long time before speaking. 'Well, I'm glad you're sitting down,' she said, placing Hermione into the little hospital crib next to her. 'I should probably start this off with a "once upon a time", isn't that the way most fairytales begin?' She smiled, but there was a sadness in her eyes as she looked down at her daughter. 'I'm glad Seamus isn't here, the last thing I want to do is remind him of how seriously screwed up my family is. I honestly feel like I struck gold with him, and that we managed to build our own little world over the bridge away from the crazies.'

'That's what Ben said he was trying to do in the Village: he wanted to build a new world there, a new life for Grace, until I shattered that illusion for him.'

A crease furrowed Nikki's forehead. 'How?'

'I let Alistair into the house.'

I had wanted her to roll her eyes, say how preposterous it was and agree with me that Ben had to forgive his brother. So when her face grew solemn, I began to worry.

'You let Alistair into Ben's house?'

'Just briefly, he didn't want me to say that we had met because he wanted to surprise him,' I added quickly.

Nikki looked furious. 'I bet he did,' she bit out.

'Ben really blames Alistair for Caroline's death, doesn't he? I have never seen him so mad.' I swallowed. 'Is it also something to do with Holly?'

Nikki straightened the blankets on her bed, as she sighed wearily, her limp, ash-blonde hair highlighting the circles under her eyes. 'Once upon a time, there was a girl called Holly.'

I sat up straight.

'Holly was madly in love with Alistair, and he was madly in love with her. Alistair was the youngest and wildest of all the Worthingtons, so finding someone as nice and sensible as Holly was somewhat of a win for our family. No more embarrassing headlines and scandals, because Alistair was under the thumb. Oh, how Mother rejoiced – we all did. We could stop worrying and we did, for a while.' She looked out the hospital window, thinking back to those days.

'Then something happened that had you worrying again?' I was sitting on the edge of my seat, my heart pounding against my ribcage as I waited for what I had already suspected, that Ben had come between Alistair and Holly. It was all so clear to me now, and I felt stupid for not seeing it before. Alistair had returned to mend fences with his brother and Holly but Ben was stuck in the past. I could feel an old anger rising in me.

'Well, so begins another story,' said Nikki, sitting back against her pillows. 'Once upon a time there was a girl called Caroline. She was beautiful, and smart and she loved Ben and he loved her.'

I knew how this story ended, but I let her continue.

'But sometimes love isn't enough, and Caroline became distant and cold toward Ben. We worried for them, but thought if anyone could work it out, they could. And then of course the ultimate blessing came. Caroline fell pregnant, she was going to bring a beautiful little Worthington into the world. And she did, born with a mop of black hair and her father's eyes. Grace was a Worthington through and through. There was such love for her, you could see it in the way Caroline looked at her daughter when she held her in her arms. You would never have suspected, and we didn't – until that day.'

'That day? As in the day she died?'

'The day Holly found the letter from Caroline,' Nikki said.

I sat so immobile, barely breathing.

'Holly was on our doorstep, hysterical. Seamus and I couldn't make sense of what she was saying, she was so upset. I remember Seamus reading over it, the way he glanced at me, like his first instinct was to protect me, but then he turned to Holly to ask her if Ben knew.'

My heart sank. 'Knew what?'

'The truth.'

'She didn't want to have a baby with Ben?'

Nikki shook her head. 'She didn't want to have a baby with Alistair.'

I shook my head, my eyes wide, disbelief flowing through my very being. I had misheard her, of course I had.

'That can't be, Grace has Ben's eyes, she's his daughter.'

Nikki began to tear up as she shook her head. 'They're Worthington eyes, Sarah, but they don't belong to Ben. Holly found the letter in Alastair's pocket.'

A stray tear ran down my cheek as the horror and realisation washed over me. 'Does Ben know?'

'Holly showed Ben the letter first.'

'What did it say?'

'As much as I hated her, it didn't seem real. Caroline was such a confident, together person, but on the page, her writing was so desperate, so needy. Begging Alistair not to tell anyone about their affair, that she stood to lose everything if people suspected the baby wasn't Ben's.'

'Oh my God.'

'Grace was born, and although it was certain she wasn't his, Ben refused a paternity test. He cared for her as if she were his own, loved her despite the truth. How hard it must be to look into her eyes knowing of such a betrayal.'

'And Alistair?'

'He promised to stay away, that the affair was over and that he wasn't ready to be a father.'

'But it wasn't over, was it?'

Nikki shook her head. 'The day of the accident, Alistair was driving Caroline back to the Village, but they never made it. Ben had to deal with the loss of what he believed was his daughter, the loss of a wife and the loss of a brother. You can't imagine how many times a man could be broken, be betrayed by the people who were supposed to love him. It was cruel enough losing Caroline, but to know that it happened while they were still going behind his back, even after all the pain he went through when he found out about Grace. Well, you can imagine.'

I shook my head. 'What have I done?' I thought of Ben's face as he lifted Alistair's jacket, the look of anger in his eyes knowing that his brother had come into his house, how he'd wanted to protect his daughter. I had jeopardised that. Then I remembered the night Holly was downstairs crying in Ben's arms, and how he had made her promise not to go back to him.

There were multiple victims in this story. Holly, heart broken by Alistair; Ben betrayed by Caroline, with his brother the ultimate betrayer; and now Ben was destined to live a life that would involve ghosts and secrets so awful there was no wonder he wanted to shut himself away from the world. Well, he wouldn't shut himself away from me – I wouldn't let him.

'Sarah, I'm sorry you've been dragged into this mess. What must you think of us?'

'I think there is always a hero and a villain in every story,' I said. 'The biggest battle is not knowing who is who.'

Nikki nodded, looking at me with hope. 'And now you know.'

'Yes.'

'So how about you go rescue that hero? I think he could do with a happy ending.'

I didn't know how to answer that; I stood and gave her a hug. 'I'll try,' I said.

Because it was all I could do.

Chapter Thirty-Four

I knew Nikki wanted me to fight, but every way I tried – phone messages, long-winded emails, and even physically going to Lafayette Street – I found a brick wall and I banged my head against it.

I didn't get past the entrance of the Lafayette foyer; Ruth's smug voice called down to me that Mr Worthington was not taking calls. She was getting her revenge, I thought as I slunk away to Dave's car. Dave's big brown eyes asked the question in the rear-view mirror.

'Back to the Village, Dave,' I said. I had some packing to do.

As we pulled away from the kerb, edging our way into the busy New York City traffic, it finally hit me: I was no longer Grace's carer. I had lost that right by letting in the one man who had torn the family apart, who had run away from all responsibility, who was as charming and carefree as ever despite the betrayal of his brother, despite the tragic repercussions of his careless actions. He may have had kind eyes and a charming smile, but I would trade those for Ben's stoicism and harsh, honest eyes in a heartbeat.

I ached at the thought of never seeing him or Grace again. Here was a man taking on a baby who was not his own, working to protect her, to give her everything, even if it went against every natural instinct. Grace was the symbol of Alistair and Caroline's betrayal yet he loved and cared for her regardless.

Ben Worthington was the best man I had ever known.

I looked out the window, hoping Dave wouldn't see my tears. 'Dave, do you mind if we make a little detour?'

'I have no prior engagements, Miss Williams. Where would you like to go?'

'I just need to pick up something from the Village.' I couldn't believe I was about to say it. 'Then take me to Penny Worthington's.'

For the first time since my interview I wasn't nervous about standing in Penny's expansive foyer, waiting to be summoned into one of her stark parlours. I clutched a letter of resignation, and draped over my arm was Alistair's jacket. I couldn't wait to hand both things to her and leave, never to return.

'Excuse me, Miss Williams, this way please.'

Frieda was waiting to lead me down the hall in a direction I had never been before. How many rooms for entertaining did one woman need? Our heels clicked on the polished marble floor as we approached a large wooden door. I could see Frieda preparing herself to enter, almost as if she was anxious. It was a rather contagious feeling. Where was she leading me, to a firing squad?

Frieda reached for the handle with an apologetic smile. 'Mrs Worthington is not at home, but Mr Worthington will see you now.' She said it quickly before opening the door.

'Wait – what?' I protested.

But it was too late, I was waved into the room and the door was closed behind me. I stood with my back to it, my wide eyes roaming the room. It wasn't white or barren. It was a deep burgundy colour with wood panelling and edged with floor-to-ceiling bookshelves and a rather strange collection of African-inspired statues and ornaments. A leopard-print sofa that was most definitely not Penny Worthington sat at the back of the room. A fully stocked bar was close to a pool table that was lit with rich gold lighting – the main feature of the room – and the smell of tobacco and whisky lingered.

'Welcome to my man cave,' said a voice.

My head swivelled, struggling to determine where it had come from in the dimly lit room. I walked tentatively toward the lounge. The only sign of life was a puff of smoke billowing from a wing chair and a crystal tumbler on the coffee table filled with a shot of whisky. It was then I heard laughter – no, it was more like a dark chuckle – and I thought that maybe I had entered a vampire's lair, and I was on the menu.

A man in a navy knitted sweater, slacks and slippers sat in the chair, holding a cigar in one hand and an iPad on his lap, with one earbud in, laughing at – I tilted my head – a funny cat video?

He wiped a tear from his eye, trying to gain some composure. 'That is the best. Now, if I want to share that on my wall, how do I do that?' he asked, looking over his glasses on the edge of his nose.

'Um, as in, on Facebook?'

'Yeah, that's it. How do I do that?' he said, lifting the iPad to me.

I blinked against the cigar smoke, looking at the screen and pointing to the share button beneath the video post.

'Great, thanks,' he said. I could not be more confused about what was before me. I don't know what I'd pictured when it came to Nicholas Worthington. He was a handsome man, in a silver-fox way, his eyes the same unmistakable blue-grey as his children's, more striking perhaps than any of his offspring's. He took his glasses off to look at me.

'So how can I help you, Sarah Williams?'

I was surprised he knew my name. I hadn't thought he would be kept in the know. 'I just wanted to give this letter to Mrs Worthington,' I said, holding it out.

He placed his cigar in the ashtray to his side and took the envelope from me with interest. 'Anything I can help you with?'

I wanted to say, 'Keep your family in fucking check,' but resisted. I smiled politely and shook my head. 'No, it's all in there,' I said, turning for the door.

'You shouldn't give up on him so easily.'

His words halted me. 'Sorry?'

'He's a good man; stubborn but good.'

'He says that comes from you.'

The chair creaked as Mr Worthington leant around the side to look at me. 'Stubborn, yes, but good? *Never.*' He winked, and it was then I realised what a wonderful combination Penny and Nicholas Worthington could be. 'I see you have my young son's jacket with you, did you want me to hand that over too?'

I looked at the jacket slung over my arm. I'd been so distracted I had all but forgotten I'd wanted to return it.

'What is it with this jacket? How does everyone know who it belongs to?' I said, mainly to myself as I looked for an embroidered nametag.

'I can spot that purple silk lining from a mile away; he says it's his signature colour, whatever that means.' Nicholas rolled his eyes, and with that simple gesture, I knew I liked Ben's dad.

I smiled, before turning to make my exit, ready to leave the jacket on the bar and this mixed-up family behind, when the double doors burst open and in walked —

'Father, I'm heading to the Hamptons for the weekend, do you thin—' Alistair stopped dead in his tracks at the sight of me. 'Sarah? What are you doing here?' He smiled, charming and carefree, seemingly glad to see me.

My blood boiled as I gathered his jacket, scrunching it into a ball and thrusting into his chest.

His eyes narrowed. 'What the hell?' he said, juggling his jacket and brushing out the creases. 'Careful, Sarah, this is expensive.'

'I just thought I'd return it seeing as you left it on the floor in my room, but I guess you're probably used to people cleaning up your mess for you.'

Alistair glanced at me: gone were the charming depths, replaced by what I could only imagine were his true colours. I heard a snort from behind me but I couldn't be certain if Nicholas was laughing at me or another cat video.

Taking no notice of his father, Alistair shook his head in amazement. 'I see Ben is set on poisoning you against me. That didn't take long.'

'You are something else.'

'What? How am I always the villain in this story? I've lost too, I've sacrificed too!'

'The Hamptons, huh? Sounds like you're really roughing it.'

That cocky grin creased the corner of his mouth. 'Come on, Sarah, you have to admit it's for the best. I can't have a baby – I'm in the prime of my life. Plus, it wouldn't hurt to soften Ben a bit, the cranky old bastard. I think I've done him a favour.'

I don't know how it happened, or where the urge to hurt him came from but, before I knew it, my fist had connected with his nose. Alistair's head flung back and I bounced on the balls of my feet, shaking my fist. Shit, that hurt!

Alistair smothered his nose, groaning in agony. 'Sarah, what the *fuck*?'

I was just about to tell him exactly what the fuck when uproarious laughter broke out behind me.

Nicholas Worthington stood from his chair and began to clap. 'Young lady, you have just done what many have wanted to do for years.'

'Oh, that's nice.' Alistair winced, flicking a hanky out of his pocket to block the blood coming from his nose.

'Five minutes back in New York and you're already causing trouble again.' Nicholas's voice was like thunder, rolling over the room and commanding respect. It had me stepping aside, and it gained Alistair's attention as he straightened. The full weight of his father's stare was his problem now, more so than a potential broken nose.

'Time we reevaluated your travel plans, I think.'

'But, Father, I —'

'Oh, I know, you're in the prime of your life,' Nicholas said mockingly as he walked over to a desk in front of his library. 'All the more reason to send you somewhere where you can be a help more than a hindrance.'

Alistair looked dismayed. 'I'm not leaving New York.'

'Now, Alistair, I have it on good authority that one of my most trusted and valued friends is setting up a medical practice in Slovenia, and could certainly do with a helping hand while his wife cares for their young children. Seeing as you have such tremendous people skills, I thought you would be a fine help to the cause.'

'Slovenia?' Alistair and I said at the same time – Alistair in horror, me in surprise.

I thought about the hardworking, no-nonsense Liebenbergs, and the remote rural setting where Alistair might stand to learn something of value, and smiled broadly at Nicholas Worthington.

'You are familiar with Slovenia, Miss Williams?'

'Oh, you know what they say,' I said, turning a smug smile to a glowering Alistair. 'Slovenia is always a good idea.'

Chapter Thirty-Five

packed my belongings and sat them near the front door. I'd booked driver Dave the day before to ensure I'd make my flight home. I had spent the evening cleaning and prepping the house to leave it exactly how I had found it: soulless, unlived in and unloved. I had almost believed that, in the past weeks, I could feel a shift in the house, a change, but it was not to be. I'd gotten up early with the sole purpose of writing Ben a letter, to thank him for allowing me to be a part of their beautiful little family, but with three days gone and not so much as a word from him, I'd reconsidered, thinking it best to do as he had asked, and leave.

I had one thing left to do. I would never get to say goodbye to Grace, so as much as I knew I would never forget her, I wanted to leave her with something to remember me by.

I stood back, tilting my head to the side to survey the scene before me. In a series of white, wooden A4 frames,

I had created the ultimate New York City scene on Grace's blank bedroom wall. Illustrations in full colour of a girl venturing to Times Square, strolling past Tiffany's, standing near the fountain of Washington Park, sauntering through a leafy Central Park landscape. A whole array of New York scenes telling of a girl's love for the city and for the family she had lived with. I could think of no better way to tell Grace my story. Even if Ben tore them down, I wanted him to see them too, to know that regardless of how things ended, in the short time I had been here, I had seen and discovered so many things.

I took one last look and smiled, before switching off the light and closing the door behind me. I went downstairs, lingering in the hall, not wanting to take that final walk through a house I had become attached to, not just because it was beautiful, or because of the warmth I had come to discover in the least likely of places: Grace's smile; Ben's arms. This had somehow, without me even realising it, become my home. And now I was leaving it behind.

I grabbed my bag and opened the door, dragging my suitcase out behind me. I sat on the steps and waited for Dave. New York always inspired such romantic endings in movies, where the hero would come chasing after his leading lady, kissing her in the rain or meeting her on the rooftop of a skyscraper. Everyone lived happily ever after, but as Dave finally pulled up out front, greeting me with a smile and putting my things in the car, I knew that this wasn't a movie. Ben wasn't coming for me, and I would just have to accept it.

Dreading the long flight home and feeling at my self-pitying best, I lay down in the backseat, no longer able to watch the commotion of New York streets whizz by; it would only make my heart ache for all the things I could not have. I closed my eyes, letting the hum of the car soothe me into calmness.

'How long does it take to get to the airport, Dave?'

'It's quicker than you think,' he said.

'Oh, secret shortcut?' I said. 'Very good.' I pulled myself up on one elbow and looked out the window. 'Dave, we don't go anywhere near Lafayette Street, do we?' I asked in a panic.

He looked at me in the rear-view mirror. 'No, Miss Williams.'

I nodded. 'Good.' I lowered myself down and closed my eyes.

~

The car came to an abrupt halt, shunting me out of my sleep. A horn blasted and my hands clawed at the leather seat to prevent me from rolling off as I tried to get my bearings and wiped the sleep out of my eyes.

'Are we there?' I asked, hearing the sound of the horn again. 'What the? Have you stopped in a loading zone or something?' I croaked, twisting onto my stomach, trying to find my shoe on the floor.

'Yeah, something like that,' said Dave, getting out and yelling at the driver behind. 'Ha! You tell 'em, Dave,' I muttered as I located my shoe. Then I worked to control my bed hair and straighten my clothes. Dave opened the door, causing me to squint against the light that streamed in.

'Hurry, miss, we're holding up traffic,' he said, offering me his hand and helping me get out; it was difficult to find my feet with one leg asleep, but I soon forgot the hindrance as I stood beside the car. Dave slammed the door behind me.

'Dave? Where's the airport?' I asked, looking around, dumbfounded. 'This is definitely not the airport.' I heard another car door slam and Dave was back behind the wheel again, shrugging and yelling, 'I'm sorry!' through the open window. The other car blasted its horn again, causing him to put his foot on the accelerator and leave me in the middle of the road.

'Hey, lady, out of the way!' the cab driver shouted, and I quickstepped onto a familiar red-brick paving. I stood right before a grand stone staircase leading down to the Bethesda Terrace. Was Dave trying to kill me? Rip my heart out, set it on fire before stream rolling it? I was going to miss my flight. Looking up and down the terrace drive I wanted to scream.

He had my fucking suitcase!

Why hadn't I taken my phone? I had left it and the house keys with Dave, feeling the need to cleanse my life, but now I was screwed.

I walked along the terrace. 'Excuse me, do you have a phone I could borrow?' I asked a family. They seemed to flinch at my manic request, the mum and dad ushering their children away and smiling apologetically. Ugh, where was Penny when I needed her? *Don't mind her, she's Australian.*

I moved onto a man standing on the edge of the terrace balcony overlooking the fountain, lake and woodland, photographing it all in the golden hour.

'Excuse me, sir, sorry to trouble you but do you have a pho—'

My words fell away when I glanced down to the plaza paved in an intricate circle. Standing in the centre of the circle was the lone figure of Ben.

As if he knew, he turned from the lake, and our eyes locked.

I swear my heart stopped.

'Are you all right, miss, do you need some help?' asked the photo enthusiast.

I shook my head, unable to tear my eyes from Ben, afraid that if I did, the vision might change.

'No, thank you,' I said, peeling away, running my hand along the top of the balcony's balustrade, banging into a couple of tourists before running down the stone stair-case that led to the lower level plaza. I moved so fast I thought I might lose my footing and wouldn't that be a grand entrance. I tried to slow my pace the closer I got.

Ben hadn't moved, had only turned to watch me come down the steps.

Dodging more tourists, I made my way over to where he stood. Seeing those cold eyes, I had a good mind to keep walking, maybe punch him in the mouth for his silence. I was so tired – of the secrets, the uncertainty from day to day of a man who could be so cold, and then look at me with a fire that burned. How could I be sure of what it would be today?

I looked into his eyes, so impossible to read, and I when I reached him, I stood in silence.

'Getting dropped off to mix with the undesirables?' he said.

'It wasn't by choice,' I replied, trying my best to keep my emotions in check.

'Was breaking Alistair's nose your choice?'

Keeping my poker face was harder than I thought, especially when he was looking at me the way he was.

I lifted my chin. 'Yes, it was. But what does it matter? There are far too many secrets in your family, and it may be the way it has always been, but I want no part of it. It's toxic and ugly, despite the lovely things you surround yourself with as you dig your head in the sand. I am done.'

I used the thought of the all things that angered me to walk away, but Ben reached out for my arm. My chest tightened at his touch, the feel of his skin on mine like a hot brand. The last thing I could afford to do was turn to him, but he was pulling me around.

'What if I told you there was only one more secret, and that was all? No more, not ever.'

I shook my head, fighting against the feelings he evoked in me, the way his thumb stroked against my arm as if to quietly comfort me.

'Just one more,' he whispered, stepping to me.

My chin trembled. 'I can't.' And just as I was about to pull away, I heard a sound that stood out from all the bustling crowds and street music, a distant cry that I would recognise anywhere. I searched for it, looking past Ben's shoulder, and saw Ruth pushing a stroller.

'I am sorry, Mr Worthington, but Grace is not going to settle,' she said, unclipping and handing the baby over to Ben.

'Heeey, what's the matter?' he said, lifting Grace up and kissing her before rocking her into instant happiness.

'Have you told her yet?' Ruth said.

'Ruth,' he warned.

I glanced between the two of them. 'Told me what?'

Ruth rolled her eyes. 'What have you been doing all this time?' she chastised him before turning her deadpan expression to me. 'The secret is he loves you and he wants you to stay; honestly, you people are just so utterly ridiculous,' she snapped.

Ben, Grace and I watched her roll the empty stroller away toward the fountain, mumbling and shaking her head.

We turned to each other.

'Annnnd that's how you kill a moment,' Ben said.

I stood, stunned, waiting for him to clarify Ruth's statement, to hear the words from his mouth. Only then would I believe them. Grace began squirming and whinging, leaning out to grab me, and it was a welcome distraction. I took her into my arms, holding her to me, breathing her in and kissing her temple.

'Hey, Gracie girl.'

'No more running away,' he said. His expression deathly serious. Was he going to say it? Repeat what Ruth had just said, or was she just being cruel? 'No more nights at Lafayette, no more dinner parties with people we don't like.'

'No more secrets,' I added quickly.

Ben smiled. 'Not any more.'

I swallowed. 'So, when Ruth said that you—'

'From the moment you promised to love and care for my daughter, the same meeting when you stood in my office questioning my parenting skills.'

I cringed. 'I did, didn't I?'

'You most certainly did,' he said.

I felt my stomach do a little flip watching the lightness in his eyes. I felt the full weight of that stare. He was telling me that he loved me, even if it had been interrupted by Grace's cries and Ruth's deep sighs and eye rolls, but I was used to that. Plans changed, moments got interrupted and I always had to think on my feet, just as I was doing now. How could I possibly put into words how he made me feel, how any time he walked into a room my heart beat faster, or that when he looked me in the eyes the rest of the world fell away? I adjusted Grace's weight on my hip as I tore my eyes from her beautiful, happy, flushed face to Ben's. I wanted to look him in the eye so he understood I meant what I was about to say.

'You asked me why I chose to stay. I told you I stayed because I loved Grace. I said I stayed because I loved New York.'

Ben was silent, watching me intently.

I shifted, swallowing and trying to keep my thoughts together. 'But aside from those two very good reasons, I need you to know that, despite everything, I also stayed . . . because of you.'

I could see the most delicate shift in him, as if relief was flooding through his squared shoulders, as though he wasn't able to control his reaction.

Then, ever so slowly, Ben's lips turned up. 'It was the grilled cheese, wasn't it?'

I burst out laughing, readjusting Grace in my arms as I stepped forward, looking at the man I had come to love. Through all the days and nights that I had been in this city, I had never known such frustration, such chaos, such tenderness – such love. I knew it in the way he looked at me now, and I felt it in the warmth of my arms holding Grace, who happily chewed on a strand of my hair.

In the movies, now was the time when the man leant down and kissed the woman, taking her breath away with an embrace and promising her the world. But this wasn't a movie, this was us, and although I made the first move, he met me halfway, circling his arms around us, kissing me tenderly in the heart of Central Park.

I pulled away, cocking my brow at him, as he waited for my answer.

'That, Ben Worthington, simply sealed the deal.'

'The grilled cheese or the kiss?'

I smiled broadly, looking at him in the dying rays of the New York sun and running my hand along his freshly shaven cheek. 'Both,' I said, reaching up on my toes and kissing him once again. 'Ben?'

'Sarah?'

'Let's go home.'

Ben laughed, glancing from me to Grace and back, before breaking into that infamous crooked smile of his as he leant in, kissed my forehead and whispered, 'Right where we belong.'

IF YOU LIKED *NEW YORK NIGHTS* YOU WILL
LOVE THE OTHER BOOKS IN C.J. DUGGAN'S
HEART OF THE CITY SERIES: *PARIS LIGHTS* AND
LONDON BOUND.

Read on for a preview of *Paris Lights*.

Chapter One

I genuinely believe that aside from your place of birth there is somewhere else you belong: a place you're guided to by your heart. Some people might spend their entire lives in search of such a place, but all my life, throughout my travels, I knew which place was waiting for me.

Paris.

I had fed my love of Paris by having the Eiffel Tower plastered on my bedspreads and cushion covers, by buying kitchen accessories and placemats with *Rue Du Temple* scrawled across them, and hanging a cute *Bon Appetit* sign in my kitchen. I'd tried to explain to my boyfriend, Liam, that it wasn't really an obsession, I had just adopted a French Provincial style of decorating for our home. He seemed unconvinced.

Everyone wants to go to Paris. To fall in love, eat smelly French cheese and drink good local wine while toasting to the Eiffel Tower. It was more than just our home's décor and my Chanel lipstick collection that strengthened my bond. Paris is the art capital of the world, with tourists flocking from near and far to catch a quick glimpse of Da Vinci's *Mona Lisa* and wander the vast halls of the Louvre. But, while many people believed the Louvre to be the pinnacle of the Parisian art museum scene, there were so many other museums to see. With much excitement, I had rattled off the list of must-see locations to Liam as we'd planned this long-awaited weekend in Paris.

'We could head to the Centre Pompidou, Paris's bastion of modern art. We'll need a good couple of hours to wander through all the amazing rooms with world-famous works of – oh my God, we'll be able to see Picasso, Klimt, Miro and Kandinsky!'

Liam's face had twisted in horror, and he'd said, 'Claire, I would sooner claw my own face off than spend an entire weekend in art museums.'

I had laughed it off, but my heart sank knowing that he wouldn't budge on this. I would have to settle for compromising on the art so we could both enjoy the trip.

Liam had insisted we save the Eiffel Tower until our last day in Paris. He'd said we shouldn't conform to the typical tourist itinerary, that we should discover other parts of the city first. He was so smart, so romantic.

We battled the crowds at the Louvre for a date with Mona Lisa, strolled hand-in-hand through the Jardin de Tuileries, dodged pigeons and love-lock sellers near Notre Dame, and, of course, no trip to Paris would be complete without a visit to the famed Moulin Rouge.

And this morning, stepping from the bus, our heads had craned upwards, my mouth ajar as Liam clicked away on his expensive Canon camera, snapping the iron beast before us. Except it wasn't a beast. The Eiffel Tower was a lady – strong, imposing, beautiful – but I couldn't have said so to Liam. He would have just rolled his eyes.

We'd lingered around the edge of the crowds, taking it all in. It was incredible how something that stood still could evoke as much excitement as a themed rollercoaster at Disneyland. Hordes of tourists surrounded us in a blur of excitement and delight. Despite the wonders around me, though, my attention remained on Liam. I only had eyes for him.

I tilted my head, admiring my gorgeous boyfriend: his dark, unruly hair, his five o'clock shadow, his charcoal-grey jumper and dark jeans that made him look like he belonged here; a true Parisian. Liam had been acting strange for days. Twitchy, antsy, a bit snappy. As he stood beside me, rubbing his unshaven jaw, I could see the cogs turning in his head, no doubt wondering what to say, how to do it. He is such a stickler for details; it's one of the things I love about him.

My chest expanded as I breathed deeply. I tried to hide the knowing smile that twisted the corner of my mouth. *This is it; this is really going to happen.* It was all clear to me now: the impromptu visit to Paris; saving the tower till last.

This is my moment.

Wait until everyone back home finds out about this.

I stood in the heart of the square and waited for Liam to speak. Waited for him to ask the big question, to go down on one knee in front of all these people, and ask me to be Mrs Liam Jackson.

My chest tightened as he turned to me. His focus was on me and me alone. In this moment, under the massive iron structure, the world around us didn't matter. It was as if we were the only ones on the planet and that the tower had been built for us alone. I could feel my skin prickle despite the warm air that swept over us.

'Claire.' Liam swallowed nervously. I could feel my eyes watering as he reached out and grabbed my hand, a hand that had been nervously tapping my thigh.

'Yes?' I breathed out, my heart beating a million miles an hour. *Yes, yes, yes* had been echoing in my mind all morning.

The dark, hypnotic pools of Liam's eyes made me breathless as he gazed intently at me.

This is it! This is what I've been waiting for. The perfect end to a perfect weekend.

He squeezed my hand. 'I think we should see other people.'

I didn't think I'd heard him correctly; the sound of a record scratching in my head might have prevented me from understanding. Or maybe it was the tourists, talking and pointing animatedly as they took selfies with the tower. Even the traffic noise seemed painfully loud right now. I tilted my head as if to listen more intently, my eyes blinking in confusion.

'Sorry?'

Liam's eyes seemed less romantic now, and his face was twisted in pain. But it wasn't pain caused by the inner turmoil of working on romantic perfection like I had thought. It was another kind of pain entirely.

'I said, I think we should—'

'No!' I shut off his words, afraid that he would only repeat himself. 'No, no, no, no!' This was not how it was supposed to go.

I had planned it all in my mind: Liam on one knee, a box appearing from his pocket (preferably from Tiffany), applause ringing out across the square as I cried and said, *Yes, yes, YES!* I had envisioned how to pose with my ring for Instagram, adding the witty caption: 'I said oui oui.' I had even picked out the appropriate filter for our selfie. It was all so perfect – in my head.

'Claire, I'm sorry.' His brown eyes were sorrowful, as though his heart was breaking. It was like I had just said the words that would tear us apart, not him. 'I never meant to hurt you.'

I felt my fists clench. My shock, my disbelief, was morphing into something else, even as the hot tears pooled in my eyes.

He never meant to hurt me.

'You're breaking up with me!'

Silence.

'In *Paris*.'

He looked away.

'Under the Eiffel fucking Tower!' I screamed, attracting the attention of those who were unlucky enough to be standing nearby.

Was there any feeling worse than this? A punch in the face on a gondola in Venice maybe? He might as well have punched me – it felt like all the air had been sucked from my lungs.

My admiration for him, my total and utter besotted and blind obsession with Liam, died. I could feel my heart darken; my soul was so black it scared me. We had been together for eighteen months, had moved from Melbourne to London so Liam could follow his path in life – whatever that had meant; he'd never actually clarified it. If he meant we were both always strapped for cash and working double shifts in the dimly lit London pub, then we were following his path all right. Living the dream! We had been so determined to find our way and make a new life in a foreign land, despite Liam's rather lacklustre path in London. I had been certain we knew each other's dreams and fears. And that's what was burning a hole in my heart, because at the crux of it, I don't actually think Liam knew me at all. Because anyone who ever did know me knew that coming to Paris had been my lifelong dream. I had mentioned it often enough. The city was so close to our new home, but until this weekend we had been too busy to make the trip: there was an excuse, there was always an excuse. So when Liam not only agreed, but instigated this trip, I had convinced myself that this was the moment. Why else would he bring me here?

I shook my head. 'How could you?'

I broke away from his hold. He was trying to explain, but I couldn't listen to his reasoning. I stumbled away, skimming past people as I made my way toward the bus that would take me back to the hotel. Everything was a blur. I sat on the top level of the double decker, my eyes forward, staring aimlessly at a balding Italian man and his wife. I couldn't look back to the tower for fear of catching a glimpse of Liam. I didn't hear Liam calling my name, pleading for the bus to stop as it pulled away. I'm not sure if I was more relieved or hurt by the fact he didn't pursue me, but I guess those kind of dramatics only happen in movies.

The sky was grey and ominous. I swear it had been blue when we arrived. That's how quickly things had changed. My bus rolled on, pausing only to give happy, snapping tourists one last chance to take a shot of the tower. I couldn't even bring myself to look at it, not that I would have been able to see it anyway through my bleary vision.

Maybe one day I would forgive Liam for breaking my heart. But tainting Paris, and ruining my experience of this city, that was something I could never forgive – ever!

~

Apparently Paris is especially magnificent in the rain. I had yet to experience the pleasure in my short stay, but as soon as I stepped off the bus, the heavens opened up, soaking me to the bone. It seemed a fitting finale to my disastrous afternoon. In a moment of complete self-indulgence to my misery, I had refused the complimentary plastic poncho from the tourist bus, opting instead to let the rain pummel me. Ordinarily a person might squeal, laugh and run for cover, delighting in the glorious downpour in a foreign city. It was, dare I say it, romantic. But let's face it, romance was dead, as was my ability to feel anything.

I walked along the pavement from the bus stop to a pedestrian crossing, squelching a slow, sad path in my ballet flats, my pleated skirt clinging to my thighs, my long brown hair plastered to my face. Mercifully, the droplets of water disguised my tears. Our hotel was a few blocks away on Rue Lauriston. We were ideally located between the Arc de Triomphe and the Eiffel Tower. It only seemed like yesterday that we had booked the last room available with great excitement.

Our hotel that *we* had booked.

I guess I had to stop saying things like that now. In one afternoon, the life I'd thought I had had became completely redundant. Was that even possible? Had I stayed to face Liam's explanations I might have found out more. If I'd challenged him, fought, screamed, demanded answers. But 'Let's see other people'? That was like a dagger to the heart, almost as bad as 'I'm seeing someone else'. I tried not to entertain the thought that that could have been the reason behind his decision.

I let my feet guide me along the narrow path, through the neighbourhood that seemed amazingly familiar to me even though I'd only been here for a short time. The past three days I'd been wide eyed, drinking in every detail of the impressive Haussmann-designed apartments and buildings; watching the locals go about their daily rounds to the butcher, florist or bakery in their effortlessly stylish way. The air felt thick. I fixed my gaze on the ground, willing my feet forward, telling myself that my reward would be to lock myself away in my hotel room and let my defences crumble down and scream and cry into my pillow.

The red sign of our hotel was mightier than any beacon. I battled on, each step becoming more perilous as the soles of my shoes fought to gain traction on the wet footpath. It took immense concentration to quicken my pace without breaking my neck, but I was determined. That's when I heard the distant sound of a fast-approaching car.

It slid around the corner, the revving engine of the black Audi echoing in the small street, disturbing the peace and quiet, slicing its way through the dying light. It was enough to distract me, annoyed as I was by the reckless-ness of its approach as it sped along like a rally car, and in wet conditions too.

I made sure to glare at the driver.

'Bloody maniac,' I grumbled.

Stepping back from the kerb, I gasped as the car sprayed up a wave of putrid gutter water. Now I was mad. Madder than hell.

I watched as the very same car pulled up in front of my hotel.

'Right,' I said. I was in just the mood to give the flashy lunatic behind the wheel a piece of my mind. And sure, there was a good chance that he wouldn't understand a word I was saying, but if all else failed, flipping the bird was a pretty universal gesture. I neared the car, sleek and beaded with droplets of rain, the windows so heavily tinted it was impossible to see inside.

'Hey!' I shouted, knocking on the driver's window angrily.

There was no response; the only sign of life was the heat that radiated from the vehicle itself. I glared at the window where I imagined a person's head might be. Feeling pretty satisfied at showing my displeasure, I sacrificed the unladylike gesture of flipping the bird and thought it best to just head into the hotel, leaving a watery path behind me.

And I was about to do exactly that when the unexpected happened. The driver's window slowly edged its way down, revealing a pair of intense, angry blue eyes that seemed to stare right into my soul.

Yep, my day was about to get a whole lot worse.

Chapter Two

If I could have, I would have glued all Liam's undies to the floor and set his favourite pair of jeans on fire, all the while tossing his other possessions over the balcony. Instead, with much less drama, I quietly spoke in a croaky voice to the doorman by the front entrance.

'Can you please come and collect some bags from room twenty-five?'

I was wet and deflated and completely rattled from the death stare the Audi driver had given me, which had sent me fleeing into the hotel. Guess I wasn't as tough as I thought. I certainly didn't feel it right now. What's French for fragile?

If it hadn't been for Cecile, the warm, bubbly lady at reception, I would have sworn everyone in Paris hated me.

'Bonjour!' she said, beaming, showing the gap between her extremely white teeth. Her bright blue eyes lit up and I knew I had her full attention like always. 'Oh, Mademoiselle Shorten, you got caught in the rain?'

I sheepishly examined the squelchy footprints I had trekked through reception.

'Next time, take an umbrella by the door,' she added helpfully.

Ha! Next time. There won't be a next time. I am done.

Despite the bitter edge to my thoughts, I smiled. It was strained, but no matter how bad I was feeling I could never take it out on sweet Cecile; she had, after all, been one of the very few highlights of my weekend.

'Merci,' I said, one of the very limited words I knew the meaning of, even after listening to the audio translator on the Eurostar from London three days ago. My memory for language was not great; I had managed to remember that paper in French was 'papier', and the door was 'la porte'. Neither was going to get me out of a bind.

My watery trail followed me across the foyer to the lift. Pressing the button to summon the slowest lift in Paris, if not the world, I brought the edges of my soaked cardi together, the chill from my wet clothes starting to work its way into my bones. The screeching, rackety shoe box–sized lift groaned its way down to reception, the door struggling to open as the tiny cavity of doom presented itself to me. I tentatively stepped in and, like every other time I had done so, I wondered if this would be the time I would be trapped in here. Would today be the day the lift gave up the ghost? With my current track record, I wouldn't be surprised – it would be the icing on the bloody cake.

The lift screeched its way up to level four, its doors sliding painfully slowly to the side, releasing me to freedom on the narrow landing. I couldn't get out quickly enough. I would live to see another day.

I walked down the narrow carpeted hall to our room. The dated, awkward spaces that had once seemed so quaint to me now just seemed dingy. It made me feel less bad about leaving marks on the already worn, rose-coloured carpet. In the short time that I had stayed here, I had realised that our door required a particular lift-twist-and-shimmy action in order to open it. Still, it took me three goes to get it open, with a few swear words to aid the cause. After finally hearing the magical click of the lock, I shouldered my way through, the door hitting one of the suitcases in the light, tidy yet small room. I negotiated my way through the mess of our bags and clothes to the bed. Side-stepping around it I went to the balcony door, wanting nothing more than to let some fresh air in.

As I opened it, the balcony door hit the edge of the bed, allowing barely enough room to go out; it was something Liam and I had laughed about when we opened it the first time. Every new, quirky discovery had been met with carefree laughter because, after all, it was Paris: there could have been a rodent watching TV on our bed and it would have been okay. WE WERE IN PARIS! But now, as I shifted awkwardly through the small opening and onto the little rain-dampened balcony, I didn't feel any form of whimsy or lighthearted joy at all, even though my heart never failed to clench at the sight of the beautiful apartment buildings lining the street. Opposite me, a slightly damp black cat lazily washed himself on the balcony, the window left ajar for him for whenever he was ready to return.

Despite the traffic noise and the sound of a distant police siren, my mind was alarmingly quiet. My legs, which had felt like jelly, no longer shook, and although a breeze swept across me I didn't feel cold. If anything, my cheeks felt flushed and my heart raced; was I getting sick? Was this a normal reaction to heartbreak? I couldn't tell as I had no experience with being dumped, apart from David Kennedy ditching me in Grade Four for Jacinta Clark. Liam had been my first serious boyfriend and heartbreak was new to me, so I didn't know if what I was feeling was normal. I felt like a robot. Was I completely devoid of emotion?

My question was answered the moment I glanced down to the street, my eyes narrowing as I saw the black Audi that was still parked out the front of the hotel. The sudden rage I felt bubbling to the surface proved I wasn't a robot. I was all right, just as furious as I'd been on the pavement, meeting those steely blue eyes boring into me through the slit of the car window. Without apology they'd stared me down, and it had worked.

'Cocky bastard,' I mumbled, my voice causing the cat opposite to pause mid-clean and look at me with his yellow eyes.

'Shut up. I wasn't talking to you,' I said, smiling as he went back to his bath time. My humour was short lived. Hearing voices echo off the buildings, I gripped the edge of the railing, leaning over to get a better look at the commotion below.

A man in a dark navy suit strode out of the hotel entrance. He seemed determined, purposeful and intent on ignoring the struggling doorman who ran after him with an umbrella in a bid to keep him dry. The man ignored him, clicking the button and walking toward his . . . black Audi. He was talking on his phone, loud and robust, as he argued with someone on the other end. He seemed passionate, and manic, his free hand gesturing animatedly, before turning to aggressively wave and dismiss the doorman, who backed away with what looked like a thousand apologies.

The suit, whose face I couldn't see from this angle, opened his car door, ended his conversation abruptly and threw his phone inside.

What an arrogant bastard. I had seen it in his eyes, now I'd heard it in his voice and watched it in his stride. I almost wished that he would look up now, willed him to do so, so I could give him the finger this time, send him a 'screw you, buddy' scowl. The thought of doing such a thing almost made me feel giddy, but of course thinking and doing are two different things, and just as I stared down at him with a knowing look on my face, the last thing I actually expected to happen, happened.

He looked up.

I didn't give him the finger. Instead, I yelped and stepped back so fast I tripped on the lip of the door and went hurtling through the narrow opening, crashing rather mercifully onto the bed, before slipping onto the floor and collecting the side table on the way, pulling the curtain down with me, the rod narrowly missing my head.

I groaned, feeling the sting of carpet burn and a healthy dose of humiliation as I sat on the floor, the sheer fabric of the curtain draped over me like Mother Teresa.

'*Sacré* fuckin' *bleu*,' I said, half laugh, half sob.

Yeah, I showed him all right, I thought gingerly, and picked myself up, using the mattress as support. I hadn't even gotten a chance to really look at his face, all I remembered was meeting those same steely blue eyes and panicking. I heard the loud engine of his car speeding down the narrow road, probably taking out women and children along the way without a care in the world. Men like that belonged on an island; an island that should be set on fire.

I got to my feet, pulling back my curtain veil, and rubbing my arm, wincing at the bruises that were sure to come. I sighed, glancing out the window. The cat was gone. It had probably been spooked by the unco tourist flailing about and disturbing the peace, just as mine was suddenly disturbed by a knock at the door.

'Luggage, mademoiselle?'

Oh shit! Shit shit shit shit.

I stepped once to the left and twice to the right, a dance that continued as I tried to get my head together.

'Ah, just a second,' I yelled a bit too frantically. I picked up the side lamp from the floor, trying to straighten the skew-whiff lampshade and wrestling with the curtain cape over my shoulders. I'm sure I looked like some demented form of the Statue of Liberty. Shoving the curtain and pushing the rod behind the bed, I quickly drew the drapes. *Nothing to see here!*

Flustered, I gave in to the one fantasy I'd had walking back to the hotel: I grabbed every piece of Liam's belongings and shoved them into his bag. Quickstepping to the bathroom I dumped his toiletries into his bag too. It kind of felt good, packing him away piece by piece. By the time I opened the door to the doorman I was breathing heavily, my hair was half dry and fuzzy and my clothes were patchy and creased. If the doorman wondered what a hobo was doing in residence on the fourth floor, he didn't say anything. He smiled and gestured to take my bag, seemingly confused when he looked over my shoulder at where my stuff lay strewn all over the room.

'Ah, just one?' He lifted his finger.

We weren't leaving until tomorrow, heading back to London on the 11.05 train. I hadn't thought beyond just wanting Liam away from me – I couldn't even face him right now. I thought that his bag at the front door was a good enough hint as any; I only hoped he didn't see the need to come and talk to me.

I nodded. 'Just one.'

The door closed behind the doorman, leaving me standing in my room, my heart beating so fast it felt like it was robbing me of breath. I felt hot and manky, claustrophobic, so I peeled my clothes off quickly, hoping that would alleviate the feeling. I sat on the edge of the bed in my bra and undies, hands on my knees, shoulders sagged in defeat. What had I done? A knee-jerk reaction was typical of me, and in this moment a new kind of panic surfaced. Didn't I owe it to us to talk? To try to work it out? After all, the biggest change in my life had been moving to London with Liam. Was I simply going to let everything go?

My thoughts were interrupted by a muffled chime coming from the crumpled pile on the floor. I bent over, searching through the damp mess, feeling the lump in my cardi pocket that was illuminating the thin fabric.

Mum.

Quickly swiping the screen to avoid the loved-up picture of me and Liam, I tapped on Mum's text.

Just saw the pic on Instagram, you FINALLY got to see the Eiffel Tower, more pics please!! Xx.

I stared at Mum's message, confused. I didn't post any –

I froze, a sudden horror looming over me. 'Oh no, he didn't.'

I swiped and tapped the screen urgently, a part of me fearing that it could be true, and just as I tried to tell myself it wasn't, there it was. Loud and proud on Liam's

Instagram profile, a picture of the Eiffel Tower – a few, actually, from different angles, different filters.

'You've got to be kidding me!'

He was so distraught at breaking my heart, he'd gone on to take photos, whack a filter on them, even fucking hashtag them: *#Eiffeltower #parislove #wonderwhatthepoorpeoplearedoing*

And he didn't stop there: seemed like Liam had a busy afternoon being quite the tourist, while I sat here in my undies, cold, battered and bruised. I glowered at the screen, tears clouding my vision, barely believing how incredibly selfish he could be.

I threw my phone down and buried my head in my hands. It was over, I knew it was, and more than anything I wished I could bring the numbness back.

I wished I was a fucking robot!

Chapter Three

I woke the next morning on top of the covers, still in only my underwear. There had been no more knocks on my door. No messages, no phone calls, no pleas from Liam for forgiveness or to be taken back. When I dressed, packed and headed downstairs to check out, Cecile at reception told me awkwardly, and with a sad smile, that Monsieur Jackson had booked into another room late last night.

'Thank you,' I said, putting the room key on the counter. 'Has he checked out yet?' I hated to ask but I had to know; I had our tickets for the painful trip back to London, something I could barely think about.

'No, mademoiselle.'

'Okay, well, um . . .' *Leave the ticket at reception and just go.* 'When he comes down, can you please tell him I am in the restaurant?'

Cecile nodded. 'Of course, I am very sorry to see you go. I hope you have enjoyed your stay here in Paris.' Her eyes were kind, and I could tell it pained her to do her usual checkout spiel, knowing full well that Paris was not going to be the city of love for me – far from it. I had hoped to take to the city like a true natural and that maybe Liam and I could return here every year for the anniversary of our engagement. But now I thought if I never saw that tower again, it would be too soon.

'I did,' I lied. 'Thank you for everything. You have been very kind.'

Cecile's beaming smile was back once more, her eyes alight as she stood tall with pride.

'*De rien, merci beaucoup.*'

I smiled. 'Am I okay to leave my bags here?'

'Oui, I'll have Gaston take them for you.'

'Merci,' I said, quietly. I felt like I was annihilating such beautiful words with my accent.

In the restaurant I was greeted by the familiar sight of Simone, a bored waitress from Tottenham who wore her hair in an impossibly high topknot bun. From the intel I had gathered over the weekend, she had been working at Hotel Trocadéro near on three months, didn't speak French but made it work, seeing as a lot of tourists stayed here. Cathy, the other breakfast girl, was a local.

'Fake it till you make it,' Simone said with a wink. 'Where's your man?'

'Oh, um, he's in the shower,' I said, masking my lying mouth by sipping my coffee.

'So you heading back then, to London?' she asked.

'Yeah, and you?'

'Oh, don't even, I'm trying to stick it out just to prove to my ex that I can live without him.'

That got my attention. 'And how is that working for you?'

'He's here every bloody weekend.' She laughed, rolling her eyes.

'Oh.' My shoulders sagged. I had hoped she was about to tell me a heroic tale of girl power and self-discovery, not weekend booty calls, mid-week mind games and text arguments. I zoned out after a while, a glazed look in my eyes, until they refocused on a figure standing at reception, talking to Cecile.

Liam smiled at Cecile, thanking her for what could only be assumed was the message she had passed on for me, then he tentatively turned to the restaurant and approached me. Simone had mercifully moved onto the next table to address a dirty spoon crisis, as Liam arrived before me. His dark eyes glanced at the empty chair, silently asking permission to sit.

When I didn't respond he took it as a yes and pulled out the chair. I looked straight into his eyes with a deadpan expression; I wanted him to feel my pain, my disappointment, my heartbreak.

'I've ordered a taxi for ten fifteen,' he said.

I lifted my chin, giving nothing away.

'Do you have everything?' he asked, like he always did. Always the control freak.

'Of course,' I snapped.

'Well, I think the trip home will give us the chance to . . . talk.'

I shrugged. 'Why wait?'

Liam sighed. 'Claire, please don't be—'

'What? Difficult? Sorry, but you don't get to call the shots, not on this.'

Liam shifted in his seat, smiling painfully at the couple at the next table, before he turned back to me, leaning forward. 'The taxi will be here soon.'

'Okay, well, until then we have some time to kill.' I wasn't backing down on this, no way, no how. I crossed my arms and sat back in my chair, staring him down, much like the suited Frenchman had done to me yesterday. Who'd have thought I would actually be grateful to him for showing me how it's really done? Liam swallowed, shifting once more in his seat.

Ha! What do you know? It really does work!

Truth be known, I didn't really want to talk, not here or on the train. I had nothing in my head, no begging requests for him to take me back, no heartfelt speech to give; nothing. But seeing as the ball was in my court, a situation that was so rare in our relationship, I wanted to at least say something, and the only thing that had sprung to mind was the very same question I had asked myself on the long, rainy walk back to the hotel.

I looked at Liam, my hard stare finally faltering. 'Why?'

It was the simplest of words but held the most meaning, and I knew it was the very question that Liam had been dreading, if the look on his face was anything to go by.

COMING SOON,
THE THIRD BOOK IN
THE HEART OF THE CITY SERIES:

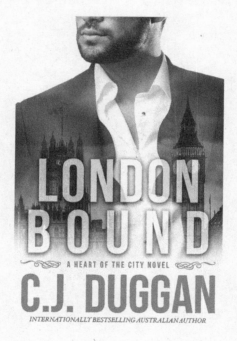

C.J. Duggan is the internationally bestselling author of the Summer, Paradise and Heart of the City series who lives with her husband in a rural border town of New South Wales. When she isn't writing books about swoon-worthy men, you'll find her renovating her hundred-year-old Victorian homestead or annoying her local travel agent for a quote to escape the chaos.

CJDugganbooks.com
twitter.com/CJ_Duggan
facebook.com/CJDugganAuthor

ALSO BY C.J. DUGGAN:

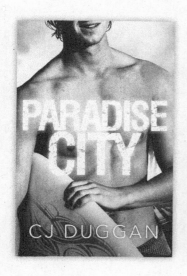 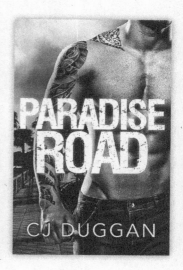

THE PARADISE SERIES – SEXY AUSTRALIAN
NEW-ADULT ROMANCE FULL OF SUN, SURF
AND STEAMY SUMMER NIGHTS. THERE'S
BOUND TO BE TROUBLE IN PARADISE . . .

Stories that make you feel

Books with Heart is an online place to chat about the authors
and the books that have captured your heart . . .
and to find new ones to do the same.

Join the conversation:
(f) /BooksWithHeartANZ • (y) @BooksWithHeart

Discover new books for **FREE** every month

Search: Books with Heart

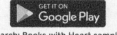

Search: Books with Heart sampler

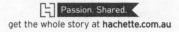

get the whole story at **hachette.com.au**

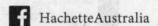
hachette
AUSTRALIA

If you would like to find out more about Hachette Australia,
our authors, upcoming events and new releases you can visit
our website, or our social media channels:

hachette.com.au

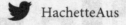 HachetteAustralia

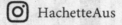 HachetteAus

HachetteAus

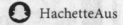 HachetteAus